VINTAGE

A CLEAN SMALL TOWN MECHANIC ROMANCE

PRICE FAMILY ROMANCE

LUCINDA RACE

MC TWO PRESS

BOOK 4

Vintage
Price Family Romance
Book 4
By
Lucinda Race

INSPIRATION

The first kiss and the first glass of wine are the best.
Marty Rubin

1

———

QUICK NOTE: If you enjoy Vintage, be sure to check out my offer for a FREE Price Family novella at the end. With that, happy reading!

Leo parked his truck in front of Black River Restoration. The bright mid-April sun filled the cab. He turned in his seat and looked at his nephews in the back. Nine-year-old Johnny and George, the instigator at age eight, were punching each other in the arm and laughing.

"Do you remember what we talked about before we left your house?" He gave each boy his best stern look. "I have to see a man about a paint job and they've been closed for the last few days, so I need for you to be on your best behavior. No horsing around or fighting. After I'm done, we'll do something fun until Mom gets home." Normally he wouldn't bring the boys, but Saturday was always a busy day for his twin sister and today he was on kid-sitting duty.

"Uncle Leo, the last time, it wasn't my fault." Johnny crossed his arms over his chest and frowned.

"Johnny, you knocked over an entire display of oil filters when we went to the auto parts store." He struggled to keep a straight face. No matter where he took the boys, trouble followed. "You two are going to sit in a chair and, if necessary, sit on your hands. I'll be less than ten minutes. Understood?"

George nodded and poked Johnny. "Don't worry, Uncle Leo. Mom said if we didn't leave a trail of chaos behind us today, we'd have pizza tonight."

Leo took the keys from the ignition. Was that the way to mitigate damage? Bribe them with their favorite food? It was worth a try. "If we get out of here unscathed, I thought we'd have milkshakes with lunch."

"What does that mean?" Johnny scrunched up his face.

Leo caught his eye in the rearview mirror. "We leave the place in the same condition it was when we walked in the door."

He slid two comic books into his back pocket in case they needed a distraction. The boys brightened and began to talk about what flavor of milkshake they were going to get. Leo opened up the back door and they hopped out with an ear-piercing yell.

He growled. "Guys, not the best way to start this meeting."

Johnny stopped and looked up. His large brown eyes and blond hair made him the spitting image of Leo, whereas George had Leo's twin sister Liza's hazel eyes.

"Sorry." He gave Leo a gap-toothed grin.

Leo ruffled the boys' hair and jerked his head toward the door that said ENTRANCE.

"Come on."

They stepped into a large metal and glass lobby. Sunlight bounced off every stainless-steel surface. It was bright enough for sunglasses; he noticed the window blinds could be tilted to reduce the glare. The counter-height desk was directly in front of them. Behind it was a door that must lead to the shop. Leo was surprised to see it had a swipe card access only. But they only dealt with high-end clients, so it made sense. He admired Eddie James. He was someone Leo aspired to be like, an honest businessman and one helluva body guy. Leo was good but this guy was the best and the people who worked for Eddie were trained by him personally. Leo might even learn a few things from him. If nothing else, he'd deliver for his client. To the right was a hallway, and the floor had the same black-and-white tile in the lobby. He surmised it must lead to the business offices.

He jabbed a finger at two leather and metal chairs. "Boys." It was then he noticed a display of model cars behind the chairs, and he cringed. All he would need is for the boys to spot them and decide to investigate. Hopefully he could make this quick.

Johnny and George sat down and Leo pulled the comic books from his back pocket. "Read these."

"Wow. The new Avengers." George grinned.

Johnny said, "Cool."

Leo looked around. It was pretty quiet for a Saturday morning, and he'd thought there'd be guys working today, since the shop had been closed earlier in the week. He had come over midweek, and there had been a sign on the door stating they were closed for a couple of days. He should have checked social media to see what was going on but he just didn't have the time. He had decided to take a chance today since the website said they'd reopened, and he was anxious to talk to Eddie. The paint job he needed on the '67 Chevy Chevelle was beyond his skill set and he knew subcontracting it out was the best thing for his customer. Eddie had a reputation as a top-notch classic car restorer.

Five minutes dragged by with no one coming to the desk. He looked out at a parking area that said Employees Only. There was an impeccably restored, deep-blue Ford Bronco. He guessed it was a '75. Had to be the owner's, but where was he? It was like a morgue around here. He leaned over the desk and saw a pad of paper and a pen. He'd just leave a note asking Eddie to give him a call; surely, he'd remember him.

The boys were passing the comic books back and forth. He wrote a brief message and had added his phone number and returned the pad to the desk when he heard a loud crash down the hall.

"Boys, stay right here!"

He jogged down the hall. Now it sounded as if someone were trashing an office. Shit, maybe he should have called 9-1-1. Too late now. He eased around the door and stopped dead in his tracks.

A woman dressed in a severely tailored black pantsuit and cream-colored blouse was standing surrounded by what resembled the aftermath of a small tornado. She looked at Leo. Her dirty-blond hair had been pulled off her face in a sleek ponytail and a trail of mascara ran down her cheeks. But it was her eyes—deep-gray eyes filled with grief and fear stared back at him. Despite that, she was beautiful, polished, and out of his league. A soft floral scent teased his senses and something tugged at his heart—his desire to wrap his arms around her and hold her while she cried.

She picked up a thick book and held it as a weapon. In a shaky voice, she demanded, "Who are you?"

"Leo Price. I was looking for the owner." He took a step closer. "Who are you?"

Her gaze swept the room, and then she sank into a chair, shoulders slumped. "The owner."

Now he was confused. "I'm looking for Eddie James."

She gave a half nod. "My father."

He wasn't quite sure what was going on. Was she pissed at her dad and taking it out on his office? Then the pieces started to come together. The clothes, the mascara, and those eyes. Something terrible had happened.

"Ms. James?" He took another step closer. "Is there something I can do, or maybe call someone for you?"

She dropped her head to the desk. "No. There's no one."

The way she spoke caused his heart to ache for her. He leaned over and picked up a stack of folders and set them on the desk.

"I left a note out front. If you're okay, I'll leave."

She didn't look up or answer him. Before leaving the office, he paused at the door, wishing there was something he could do to help.

George's voice reached his ears; he was telling Johnny they were going to get in trouble. Oh, that wasn't good. Not at all.

He rushed to the lobby and found Johnny perched on the arms of the chair that he had angled directly in front of the display of models.

"Johnny. No..." He didn't get to finish his sentence before the boy fell forward into the open display case.

The shelf, models, and Johnny crashed to the floor. He immediately started crying and holding his head as blood seeped between his fingers, dripping onto the floor.

Leo lifted him up and set him on another chair. This day was not going as he had expected. First he found a beautiful woman heartbroken, and now his nephews had damaged her property. What's next? He pulled a bandana from his back pocket and held it over the gash above Johnny's eye. "Hold on, John. I'll take a look at it in just a sec, okay?"

"I'm sorry." He dropped his head. "I just wanted to see the truck."

George was busy picking up cars and trucks and putting them back in the case. He held up a replica of the Bronco. "This one broke."

Leo glanced over. Under his breath, he muttered, "Set it down. I'll take a look in a minute. I'm sure I can fix it."

"Here." A wad of gauze appeared in his side vision. "Use this." Ms. James had an open first aid kit in her hand. "It's sterile." She hiccupped, more than likely a leftover from crying.

He glanced up. Her face was blotchy and she still had dark smudges under her gray eyes. "Thanks." He eased the bandana away from the cut. Carefully, he dabbed Johnny's head. "It doesn't look too bad, kiddo."

Ms. James knelt down. She pushed the sleeves up on her blouse and Leo noticed an expensive watch on her wrist, like the one his brother Don gave to Kate on their wedding anniversary, and Leo paused, impressed. She wore it casually like it was no big deal. "Can I clean that up for you?"

Johnny bit his bottom lip. "Okay."

She placed the kit on the floor, opened an antiseptic wipe, and said, "This might sting, but just hold on a minute."

He nodded and sat like a stone, but he did grimace as she cleaned the cut. Then she opened a single-use packet of antibiotic cream. Using a Q-tip, she smeared it over the cut. "What's your name?"

"Johnny."

"You're doing great. It's going to hurt for a bit, but it's just a small cut. I'll bet it won't even leave a scar."

Leo was amazed but pleased that Johnny let a stranger tend to his cut. The kid was starting to grow up. Leo's thought was cut off with a quick glance at the havoc he'd made of the display shelves.

"I'm going to use a butterfly bandage."

Johnny scowled. "Huh?"

She gave him a tentative smile. "It's a kind of bandage that holds cuts together better than a regular one. All of our mechanics use them."

"They do?" Leo could hear in Johnny's voice that he thought that was a cool idea. "Do you have them too?" He looked at Leo.

"I do, in the cabinet in my office."

Johnny wanted to be a mechanic; he thought cars were the best thing in the world.

"And our guys use them too." The woman smoothed the tape down and said, "There you go."

"Thank you." He looked up. "Sorry about the models."

Leo watched in horror as a look of distress passed over her face as she realized the extent of the damage. Models were strewn across the floor and at least one was broken.

"It was an accident. Really," George interjected. "Johnny wouldn't do it on purpose."

"I can fix them." She flipped the lid closed on the first aid kit and stood up.

"Ms. James." Leo took a step forward and extended his hand.

"Stephanie." She shook it, her voice all business.

"I'll take the model with me and repair it."

George held up the broken Bronco. Leo went to take it, but Stephanie touched his arm, stopping him.

"No, that's alright. I can fix it. Dad and I used to build them together."

She held out her hand. George glanced at Leo before handing it to her. He dropped his eyes to the floor and dug into the pocket of his jeans. He pulled out a five-dollar bill and thrust it toward Stephanie.

"I got my allowance this morning and you can have it."

Johnny slid off the chair and did the same. "Mine too."

"Thank you, boys, but it's not necessary."

George took Johnny's bill and took a tentative step closer to Stephanie. Leo watched with pride.

"My mom would be mad at us if she knew we broke something and didn't pay for the parts to fix it."

She glanced at Leo, her eyebrow arched.

He smiled. The boys might be hellions at times but deep down they knew the right thing to do. "They won't take no for an answer."

She gave them each a small hug. "Thank you."

"Boys, it's time to go." He pointed at the door.

"You left your number on the desk," Stephanie said. "I'll call you later in the week and we can talk about why you stopped in today." She stuck out her hand and gave Leo's a firm shake.

This time he looked into her eyes as their hands connected. He was surprised at how well hers fit in his and he searched her eyes. Did she feel it too? There were too many conflicting emotions sliding over her face for him to tell.

"I'll look forward to your call," he said.

She withdrew her hand and stuck it in her slacks pocket.

Leo picked up the now-forgotten comic books and tossed his bandana in the garbage can near the desk. He opened the door for the boys and took one final look at Stephanie. She looked lost and so terribly sad. He wanted to say something more but, unwilling to intrude on whatever had caused her to cry, he nodded and walked out behind the boys.

"Wait till Mom sees my bandage. Do you think she knows about this kind? I can't wait to show her." Johnny was babbling as he hopped up into the truck with George right behind him.

"Don't forget to buckle up."

Before he closed the truck door, George asked, "Are we still getting milkshakes?"

Leo waited half a second. He wanted to reinforce the good behavior of giving up their allowance to Stephanie.

"You broke something that didn't belong to you, but we'll talk about it when we get home." He closed his door and the truck rumbled to life. Hopefully Liza wouldn't be ticked when she saw her son with a new bandage.

2

Stephanie stood in the lobby and watched Leo and his boys get into the truck. She wanted to kick herself for not locking the door when she had arrived, so she did that as Leo lifted his hand in a final wave. In her defense, she did have a few things on her mind. The funeral.

She hugged her arms around her body. Her legs couldn't hold her up another minute and she sank to the floor. What would her dad want her to do? Fresh tears coursed down her cheeks. She looked at her hand. The hand that had placed a flower on her father's mahogany casket and the same hand that had taken a handful of dirt and sprinkled it over the casket after it was lowered into the cold, dark ground. The only saving grace was that it hadn't rained today.

She had stayed until the funeral director had urged her to leave. She didn't need to watch as the men from the cemetery finished laying her father to rest.

She wiped the tears from her cheeks and snorted. "Rest." What a strange way to phrase it. Her father was gone and now she was completely alone. Mom had died when she was a toddler. Steph didn't have any memories of her other than pictures in an album or framed photos Dad had in every room at the house. Now he too was just a photograph. She longed to be able to talk to him, to ask him what she should do first or even second. It had always been her dream to come back and work with him. But he wasn't there to give her advice or just listen as she talked through whatever problem she had to face.

Her legs were cramped and her butt had gone numb. The sun was coming in a set of windows on the west side of the building. With a heavy heart, she got to her feet and kicked off her black high heels. She would tidy the office and then go home. Tomorrow was a new day.

The next morning, Stephanie walked into the office wearing a simple tailored dress. It was something like she usually wore to work back home, but it also felt a bit too formal for Black River Restoration. To offset the businesslike outfit, she'd kept her hair long and loose and her makeup light. She needed to look friendly and kind; she hoped the crew wouldn't panic, thinking she was about to close Dad's shop. After all, there were at least twenty families who depended on their jobs. But what did she really know about running a high-end car restoration business? She was a sales manager with a degree in business management and supervised pharmaceutical reps. These days, her comfort zone was spreadsheets and income projections. The days of cranking a wrench and blending paint colors felt like a lifetime ago.

Based on the number of vehicles in the employee parking lot, it was a good thing she had taken yesterday to clean up the office because today, the shop buzzed with activity. She paused and wiped all expression from her face and rounded the corner. The noise level dropped.

"Good morning," she said to no one specifically. Then she addressed her father's right hand for the last five years. "Val, would you ask everyone to gather in bay one in fifteen minutes?"

The older woman said, "Certainly."

Maintaining a rigid back, Stephanie walked into her dad's office and closed the door. It was only then that her shoulders sagged. Was she prepared to tell everyone she was going to run the business for several months or so and then evaluate where they were? After reviewing the books, she had discovered some alarming facts. Dad was running very close to the red. He had always had a good head for business and before Stephanie tried to sell Black River, she had to discover what was wrong and either fix it or close it down before the business began to really lose money.

A light tap on the door interrupted her train of thought. "Come in."

Val eased open the door. She held up a mug that bore the company logo. "I thought you could use some fortification before addressing the troops."

Steph could feel the corners of her mouth perk up. "We're not going into battle, are we?"

Val came closer to the desk and handed Steph the mug. "You never can be sure. Take a slug or two."

Stephanie liked Val. She had been a friend of Dad's for years. After her husband had left her, and despite her lack of experience with a car restoration company, Dad had given her a job. Steph had often wondered if there was something more between him and the full-figured brunette than what he had told her.

She noticed the coffee was a soft tan color. "Thanks. I didn't have any cream at home." Her stomach flipped. It didn't feel like a home anymore without Dad in it. Now, it was just the house she had grown up in.

With a wave of her hand, Val said, "No problem. I brought your dad coffee every day for five years." Her mouth fell open. "I'm so sorry, Stephanie. I didn't mean to…" Her voice trailed off and tears sprang to her eyes.

"I know. It's still hard to believe that he's gone. He never told me about the cancer until a couple of weeks ago. Then it was offhand, like it was no big deal. I got home as fast as I could."

"He talked to me after he called you. Eddie said he didn't want to disrupt your life." Val's face softened. "He was very proud of your accomplishments. He was always going on and on every time you broke a sales record. But I know he was glad when you came home."

Stephanie took a sip of the coffee. It went down like it was full of day-old grounds. Not that the coffee was bad, but the thought that she had spent so much time away from Dad. Time she'd never get back. For what? The accolades of being a sales rep, moving up the corporate ladder? Maybe if she had been here, things might be different.

"I know that look, Stephanie. It's the same expression Eddie would get when he second-guessed himself about a quote."

She shuffled a stack of papers on the desk and blinked away the tears that formed.

"Hon, you can't change what was done."

She lifted her eyes to the older woman. "Did you love Dad?"

Val's eyes grew misty. "Did he ever talk about us?"

With a shake of her head, Steph smiled. "That just answered my question." She reached out and took Val's hand and gave it a squeeze. "I'm glad."

"If you have any questions or just want to talk, I'm here for you."

Stephanie pushed back the old metal and pleather office chair. "I appreciate that. For the moment, I need to talk to the staff."

"Hon, think of them as your father's friends and coworkers. It'll make it easier for you and them."

On impulse, Stephanie gave the older woman a quick hug and reminded herself to relax. Val was right; they were all friends.

*

Standing in front of a group of people she didn't really know, and a few she hadn't seen in years, was harder than she thought. It was nothing like sitting across from a doctor and pitching the latest and greatest blood pressure medicine, and even that was something she hadn't done since her promotion.

"Hello, everyone. I'll keep this brief and to the point." Her gaze roamed the group. Twenty sets of eyes were trained on her. She shifted from foot to foot. She should have worn flats to make up for all these cement floors she had to stand on. That would be tomorrow.

"I'd like to thank you again for coming to Dad's funeral. It meant a great deal to me."

A few of the guys dipped their heads. One made the sign of the cross over his chest.

She kicked off her high heels and looked around. "I need to dig out my work boots." She smiled at Dad's, no, her team. "I've taken a leave of absence from my job in Portland until October. I plan on running Dad's business in the meantime. I'll be looking to several of you for help in preparing quotes, ordering supplies, and organizing the work schedule, but I don't plan on making any staff changes."

Around the room, there were smiles of relief and murmurs to each other.

"Chuck"—she looked at the man standing in the front—"according to Dad's notes, it seems you've been scheduling the engine rebuilds, so I think we should talk tomorrow morning." Her eyes sought out Gary, the body guy.

"Gary, if you could come into the office in half an hour, we have a new potential project that I'd like your input on."

"Sure thing, boss."

She wanted to correct him, but in a split second changed her mind. "I'd like to ask for your patience as I learn everyone's name. I know I've been gone a long time, but please understand I have all of our best interests at heart."

A woman in the group raised her hand.

"Yes, did you have a question?"

"I'm Zira."

"Hello, Zira. What are your responsibilities here?"

"I turn wrenches." She paused. "You know, engine work."

Stephanie felt her lips twitch. "I know the expression." If she only knew that there had been a time when she would have pit her skills against any guy in the shop.

"Well, I'm the last one hired, so does that mean I'm the first one fired?"

Steph's heart thudded in her chest. That didn't take long.

She said again, "I have no plans to make any personnel changes unless"—she watched with a knowing look as a ripple like a fan wave at a ball game went through the staff —"you're not doing the job you're supposed to do. I won't pay people for sitting around drinking coffee and shooting the breeze. Just like when Dad ran this business, when we walk in the door, we work."

The tension in the room seemed to abate. Taking a deep breath, she exhaled. So far so good.

"Any other questions?" She waited a few seconds. "Okay then. My door is always open if you want to talk. Thank you."

The group broke up into smaller groups of twos and threes as people moved back to different areas in the building. Zira lingered, watching Steph. She took a step forward but hesitated before walking over to her.

Stephanie watched as the new mechanic made her approach. She was dressed in coveralls, thick-soled work boots, and a baseball cap with her dark-brown hair tucked underneath it. She looked like she fit in with the team but the way she carried herself told Steph she hadn't found her confidence yet and it made her wonder how she could help her and if she could mentor Zira to be the best she could be.

"Boss?"

"You can call me Stephanie."

She seemed to think about that before saying, "Sorry, but you look like a boss, dressed up and all."

She glanced down at her clothes and realized Zira was probably implying it wasn't the best choice for an auto restoration business.

"I see your point."

"Boss"—Zira flicked her a grin—"I just wanted to say thanks for not kicking me to the curb. I'll show you I deserve my place here."

"I'm not sure why you thought I would, but Eddie wouldn't have hired you if he didn't think you were talented."

She bobbed her head. "He taught me a lot too. Said I reminded him of someone, another girl who could hold her own in this man's world."

Stephanie willed herself to smile. "Coming from my dad, that was high praise."

Zira gave her a long look, and then her hazel eyes brightened. "It was you, wasn't it?"

She blinked hard. "Excuse me?"

Zira leaned toward her. "Don't worry. I won't tell the guys they've got two women who are a whiz under the hood." Her cheeks went pink. "That didn't sound right at all."

Stephanie laughed. It felt good to let go a bit. "I know what you meant. Not to worry. Just do a good job and you'll be fine."

Zira gave her a wink. "Just in case you're wondering, I have an extra set of coveralls in my locker."

Still smiling, she said, "Thanks, but I don't think I'll need them."

Gary joined them. "Boss, do you want to talk now? I have to get some paint matched for a car we've got coming in next week."

Stephanie realized she might just have to give up on the team not calling her boss. It sounded like it was set in stone and the workday wasn't even two hours old.

"Give me five minutes."

"Sure thing."

He and Zira walked toward the coffee machine. They looked kind of tight. That was good; at least she had one ally in the shop. Maybe Val could give her some pointers on where to shop for work clothes. It seemed like her pharma rep clothes weren't exactly in vogue here and she'd have to tell Maggie she'd been right; Steph should have packed casual clothes before she left Portland. A pang of sadness washed over her. Maggie was her best friend and more like a sister and the only person Steph had left in the world. That concept was going to take some getting used to.

3

Getting the jump on Wednesday, Leo was already under the hood of his current project, the Chevelle, when the office phone rang. He wiped the grease from his hands and picked up the extension.

"Vintage."

"Hello, I'm looking for Leo Price. This is Stephanie James."

An image of the lovely Ms. James popped into his mind. He smiled and wondered what had taken her so long to call.

"This is Leo."

"I wanted to call and apologize for Saturday. I forgot to lock the door and certainly wasn't open for business. And it's taken until midweek for me to call you back."

"Think nothing of it." He wanted to ask what had happened but instead said, "Are you better today?"

"Every day will get better. Thank you."

Her voice was soft. He was lost in remembering her gray eyes when he heard, "Are you still there?"

"Yes, I'm sorry. I was distracted for a moment." *Pay attention, Price.*

"I spoke with Gary, my paint specialist. After reading your note, I realized he's better qualified to answer your questions. He's in charge of our paint department and is an expert in metal flake."

"Would you be able to take this job on? The car will be ready next week. I have a little more body work to finish up and once you take it, I can work on the engine and be ready to drop it back in when the car is out of the paint booth." All details she probably didn't need, but he wanted to keep talking to her, which was odd. Most women didn't hold his interest this long.

"Would you be able to come by, talk with me and Gary, and discuss transportation needs?"

Leo glanced at the engine stand. He prayed she would give him a couple of days. He was up to his eyeballs at the moment.

She asked, "Would tomorrow at four work?"

It would take him forty minutes to get there, and figure in a shower, so he'd have to quit working by two. "Yeah, that'll work." He hoped that didn't sound as annoying to her ears as it had to his.

"Okay. I'll let Gary know and we will see you tomorrow. We look forward to working with you."

The line disconnected and the way the call ended was way too businesslike for the way his thoughts were headed. But at least he'd see her tomorrow.

S tephanie leaned back in her dad's chair and stretched her arms above her head. She got up and crossed to the door.

"Val, when you have a second, can you come down?" She went back and carefully sat down in the chair to keep it from listing to the left side. She had already flipped it over to tighten the screws, but that hadn't done a thing.

"What's up, hon?" Val pushed open the door and entered the office. "I see you've really cleaned this place up." She nodded and looked around. "Looks good."

"Thanks. I have to be able to find files, and Dad wasn't that organized. At least not in the way my brain works." She stood and wiggled her hips. With her hand on her waist, she pointed to the chair. "How did Dad sit in this contraption? There is zero padding."

"You know your father. He never wanted to throw anything away until there just wasn't a choice."

"There's frugal, and then there is life-and-limb peril. This chair falls into the peril category. Any idea where I could order a new chair and how quickly we could get it here?"

"Come with me." Val left the room, leaving Stephanie no choice but to follow her. She pushed open the storeroom door and stepped to one side. There were four large boxes labeled *desk chair*.

"If he had new ones, why on earth didn't he replace it?"

Val got a faraway look. "It was the only chair you had sat in. He wanted to keep it."

Fresh tears threatened to spill over her lashes. She struggled to swallow the lump in her throat. "I didn't realize Dad was so sentimental."

"If something was connected to you, well, you get the idea. He never wanted you to be far from where he was. Even if it was a chair or a pen. That was just the way he was."

She really didn't want to cry in front of Val. Instead, she stepped closer to the boxes to get a better look at the chair options.

Val pointed to the box on the left side. "That's your chair."

Confused, Steph said, "Mine?"

"Eddie ordered it about a month ago and said it was for you." Val placed a hand on her arm. "It was his way of planning ahead."

Anger bubbled up and over before she could keep it under control. She slammed her hand against the metal shelving. "Then why didn't he tell me he was dying sooner? I would have come home and we would have had more time together."

"Stephanie, your father didn't want to spend his last months of life with people hovering around him. That included you."

"I wish I had more than a few weeks with him." She blinked away the tears. "He went so quickly."

Val pulled her into a hug. "He waited for you to get home, and then he went on his terms."

Her breath came in hiccups. She pulled back from Val. "Thanks."

"How about we get your chair out and have one of the guys put it together for you?"

"Heck, I don't need a guy. A few tools and I'll be sitting pretty." She pulled at the box and Val grabbed the opposite side. "I'm keeping Dad's chair in my office."

"The apple didn't fall far from the tree, did it?"

Stephanie grinned. "I guess not."

⁕

The drive to Black River was uneventful. Leo pulled into the parking lot the next day and noticed that the Bronco was parked in the same spot. That had to be Eddie's ride. A few minutes before four, he strode to the lobby door and pulled it open. There was a full-figured older woman behind the desk, talking on the phone. She held up a finger and gave him a broad smile. He was surprised to see she was dressed in a pink sweater and her salt-and-pepper hair was in a short bob like his mom's. Her warm hazel eyes left him wondering if this was Eddie's wife. But she didn't look anything like Stephanie.

"Hello. I'm Val and you must be Leo." She stuck out her hand to shake. "Stephanie asked that I take you to the conference room. She and Gary will be right in."

"Will Eddie be joining us too?" He watched as her face fell and the light dimmed in her eyes. Would she cry? If she did, he could handle it; he had three sisters. He held his breath, but she exhaled and her shoulders sagged.

"He passed away last week. His funeral was Saturday."

Leo felt as if he had been gut punched. "Saturday, as in a few days ago?"

"Yes." She looked down the hall toward Stephanie's office. "She didn't tell you, did she?"

"I had no idea." He spun around and looked at the display case. The model of the Bronco was back on the shelf. "She never said a word."

"I'm not surprised. She's trying to conduct business as usual."

Leo hung his head. "I had a feeling something was really wrong when we were here."

"Don't mention to Stephanie that you know. She might mistake the work for sympathy." Val stepped from behind the desk. "Follow me."

He trailed behind her around the corner to the first open doorway. She stepped to one side. "Have a seat. Can I get you water, coffee?"

"No. Thank you." He sat down and then pulled out the paint color information for the Chevelle. He leaned back in the chair and rubbed his hands over his eyes. He had guessed something was very wrong when he went into her office, but he had never thought it was Eddie's death. Based on the one time they'd met, Leo would have put him in his mid-fifties and in good health. It made him think of his dad and his ever-present heart condition.

"Leo." A soft subtle floral scent teased his senses. He dropped his hands and Stephanie entered the room. He stood up.

"I'm glad you could make it this afternoon." She placed a folder and a laptop on the head of the table and eased into the chair. "Gary will be right in." She placed her hands in her lap and smiled. "I'm sure this meeting is a bit unorthodox, but my business background is all about meeting with a client and creating a plan for success to meet your needs."

She smiled again, but this time it didn't warm her eyes. Her focus had changed to the now-open folder in front of her. Leo could tell this was all business for her. She was faking it to make it, so to speak.

"As long as we can get the car painted and have it look spectacular, I don't mind the meeting. Besides, it gets me out of the garage on a beautiful afternoon." The company wasn't bad either.

A man came in wearing a logo collared shirt and dark pants along with work boots.

"Hi, I'm Gary. You must be Leo. I've heard of your shop in Crescent Lake, right?"

Leo stood and shook his hand. "Yes. That's right. It's good to meet you."

The men sat down on either side of Stephanie.

"Tell us about the vehicle, and it looks like you have paint color numbers for us." Stephanie took the notes Leo handed her.

"As I said yesterday, I've almost completed the body work and it will be ready for paint next week. The client wants to have black holographic metal flake. It will have a slight sparkle in the shade but in the sunlight appear to have a linear rainbow." Leo looked from Stephanie to Gary. "I can paint a car, but when it comes to the metal flake and this particular client, I want the best." He studied Gary. "From what I've heard, this is the only place on the East Coast that can do it right."

"Tell me more about the car." Stephanie opened her laptop, fingers poised over the keys.

"It's a 1975 two-door Chevy Chevelle. I've sent the chrome out and the engine is almost done after a bit more work and then, I'm planning on moving on to the upholstery while the body is here."

She tapped on the keys. "Who's doing the upholstery work?"

"I am." That was an odd question. He needed a paint job.

She nodded and made another note. "Gary, you can prepare a quote for Leo but before we agree to take the job, I'd like to add in a contingency. If we find the body work inferior to our standards, we reserve the right to"—she smiled at him in a way that pissed him off—"tweak it."

"Are you implying the quality of my work may be subpar?"

"I have zero point of reference to answer that question, but I have to think of our reputation. If we agree to do this job, we can't make a silk purse from a sow's ear."

He cocked a brow. "Meaning?"

"As an example, if you left burrs in the metal and we paint it as you deliver it, and then someone asks who painted the car, now our name is associated with a bad job."

He shifted in his chair and clasped his hands together as he leaned forward. "What are you talking about?"

"It's something my father drilled into me growing up." She cocked her head. "Never realized it stuck until this very moment."

She let go of a ragged breath and instantly Leo cooled his temper, reminding himself she had just lost her father and she was working in a business that seemed completely foreign to her.

Gary was temporarily forgotten as Leo addressed Stephanie. "I have an idea."

She gave him a sidelong look. "I'm listening."

"I'd like to invite you to swing by my place, see my work for yourself, and then if you feel you could do the job, we'll draw up a contract and I'll sign it."

She looked at Gary. "What do you think?"

"I don't have an issue either way. It might be a good idea to take some before photos too."

"Then it's settled. How about I come to your shop tomorrow, around nine, and I'll bring a contract ready for you to sign."

Leo stood up and shook her hand. She was in for a surprise. He was almost as good as anyone in her shop. "I'll see you in the morning."

4

*L*eo paced in his office on Friday morning. What had he been thinking? Another abbreviated day, all because Stephanie James questioned his skills? He had to be nuts.

He caught sight of the Bronco pulling into his parking lot. Stephanie was behind the wheel. It made more sense now.

He had the shop door open before she put the vehicle in park. She gave him a wave and pushed open the driver's door. She wore slim-fitting jeans, leather boots, and a black short-sleeved t-shirt that looked like silk, not the standard cotton.

She held up two to-go cups. "I come bearing a peace offering."

Well, this was an interesting surprise. "Not necessary, but thank you."

She handed him a cup and took in the exterior of his garage. His pride and joy.

"Nice place."

"I like it. Not as grand as Black River, but it's mine and the employees seem to like it here."

"Oh, how many do you have?"

"One."

She flushed a cute shade of pink.

His arm swept the parking lot. "One truck in the lot for one employee."

"I see that now."

Leo held the door for her and she stepped into a small entryway. Over her shoulder, she asked, "How long have you been in business?"

"Since I graduated college, so fourteen, no, fifteen years."

She set her designer bag down on the empty wood desk.

He said, "My sister has a bag like that."

"Your sister has good taste."

"Well, are you ready for the nickel tour?" He set the coffee cup aside and Stephanie did the same. "You can leave your bag. I never have anyone stop in."

She seemed to hesitate and then smiled. "Lead the way."

*H*e opened the door behind the desk and ushered her into his inner sanctum. She immediately took in the familiar smell of a garage, just like the one she had grown up in. It reminded her of Dad. She told herself she wasn't going to cry today—well, at least not in front of anyone—especially not the tall, handsome man standing next to her. He was lean with legs that would eat up the ground. His blond hair dipped over one eye and she itched to push it back so she could look deeper into his molten brown eyes. His hands were strong and calloused from working with them, but no trace of grease lingered under his nails. Just like her dad.

"The Chevelle is over here." He crossed the large space to what she guessed was his only other bay.

She walked around the car. The body work was excellent, but she wasn't going to let on she approved. At least not yet. She still wasn't sure why she had held back yesterday when Gary questioned her about why she needed to see the car; they could inspect the metal when it was dropped off. Maybe it was an excuse to get out of Black River for a couple of hours.

"I can see why the client wants the metal flake. It will look sharp."

"It took the client a bit to decide on the actual color, but now that he has, we're ready to move forward."

"How many cars a year do you restore?"

"Depending on how much is needed, a few."

He was deliberately being cagey. She had to wonder why.

"Was this a complete restoration job?"

He nodded. He walked around to the other side and she walked with him. "This car was a wreck when I was asked to work on it. Didn't run, the body was in rough shape, and the owner wanted matching numbers."

Steph was quick to calculate. Someone had very deep pockets. "Nice project." She realized there was a third bay beyond the Chevelle. She walked over to discover another car that was in process.

"That's my personal project car. I have a major weakness when it comes to Mustangs."

She flashed a grin over her shoulder. "Gotta love a Mustang convertible."

"And your ride, the Bronco. Interesting choice."

"Dad and I worked on it together when I was a teenager." The pang of longing to talk to Dad about Leo's shop was sharp. He had a good place here and she could tell he was good at what he did.

"I was sorry to hear about Eddie."

She didn't look at Leo, afraid the tears would form. "He was a good man."

She licked her lips and ran a hand over her hair, then said, "I think we can work well together. If you're still interested." She headed back to the office, and he trailed behind her. "I brought the contract with me."

When he held open the door to his office for her, she didn't mean to inhale his scent as deeply as she did. Soap and all male. If the timing were different, she might have asked him to meet her for a drink some night. But she had a business to sort out and there was no time for fun and games. Not with a six-month timeframe before she had to go back to Portland.

"I'll send Gary out with the hauler and he'll pick up the car." She pulled a few papers from her bag and Leo chuckled.

"You've got all kinds of stuff in there."

"Just call me Mary Poppins." She handed him the contract and a pen.

He scrawled his name on the first page.

"Sign the next one, and then we'll both have copies."

He did as she asked, and then she signed them too. After handing one contract to Leo, she put the other in her bag and smiled. "I look forward to working with you."

"I think it will be interesting."

She tipped her head. "Did I miss something?"

"No. I look forward to our next meeting." He walked her out to the Bronco. "Thanks again for the coffee."

"Anytime." She hopped up inside and rolled down the window.

"Can I hold you to that?"

"Leo, I don't mix business with pleasure."

"That's too bad. We would have a lot of fun together."

She laughed. "We just might have."

"If we hurry up and conclude our business transaction,

and if I asked you out for an adult beverage, would you say yes?"

She pushed her hair from her face. It was too bad he was otherwise involved. Even though he shouldn't be asking her to have a drink, that didn't stop her from flirting back. "I guess you'll never know."

The engine rumbled and she backed up. "See ya." With a jaunty wave, she drove off.

*L*eo watched as the most fascinating woman he had met in a very long time drove away. Not that he was some Casanova, but most women asked him out for drinks. She was the kind of woman he wanted to take in his arms and kiss away the sadness that came into her eyes, and she was also the kind of woman that when she put her flirt on, well, that made him want to kiss her in other ways.

This was definitely new territory for him, and one he just might enjoy.

His shop phone rang, and he wanted to get it before the machine picked it up.

"Vintage."

"Hi, Leo, it's Drew. I was wondering how the car was coming along?"

"Good news. I just subcontracted the paint job and I'm almost ready to start the upholstery. We're right on schedule."

"Good. I really want to be able to let Anna and Colin use it for their wedding. After Marie said they wanted something different, I thought lending them this car for their big day would be just the ticket."

It was nice of Colin's sister to suggest that as their wedding gift. Colin didn't seem to have Anna's love for vintage cars that Leo shared with his older sister, but from what Leo had seen so far, he did appreciate them.

"Will she be back from the golf circuit in time for the big day?"

"If I know Marie, wild horses couldn't keep her away." Drew chuckled.

"Thank heavens we have time. The wedding is still four months away." Leo glanced at the calendar. He'd make it in plenty of time.

"I need to run. But is it okay if I come over next week just to see how things are going?"

"Drew, stop in at any point. It's your car."

"Only after you give me back the keys and I give you a big, fat check."

With a chuckle, Leo said, "The price of classic car restoration, my friend." Leo hung up the phone and sat down at his desk. His operation was a far cry from Stephanie's, but that didn't matter. He did good work here and he wouldn't trade it for anything.

*

*S*tephanie had the windows down as she drove back to Black River. Her speed slowed considerably when she thought of how she had flirted with Leo Price. She had just buried her father and here she was, carrying on like life was normal. The cool wind teased her hair and she saw a sign up ahead for Sand Creek Winery. Dad never kept wine in the house, only beer, and she'd love to have a glass. Again, something normal.

She parked the Bronco, grabbed her bag, and followed the signs to the tasting room. The lights were on, so they must be open. She glanced at her watch; it wasn't even noon yet. Who goes to a tasting room before lunch?

She stepped into the spacious room. Bathed in wood tones and natural light, it made the space seemed cozy despite its size. She wandered around the perimeter, picking up bottles and looking at the descriptions of each kind of wine.

"Hello. Can I help you?"

Steph turned. The woman looked familiar somehow, but she couldn't place her.

"Hi. I was driving by and saw your sign and stopped in hopes you were open."

"I'm Tessa, one of the owners. Welcome." She took the bottle of cabernet from Stephanie's hand. "Do you like a good red?"

"I do. I'd like to pick up a couple of bottles of red and white. Do you have a favorite?"

Tessa picked up a bottle to Steph's right. "This is Fuse. It's a very special blend my husband created. We also have a nice Blanc, but if you like something with a little more oak, I'd recommend the Chardonnay."

"I'm not sure." She glanced at the large wall clock. "Would it be terrible if I asked to taste a couple before I buy? There is nothing worse than getting something home, popping the cork, and then pouring it down the sink."

"Well, hopefully you never have that issue with one of our wines, but do me a favor. If you do, bring it back and I'll replace it."

Tessa crossed the room to the oak bar. "Come on, let's sample." She pointed to a stool. "I'll be right back."

She disappeared into the room behind the bar and a few moments later came back with a small plate of sliced cheese, dried meats, and crackers, along with a cluster of grapes. She smiled. "How about an early lunch with your wine?"

"You didn't need to go to so much trouble. I could have just tasted a couple, swiped my card, and been out of your hair."

"Nonsense. Besides, I'm dying to ask you about your vehicle."

Steph looked out the window. "My Bronco?"

Tessa set six wineglasses on the bar and began to pour white and red wines. She slid the first glass of white in front of Stephanie.

"That's one of my younger brother's dream cars—or trucks, however you classify it. He'd love to see it up close."

"Driving it is a blast." Stephanie took a sip of the white and smiled. "This is delicious. I'll take a bottle of this one." She nibbled on a slice of soft cheese. "What does your brother do?"

"Which one?" She slid another glass to Stephanie. "Oh, Leo. He has a car restoration business, Vintage. It's a few miles from here."

Stephanie laughed and choked on the wine she was drinking. "That's too funny. I just left his place." She slid the now-empty glass back across the wooden bar. What an interesting coincidence that she chose to stop at another Price business. Maybe it was a sign she didn't have to be alone in the world forever. "By the way, I'm Stephanie James and I own Black River Restoration."

"Well, this is a small world," Tessa grinned.

Steph held up her glass and said, "And it's getting smaller all the time."

5

---

*A*fter loading a mixed case of wine in the back of the Bronco, Stephanie swung by the shop first for Dad's laptop. She wanted to spend some time looking over the last couple of years of financial records. Something was off and she couldn't quite put her finger on it. At least not yet.

The drive went by smoothly with the windows down and music from Journey wafting around her. Other than the heaviness that settled over her heart when she thought of Dad, it had been a decent day. Dad would have liked cruising down the road with her. It was one of the things she'd miss, either driving or riding shotgun with him in one of his hot rods.

She smacked the steering wheel with her hand. She should have asked Leo how his boys were. She remembered the distraught look George had worn when his older brother was getting his Band-Aid on. And then the boys willingly giving her their allowance said Leo was doing a very good job raising them. She wondered about their mother. She must be a nice lady too.

She ran her fingers through her hair and propped her

elbow in the open window. Meeting Tessa had certainly been a fluke, and just how many brothers did she have? It must be nice to be part of a family that had more than two people. She stopped at the four-way intersection close to the shop. Traffic was light. She clicked on her left blinker and turned. She'd make one more stop before going to the shop.

The sign for Brookview was just up ahead. She turned onto the well-maintained road and slowed down to follow the posted speed limit of fifteen miles per hour. People loved to walk their dogs, and kids rode bikes throughout the cemetery.

The throaty sound of the exhaust broke the tranquility as she drove down a never-ending narrow road. She stopped and shut off the truck. Taking a deep breath, she pushed open the door. She would never get used to this.

Her boot-clad feet carried her across the expanse of green grass, her heels sinking in slightly. She wiped away the tear that slid down her cheek. At least Mom and Dad were together again.

The flowers that sat on the mound of dirt were wilted and ready to be thrown into the garbage. It would be a couple of weeks until someone came to update the granite bench that marked the family plot. They would add Dad's name.

She stood looking at the sky. "Hey, guys. Just wanted to let you know I'm okay. You don't have to worry about me or the business. I took a leave of absence from work. So, I'll be hanging around, getting things in shape before I head out."

She had brushed off the seat and sat down when the finality hit her. *I'm really alone in this world.* She picked at a thread on the hem of her shirt. "You two are a little quiet today. Guess I need to carry the conversation. Thanks for the new chair, Pop. It was sweet of you to think ahead."

She covered her face with her hands, but the tears didn't come. In fact, she surprised herself when she started to chuckle. "I'm sorry for laughing, but I don't want to cry anymore." She stood up and brushed off her backside. "I miss you like crazy and I love you so much, but the next time I come back to check in, you'll see I'm going to be doing great things. For a start, I'm going to repaint my bedroom at home and get a new bed." She placed a kiss on Mom's name and then blew one toward the new dirt mound. She walked away without a backward glance. Grief was a personal thing and she was going to find a way to celebrate her parents' lives.

She hopped into the truck. Who was she kidding? There would be moments of engulfing grief, but getting the business profitable was the only thing she could do to honor them. It was time to get back to work.

Leo looked up as Tessa came through the office door. He gave her a smile and then glanced at the clock.

"Slow day in the wine business?"

Ignoring the question, she flashed him a grin and set a bottle of Fuse on his desk. "For you."

"Why?" He propped his feet on an open drawer and sat back in his chair, email forgotten.

"A friend of yours happened to stop into Sand Creek today and she really enjoyed this particular bottle. So..." She let the word dangle in the air.

"Sis, you need to be a little more specific than that." His feet hit the floor and he leaned forward. Now his curiosity was piqued.

She flopped into the chair opposite him. "You've been holding out on me. About your potential love life."

His mouth gaped open. "I have no idea where you're going with this but I'm not dating anyone at the moment."

"Do you deny a very beautiful woman was in your garage this morning?"

"I had a business meeting with someone whom I've contracted to paint Drew's car. Is that who you're referring to?"

She beamed. "She discovered the winery and stopped in to pick up a few bottles. I gave her a tasting"—she held up her hand—"and before you say it was too early to sample wine, I fixed her a snack to go with it."

"How on earth did you discover we knew each other and more importantly, what made you take the leap from business acquaintances to dating?" Not that he objected to the idea of dating Stephanie. She was gorgeous and obviously smart. "Did she say something?"

"No, she mentioned she had come from here and we chatted for a while. She was nice."

"Her dad just passed away. I get the impression she's here to run his business, but I have no idea if she lives here." Based on the way she was dressed, wearing business clothes suited her, not a pair of coveralls and work boots.

"Are you going to see her again?"

"Tessa, I expect something like this out of Liza, not you."

When she batted her long eyelashes, he could see the devilish smile in her eyes. "I have no idea what you're talking about. It's not like I gave her your number or anything." She got up from the chair. "Since I'm sure she already has it."

He shook his head and had to admit it would be a nice phone call to receive. "She does, since we're doing *business* together."

"You should give her the bottle. After all, it's always more fun to drink wine with someone who shares some of your same interests." She walked to the door and smiled over her shoulder. "I do believe Stephanie is a fan of our wines; she ended up buying a case."

"Tessa." He hoped his voice conveyed a gentle rebuke.

"Toodles, little brother." She closed the door behind her, and he watched as she sauntered to her car. The downside of Tessa getting married a couple of years ago was she thought everyone should be in love. Sometimes love was too elusive, at least in his experience. He had yet to find someone who gave him that nudge to fall—and fall hard.

He stared at the computer screen but found he couldn't concentrate. He picked up the bottle of wine from his desk and placed it in a bottom drawer. Maybe once the job was done, he could ask Steph out for drinks. He sure as heck wasn't about to expose her to Crescent Lake Winery. People never understood why he hadn't gone into the family business like the rest of his siblings, but then again people didn't understand the power of a great vintage car.

He dropped his cell in his shirt pocket and walked from the office into the shop. He picked up a wrench and stood in front of the engine stand. He wasn't in the mood to work so he dropped the wrench in its toolbox and placed a quick call.

After the third ring, a man answered. "Hello, Jonesy's Salvage."

"Hi, this is Leo. We talked last week about that Mustang you dug out of the barn over at Seymour's place. Are you looking to part with it?" Not that he needed two cars to work on, but he'd keep one and sell the other.

"Yeah. Wanna come over and take a look before you make me an offer?"

"I can be there in fifteen minutes."

"Anytime today is fine."

"Thanks, Jonesy. I'll catch you later." Leo slipped his phone into his back pocket. What the heck was he doing, thinking of taking on another project? He needed a distraction, and there was also a strong market for a vintage muscle car.

He went to his safe and withdrew cash to pay Jonesy. He'd accept any offer that was fair.

His cell beeped and he looked at the message.

Met your sister today. She's nice. Good wine. S-

Should he respond? He debated, then sent back, *I heard you bought some wine–good stuff*

He hit send and waited for a response. Nothing. He grabbed the flatbed keys and tried not to wonder why she had texted him.

*S*tephanie had her feet propped up on the desk as she looked at her phone. She couldn't ask him to join her for a glass of wine when he was otherwise attached. That was her problem. She always was attracted to men who were already in a relationship. The last time, she almost hadn't survived the heartbreak of finding out she was the other woman. She was not a woman who would ever knowingly come between a family.

Maybe he was divorced. He didn't wear a wedding ring. There wasn't even a tell-tale sign he had ever worn one and there were no pictures in his office; the desk had a phone, a few notepads and pens, and a computer.

She dropped her feet to the tile floor and closed her laptop. She could just as easily start reviewing the finances from three years ago at home, where she could put on comfy clothes and open one of the bottles of wine she had bought today.

"Val," she called down the hall.

Stuffing her notebook and laptop into her messenger bag, she looked up when Val popped in.

"What's up?" She cocked her head. "You look a little better this afternoon. Anything interesting happen?"

Stephanie leaned against the edge of the desk. "I was pleasantly surprised when I went by Vintage today. Leo's a damn good body man."

Val gave a small laugh. "Yeah, he does have a good body."

She could feel the instant heat flush her face. "That's not what I said and you know it."

"Hon, while you're here, you should have some fun and not spend all your time working."

"You don't need to worry about me. Besides, I got the impression he was otherwise committed."

"Meaning he's married?"

"He has two boys. He's either off-limits or things are complicated." She shrugged one shoulder. "It's not a big deal."

"In my experience, things aren't always what they appear. Don't close that door until you know for sure." Val gave her a broad smile. "Have a good night, hon. I'll see you tomorrow."

"You too, Val, and thanks for your hard work, helping to keep everything running smoothly."

"My pleasure."

The older woman hurried down the hall and Steph waited until she heard the door bang shut. She'd lock up and then head for home and tomorrow, she'd give some thought to the Leo situation.

6

It had been two weeks since the funeral, and Steph had still been meaning to look at Dad's financial records. In some weird way, it felt like she was invading his privacy, but she had to get over that. She couldn't run the business properly if she was in the dark. Today, though, was the day. With a glass of wine at her elbow to fortify herself if she needed it, she scanned the accounting files, determined to ferret out the problem. And there it was. Supplies for the shop seemed high. She opened an Excel document that Dad had used to track jobs. Depending on what was listed, she might have to pull each job for the last three years and cross-reference it to the spreadsheet and then the accounts.

She yawned. This would take months of careful scrutiny. She pinched the bridge of her nose and squeezed her eyes tight. Numbers were swimming in her head. She closed the laptop and set it on the sofa next to her. At least her suspicions seemed to be real instead of that vague feeling in her gut.

She sipped the white wine. The house was too quiet. She opened the music app on her phone and selected some soft piano music. At least there was noise. Her stomach growled. Should she call for pizza delivery or see what might be in the freezer?

Deciding she didn't want to see anyone, she padded to the kitchen, the tile floors warm under her bare feet thanks to the radiant heat Dad had installed. She studied the contents of the freezer and selected a pizza. There wasn't much to choose from, so tomorrow she'd need to do something mundane like hit up the grocery store. Her cell phone chirped.

She picked it up. "Hi, Maggie."

"Hey, stranger. I haven't heard from you in a few days and I wanted to check in and see how you're doing."

She sat down on a chair after she turned the oven on to heat. "It's good to hear your voice." She shrugged, not that Maggie could see her. "I'm hanging in there." She could picture Maggie leaning back in her red leather office chair, feet propped on her desk, in front of the biggest computer screen money could buy. She was more than a freelance editor; she was a talented children's book author and illustrator. Editing paid her expenses, and the writing filled her soul.

"Do you want me to come out for a few days? You know I can work anywhere I have internet and electricity."

"That's really sweet, but I need to adjust." The oven beeped and she got up and slid the pizza in, then set the timer and sat back down. She pulled her feet up onto the chair and hugged her legs to her chest.

"If you don't want me to come out now, how about a week or two at the end of the month? You'll have time to get your feet under you, and then you can show me around the garage I've heard so much about."

She thought it would be nice to have Maggie here, but this was a far cry from the city. "The weather isn't as nice as the West Coast. You'll probably be bored to tears." She loved that Maggie wanted to be with her, but it was better for now that she didn't come out, the business needed all her attention.

"Stephanie James, are you trying to discourage me from coming for a visit?"

"Not at all. I figure if you're going to fly across the country, you might as well know what to pack."

Maggie chuckled. "Good point. I'll check my work schedule and let you know."

"We can go to a few wineries while you're here. I stumbled onto one today and ended up buying a case."

"You know I'm a California wine girl. Was it good?"

"I'm telling you I was surprised. They rival what we usually drink. And from what I could tell, there are a few more we should definitely check out."

"Do your research and you can play tour guide."

She studied her red-polished toenails. Although Maggie had often talked about coming when Steph visited her dad, she was a city girl from the tips of her pedicure to her weekly visits to her hairdresser for blowouts. Black River was definitely small town and so not her scene.

"Earth to Stephanie."

"I'm here."

"I can tell by your lack of enthusiasm that something's on your mind. What aren't you telling me?"

"It's nothing." She crossed into the living room to retrieve her glass of wine.

"Well, now I know that something is bugging you. Spill it."

There was a familiar tone in Maggie's voice. The one that said she'd better talk or Maggie would be on the next plane to the great state of New York.

She sipped wine and walked back into the kitchen. Maggie had the patience of a saint, so there was no avoiding the question.

"I think there's something off with Dad's business. I've been going over the books and based on the work he has been taking in, his profit margin has been slowly shrinking. Four years ago, everything was great. He was socking money away, reinvesting in the business, and then the cost of supplies seemed to go up."

"Is that normal? Everything goes up and down."

"Not like this. I have to dig into each job, cross-reference that with the supply list, and I'm even going to dig into who handled the work. There has to be a reasonable explanation. Most of the people have worked here for years. Dad wouldn't have kept someone on if they couldn't do the job."

Maggie sucked in a breath. "Could someone be skimming cash? Aren't the employees all long-term?"

"We've hired a few new ones in the last year or two. She frowned into the phone. "No one has access except for a couple of people, and I can't imagine one of them would do something like that. Most of these people have been with Dad for years."

"One thing you're really good at is numbers. Give yourself some time to cope with all you have going on and remember you eat an elephant one bite at a time."

She laughed. "Do you remember that time you gave me that solid chocolate elephant? It had to stand, what? A foot tall?"

Maggie laughed. "I do. You were struggling with some paper you were writing for economics or history—"

"It was Eighteenth Century World History. What a snoozefest."

"Anyway, you got so down on yourself, saying you had no idea how you were ever going to finish the paper, and you came across that picture of the elephant in National Geographic. You taped it to the wall."

"And then you went and somehow managed to find

that chocolate one and gave it to me as encouragement to keep my butt in the chair and write the darn paper." She smiled at the memory. "And you told me it was one word or one sentence at a time, just like eating the chocolate."

"You never finished the elephant, but you did finish your paper."

The timer went off on the oven and Steph used tongs to check if the bottom of the pizza was dark brown. She loved crunchy crust, even on a frozen pizza. "I couldn't have done it without your push."

"Eh, you would have figured it out eventually. But it gave us a fun memory."

She set the pizza on the counter. "I'm going to let you go. Dinner is done and it's been a long day."

"Be looking for my email and we'll firm up plans."

"Sounds good, Mags. I'm glad you called tonight."

"Alright, I need to get back to work anyway but remember I'm always just a speed dial button away, you know?"

"Yeah, I do." Stephanie took a plate out of the cupboard and set it on the counter and then put the cutting board next to it. "We'll talk soon."

"Take care, Steph. Miss you."

"I'll talk to you soon." She set the phone aside and proceeded to cut the pizza. It would fill the emptiness in her belly but tomorrow, she really did need to buy food.

*

*L*eo backed the flatbed truck up to his shop's double doors. Loaded on the back was a barely recognizable Ford Mustang, circa early 1970. It had taken a couple of weeks to pick it up, but he was excited, as it was the Boss edition and he could already see it restored. Could this be the second in his personal collection of muscle cars? It had potential. Once the truck was close to the open bay doors, he made short work of unloading it. Double-checking to make sure the building was locked up, it was time to call it a day. He climbed into the driver's seat of his pickup.

Not ready to go home, he called Liza. Maybe she'd take pity on him and he could join them for dinner.

She answered on the second ring, sounding frazzled.

"Hey, sis. Everything okay over there?"

"Just the usual after school, before dinner madness. What's up?"

"Okay if I swing by?" He mindlessly tapped the steering wheel with his thumb.

"Sure. Feel like handling the grill? I've got some chicken and pasta salad. You're welcome to stay unless you have other plans."

He could hear the leading question in her voice. "Nope, nothing going on here. I'll be over soon." He disconnected and dropped his phone in the console. Maybe he'd swing by and pick up some ice cream on the way. The boys might just be enticed to actually eat their dinner without too much bellyaching.

*B*efore Leo could get out of the truck, Johnny and George came running at full speed around the side of the house.

"Uncle Leo!" Johnny was jumping up and down. "A bunch of bees moved into our tree house and Mom can't help. Remember she's allergic."

Leo grabbed the bag with the ice cream and handed it to George. "Run this in the house and ask Mom if she has any spray. I'll go with your brother to take a look."

George took off at a run and Leo shook his head. Did

these boys ever just walk? "Come on. Let's take a look at your fort."

Johnny looked up and squinted. "Uncle Leo, what would happen to Mom if she got stung? Would she die?"

There was no way he was going to scare Johnny. "Mom keeps her EpiPen handy. You know that, right? And you know where it is too and how to call 9-1-1 if she needs help."

His voice quivered and his chin met his chest. "I know, I just get scared sometimes, like what if something bad happens to her?"

Leo stopped and knelt down and tipped his chin up to look him in the eye. This was more than just about the bee sting. The boys had lost their dad and Liza was everything to them. His heart broke for the boys. "Mom knows exactly what to do if she gets stung, and I'm the bee slayer for Mom. Buddy, you and me are going to investigate."

The boy nodded, his face solemn. Leo stood up. "Ready?"

Johnny said, "Ready."

They strode around the garage, Leo matching his stride to Johnny's. As they drew close to the fort tucked into a stand of sparse trees, he could hear the distinct drone of bees. He and Johnny slowed their steps. His nephew looked up.

"Can you hear them?" Excitement mixed with fear tinged his voice.

"I can." The boys had never been stung and who knew if they had inherited his sister's allergy. "You stay here and I'll check it out." He approached the fort with caution. It sounded as if it was a big hive. Well, maybe that was an overestimation. He eased open the slatted wood door. In the corner was a large hive with hundreds of wasps buzzing around it. His heart thudded in his chest. Thankfully Liza hadn't come out.

He gently closed the door and pointed to the house. "Let's go inside and talk to Mom."

George came out the back door and jumped off the edge of the deck, holding a can of spray in his hands.

There was no way that little can would do anything but rile them up. Leo stopped George. "We're going inside. This job needs experts."

The three of them went into the kitchen. "Hey, sis."

"I hear you've been to the fort. What did you find?"

"That you'll need to call an exterminator. There is no way we should attempt to take care of that wasp nest. It's huge."

"Boys, I want you to stay inside for tonight and I'll call someone tomorrow. Until it's taken care of, you stay clear of it. Understood?"

"Sure thing, Mom," Johnny answered for them. They raced into the family room, leaving the adults.

Liza turned to Leo, crossed her arms over her chest, and leaned against the counter. "Tessa tells me she met a friend of yours and she happens to be very pretty and in the same business as you."

He dropped his head, frustrated. "You too?"

She grinned. "I heard from two other sources that she is pretty."

"She is." He was going to have to chat with his nephews about the bro code.

She beamed. "Ah, so you *do* like her?"

7

A couple of days later, Leo stopped at Liza's to check on the wasp nest. After he confirmed the fort was wasp free, it was time to either talk to the boys or forget they had told their mom about their encounter with Stephanie. He was on his way in his sister's back door when he decided to just leave it alone.

"Anyone home?" His voice echoed in the kitchen. Liza's minivan was in the driveway, so they were here somewhere. "Liza?"

A muffled response that sounded like "In here" came from the front of the house. He strode through the kitchen into the hall and noticed an old set of folding wooden stairs were dangling from a hole in the ceiling. It was being held in place with one bolt. His sister was standing on a six-foot metal ladder with sneaker-clad feet dangling in her face as she looked up through the ceiling.

"What's going on?" He came closer to get a better look.

"The boys were helping me get stuff down from the attic and they discovered this old access. We never fixed the stairs because we just don't use this entry anymore. George decided that since this was closer than the new doors, he'd take a shortcut down this way and now he's stuck and I'm not even sure what it is."

Assessing the situation, Leo said, "I'll go upstairs and pull him back while you wait here." He glanced around. "Where's Johnny?"

"He's on the other side, trying to unhook George's shirt from whatever it's stuck on."

Leo didn't like the sound of that. He rushed through the house and took the new attic stairs as quickly as possible. He found Johnny crouched next to George, whose shirt was acting like a lasso around a thick wooden peg in one of the rafters. John was trying to pull George's shirt off over his head. He could see once George took the shirt off Liza could get him down.

Reaching his nephews, he knelt down. "Hey, guys. Whatcha doing? Just hanging around?"

"Not funny, Uncle Leo." George looked at him. "My shirt is caught and Johnny can't get it undone." The neck of the t-shirt appeared to be cutting into his throat; his voice was strained and his face was a deepening shade of red.

Leo grabbed the fabric and was ready to just tear it loose when George said, "Wait!"

"Buddy, I need to rip the shirt."

"No, you can't."

"I'll get you another one."

"Uncle Leo"—his voice had a distinct wail to it—"please don't tear it."

"It's just a shirt."

Johnny put a hand on Leo's arm. "No. Please?"

Now was not the time to debate it, but it was clear he couldn't rip the shirt. "Johnny, how about you go on the other side of George and we'll take his shirt off over his head, one arm at a time." He leaned toward the small opening so he could tell Liza the plan.

"Alright, now George, I'm going to ease the shirt off

over your arm, so you'll have to push up from the opening."

George clung to the wooden trim around the old opening. His fingers, Leo thought, looked too small to hold up a kid as energetic and always in motion as George was.

"After I get one arm out, then I can do the same on the other side and other than maybe getting a scrape, you'll be able to let Mom take your weight or I can pull you up this way."

"Pull me up. I don't want to fall on Mom."

The concern in his voice made Leo proud.

"Thank you, George, but I've got you, you can always count on me."

With quick movements, the shirt was off and George had his feet firmly planted on the attic floor. The boys wrapped their arms around Leo and mumbled thanks.

He ushered them to the new stairs. "Be careful going down."

Johnny went first with George following at a slower pace. George's shirt slung over his shoulder, Leo followed them. He'd check out the other access and fix it so this wouldn't happen again.

Liza was hugging her sons when his feet hit the floor.

"Would someone mind telling me what possessed you to try and go through the little trap door? Shortcuts aren't always the easiest path."

The boys shrugged, looked at the floor, and muttered, "I dunno."

Liza gave a shake of her head like she didn't want to get on their case. The look of relief in her eyes said it all.

He placed one hand on one shoulder of each boy trying not to think about what might have happened if he hadn't stopped over. "Do me a favor. The next time you want to explore, give me a call and we'll do it together. Okay?"

Two sets of eyes rose to meet his. "You're not mad?"

"No, I'm not. However, I would like you to think before you jump into something that you don't know what the consequences will be." Johnny furrowed his brow. "Do you understand what I'm trying to say?"

They shook their heads.

"Sometimes you might get into big trouble or get hurt by doing something risky."

"You mean like coming down through the hole with a broken ladder?" Johnny asked.

"Exactly." He ruffled their hair. "Toss this shirt into the laundry and put on a clean one. We'll go get ice cream."

"Yeah!" The boys ran out of the room toward their bedrooms.

"Next weekend I'll come over and close that hole off." He pointed in the direction of the broken ladder and hole in the ceiling. He waited until the boys were upstairs, then he turned to Liza. "What's the story with the shirt?"

"Steven bought it for Johnny when he was going through his dinosaur phase and even though it's too small for George, he keeps wearing it."

"Ah, now it makes sense. Well, I'm glad it didn't get ruined."

Liza grinned. "Can I come for ice cream too, or are you just interested in spoiling the boys?"

"Isn't that what uncles are for?" He wiped a streak of dirt from her cheek and grinned. "Go wash your face. Looks like the bottom of George's sneakers were dirty."

Tired of looking at endless columns of numbers over the last week, Stephanie stretched her arms above her head and squinted at her watch. Her stomach grumbled, reminding her lunch was a distant memory—if she could call a handful of nuts and a banana a meal. The sun streaming in her window and the deep azure sky reminded her of the days when Dad would take her to this ice cream place on the way to Crescent Lake. It had the best homemade ice cream. She would always order a chocolate shake, and it had been so thick, she'd get a brain freeze on the first sip.

She put her laptop aside. The place was still in business; she had noticed it when she drove out to Leo's garage. It couldn't be that crowded at this time of day.

After a quick look in the mirror, she decided she was presentable to the world. She hurried out the door, spreadsheets forgotten in the glory of escaping for a little while. With the windows down, she drove slowly. This was nothing like driving on the West Coast which was full of fog and clouds and rain and not the gorgeous sunshine like today. She had forgotten how much she loved this place. The peaceful feeling she woke with each day was definitely a contributing factor to the smile on her face. Despite what had brought her home, the loneliness was bearable when she did things like this.

She flicked on her blinker and slowed, then turned into the ice cream stand's gravel lot. Just as she thought, there weren't too many cars in the parking area. A couple of minivans and a dark truck, and she noted a bunch of kids hanging out around the picnic tables. She'd grab her shake and sit in her Bronco. No sense in trying to mingle with mothers and their kids.

She hopped out, leaving it unlocked, and strolled to the small white building. It now had deep-purple trim instead of the pink and red she remembered. She stood in line behind a group of high schoolers, a family in front of them.

One of the boys in the group said, "Ma'am."

Inwardly, she cringed. Was she old enough to be called Ma'am?

She gave him a bright smile. "Hello."

One of the boys in the group looked at her left ear and said, "You can go ahead of us."

The boy's voice cracked with what she guessed was oncoming puberty. "I don't mind waiting." She continued to smile. He was a very polite kid.

The boy and his friends moved aside to let her pass. "Really, it's okay."

She took a step forward and stuck her hands into her jeans. She looked around and was taken aback when the boys in front of her turned and grinned. She instantly recognized Johnny, the mini whirlwind who had toppled her model display.

"Hi. You're the lady with the cool model cars." George nudged the woman in front of him. "Hey, Mom. This is the lady who bandaged up Johnny."

The woman turned. She was so pretty. She had smartly styled shoulder-length blond hair and hazel eyes with deep-gold flecks. A smile instantly splashed across her face. She extended her hand. "Hi. It's nice to meet you."

Before she could answer, the man standing next to her finished paying the perky teenaged girl working the counter and turned. She sucked in a shallow breath.

"Stephanie. What brings you out for ice cream?" Leo's smile warmed his dark-brown eyes.

She stammered and pulled her gaze back to the boys' mother. "It's nice to meet you too."

Leo passed the boys single scoop chocolate cones with rainbow sprinkles. He handed a vanilla cone to the woman.

"This is Liza and, I'm sure you've guessed by now, the mother to these two angels." She could hear the laughter in his voice.

She smiled hello. This was interesting—Leo, his boys, and their mother. His wife or girlfriend? "Um, well, I've been looking at spreadsheets most of the afternoon and decided I needed a reward for slaving away over numbers, and here I am."

Leo and Liza told the boys to grab a picnic table. They raced at full speed, trying to see who would get there first.

She couldn't help but grin. "Do they always have that much energy?"

Liza laughed. "I swear they get it from Leo. He has more than enough for three people." She took a step away from the line. "Come sit with us." Liza followed the boys to the table, leaving Leo standing with her.

With a shake of her head, she said, "No, I wouldn't want to intrude." She leaned in and ordered her chocolate shake.

"Good choice."

It was then she noticed Leo was holding a milkshake cup. She really wanted him to go and join his family.

"Will you come sit?"

"No, thank you. I'm just going to take it home and get back to work."

"Liza will kill me if you leave. I think she really wants to thank you for not being angry with the boys about the model."

Her heart skipped in her chest. She really didn't want to sit with this happy little family. Especially now that it really did burst her bubble about Leo being involved with someone else, with kids to boot.

He gave her that killer smile and handed the girl money for her shake and passed the drink to Steph. "Please, just for a few minutes. You might just discover the boys aren't completely wild. They actually sit still while they eat."

Hesitating again, she relented. "I guess I can spare a few minutes." She fell into step as they walked toward Liza and the boys, who were currently sitting in one spot, talking about the best parts of eating a cone. "Oh wait, I need to pay."

Leo gave her a side-glance. "It's all set."

She dipped her head. "Thank you."

Johnny's face lit up as she sat down next to him. "Hey, what did you get?"

"A chocolate milkshake." She deliberately slurped the drink.

He laughed loudly. "Is that your favorite?"

"It is. When I was your age, my dad used to bring me here as a treat."

Johnny looked around the parking lot. "He's not here now."

Chocolate ice cream dripped onto the table. She wiped it with a napkin, willing herself not to tear up again. "No, he's not."

"He's going to be sorry he missed it."

The vise tightened around her chest.

Leo said, "Hey, John, Stephanie's dad went to heaven."

Why on earth would he say that to a child? He looked at her with big, solemn eyes, wise beyond his years. "My dad is in heaven too." He perked up a little. "Maybe they're friends now and they can have ice cream together like we are."

She looked from Leo to Liza. They weren't married. But they were close. It was obvious.

He licked another drip before it leaked from the bottom of the cone. "Right, Uncle Leo? Don't you think my dad and Steph's dad are friends now?"

"I'll bet they are, kiddo." Over the boy's head, he gave her a small lopsided smile as if to apologize for Johnny being so matter-of-fact.

She took a deep breath and exhaled. Uncle Leo.

8

This was a nice turn of events. But did that mean Leo was completely single? He was a doting uncle and a good brother. Admirable qualities in a man.

"Is that model we broke okay?" The way George chomped on his cone caused melted ice cream to land on the front of his t-shirt. It left a nice drip of brown down the center.

She liked how he hadn't singled out his big brother even though she suspected it had been a solo caper until the crash.

"I had to order a couple of replacement parts, but it's easy to fix." She sipped her shake.

She could feel Leo watching her talk with the boys. "I could repair it for you," he said.

She gave him a smile. "It's fine." What she didn't say was she and Dad had built it after they finished the restoration of her full-size Bronco about twenty years ago. To let someone else help her would somehow diminish the memory of time spent with him. "It'll give me something to do when I need to escape my computer work."

Johnny finished his cone and shoulder-checked George. "Wanna go play on the monkey bars?" He pointed to the small fenced-in space with a few swings, a slide, and a jungle gym, complete with the bars.

Liza stood up and chimed in. "I'll go with you, just to make sure you don't get into trouble."

"Mom," George groaned. "If we fall, it's all cushioned under us."

Liza smiled at Leo. "Take your time."

Stephanie marveled at the boys' energy. They were already swinging from bar to bar and the sounds of their laughter gave her an unexpected jolt of emptiness. Would she ever be lucky enough to have kids? "They're fearless, aren't they?"

Leo grimaced. "Pretty much. From the minute their feet hit the floor until Liza informs them it's bedtime, and even then, they still resist. I do what I can to be an involved uncle and role model, but they're determined to explore the world until their heads hit the pillows."

"I envy kids. The energy, the joy in simple pleasures like an ice cream cone, and then sound sleep." She gave a short laugh. "It's all wasted on the youth."

"I hear ya. But I'll have to admit I try to take a page from their book occasionally. Like now."

"What do you mean?" She turned on the wooden bench and looked at him. His chiseled features, strong jawline, and deep-brown eyes were just as she remembered. Her heart quickened. He really did make her long for something more. But she had a full and happy life in Portland, and with Dad gone, this was no longer her home.

"Spending time with the kids, not just Johnny and George but all my nephews and nieces, reminds me to treasure the moment I'm in. Like right now."

His words were sweet. She could feel the heat rise in her cheeks. "Eating ice cream?"

"No. Being here, with you."

Her mouth opened, but she had no words.

"I know you said you wanted to wait until our business together was over, but treasuring the moment makes me want to ask you to have dinner, or lunch, or even coffee with me. Would you reconsider?"

She stuttered, "You want to go out with me?"

He gave her that charmingly lopsided smile of his. "Yes."

"I'm not sure." She wanted to say yes, but why should she start something when she was leaving in October?

"I'm sorry if I'm overstepping but if you're seeing someone or is it because we're still working together?"

"No, it's not that. I'm going home to Portland. Once I get the business on firm footing and I think I can run it from there."

"Don't you want to have some fun while you're here instead of being all business?" His hand accidently touched hers as they reached for a paper napkin. A shiver of excitement flowed through her.

Pushing aside her reaction to his touch, she said, "I guess we could have lunch."

Leo sat up a little straighter. "How's Saturday? If you don't have other plans already."

"That sounds nice. Do you want me to meet you someplace closer to Crescent Lake?"

"How about going to O's Diner out near you? The food is great and it will give us the opportunity to get to know each other." He grinned. "And rumor has it they have amazing milkshakes."

"Do you think the way to my heart is with a chocolate shake?"

"So, there is a way to your heart?" He chuckled low and sexy. "I'll remember that."

"I guess you'll just have to find out." She looked him

directly in the eye. "What is your weakness?" She wasn't the kind of woman who usually flirted when there was no future, but something about Leo kept her wanting to get to know him better. He reminded her of Dad in some ways and for now, it helped her miss him less.

"A beautiful woman who knows what a wrench is and how to use it." His look challenged her to deny her ability under the hood of a car.

It had been a long time since she had a wrench in her hands. That was a different life. She finished her shake with one final and definitely unladylike slurp. "I have to get back to the office. There is a spreadsheet calling my name." She stood up and brushed off the seat of her jeans. "What time should I meet you at the diner?"

"I'll pick you up around twelve thirty."

Did she want him to know her home address yet? "I'll be at the garage. Would you mind picking me up there?"

"Not at all. I'll shoot you a text when I park."

"Perfect." She stuck out her hand. Why the heck did she do that? This wasn't business. It was personal.

Leo clasped it and applied a slight amount of pressure. "I'll see you Saturday."

She stared at him, dumbfounded by the desire to press her lips to his. She nodded. "Okay." It sounded lame to her ears.

He held her hand for another moment and then released her. She gave him a small smile, glanced at the ground, and tossed her cup in the trash can, aware of his eyes following her. With a quick adjustment to her ballcap, she slid behind the wheel. In the rearview mirror, she saw him wave. She smiled to herself and, without looking back, lifted her arm in acknowledgement. The weekend was definitely looking up.

eo watched as the blue Bronco drove out of sight. He joined Liza and the boys in the play area, where his sister was beaming.

"I like her. Did you ask her out?"

Feeling pleased Steph had said yes, he grinned back. "As a matter of fact, I did. We're going to have lunch on Saturday."

"Really?"

He narrowed his eyes. "Why are you so excited?"

She glanced at the boys and said, "I like her. Tessa said she was really nice and I just have a feeling she'd be good for you."

"Stephanie in particular or just any girl I wanted to date?"

"Maybe anyone, but I do like her, and she is so sweet with the boys." Liza cringed and called out for George to stop horsing around before turning her attention back to Leo. "It's been a long time since I saw that smile you had plastered on your face earlier."

He knew what she was talking about. He could feel the difference, the way his insides reacted to Stephanie and how her eyes danced when she talked with him. And Liza was right; she did have a way with the boys.

"Where are you taking her?"

"O's Diner on Old Route Eight. It's closer to Black River and I thought—"

"A diner for a first date? Are you crazy?" Liza shook her head from side to side. "That's an awful idea."

"Are you saying that because you wouldn't want to go there? What would you consider a first date?"

"A bistro, a picnic, or dinner."

"That's your style, sis, not mine. The food there is exceptional, it's low-key, and we can just relax and get to know each other."

"How did Stephanie react? Like it was a good idea or just meh?"

He replayed the conversation and her reaction. "She's cool with it. It'll be fine." But had she just gone along with it to be nice? Damn Liza for planting that seed of doubt.

"You could take her to lunch at CLW. We know she likes wine, so it would suit."

"No." He shook his head. "There is no way I'm going to take a first date to our family's winery so I can have an audience and have to introduce her to everyone who happens to just walk by. Not going to happen."

She crossed her arms over her midsection. "I guess you're right. That would be way too much to handle without warning. And besides, I wouldn't want her scared off."

Leo chuckled. "The family can be a bit overwhelming. There are certainly enough of us. Five brothers and sisters, spouses, and kids."

Liza glanced at her watch. "We need to get home. The boys have showers and homework before dinner."

"Sorry about the ice cream treat. I guess I forgot it would change your routine."

She touched his arm. "Sometimes change is good for us all." She called the boys to get in the truck. "Leo, I want you to be happy. Find someone who makes you feel like you can conquer anything as long as she's by your side. Like Mom and Dad."

"They are excellent role models and something to aspire to."

The boys came rushing over and Johnny looked around. "Uncle Leo, where's Stephanie?"

He placed a hand on Johnny's shoulder and turned him in the direction of the truck. "She had to leave."

George fell into step with his brother. "You should ask her to come over. We can cook out, right, Mom?"

"Boys, let Uncle Leo make his own plans with Stephanie." She glanced his way. "It goes without saying she's welcome anytime." Liza climbed in the passenger seat and buckled her seat belt.

Leo opened the back door of the truck and the kids hopped in. He hovered in the open doorway. "Why do you like her so much?"

"Uncle Leo." He could hear the exasperation in Johnny's voice. "She's super cool. She didn't get mad when I broke her model car and she drives a super cool Jeep."

"Bronco, actually." He held back a grin when Johnny put the emphasis on *super*.

George pointed out, "She didn't even yell at us when all the models crashed on the floor. We like her."

"She's nice like Aunt Peyton and Aunt Kate," Johnny added.

"I guess that sums it up." He pointed to the seat belts. "Buckle up."

"Mom, can we have dinner when we get home? We're starving."

She sighed. "Showers first and I'll cook."

Leo closed the door and started the truck. "Before you ask, I'm going to head home."

"Why rush off?"

"I need to source some parts for the new Mustang I picked up the other day."

"I didn't know you had a new job."

"Once I finish with Drew Cameron's car, I'll have some time, and the price was right."

"Will you sell it?"

"More than likely. That year is in hot demand."

She gave him a knowing smile.

"It's nice to know that after all these years, you remember something about what I do."

She gave a playful punch to his arm. "I'll bet Stephanie will be interested in your project too."

With a chuckle, he said, "Who knows? Maybe."

9

Stephanie stood in her father's office on Saturday, arms folded across her chest while she looked out the window over the back parking lot. Why on earth did they need to order that much primer? Even stranger was that the inventory didn't match the invoice and they were short. She made a note to have Val check to see if either they ordered too much and didn't receive the product or if it was a mistake from the supplier. On Monday, she'd tackle a full inventory to see if things matched up with current open orders.

Her cell phone pinged with an incoming text. She smiled as she read it. Leo was ten minutes early. She sent him a reply saying she'd be right out. A quick glance in her compact showed her makeup was flawless. She was pleased that she had chosen slim-fitting jeans and a silk print sleeveless blouse under a hot-pink cardigan sweater. Comfortable and cute, part Portland Steph and part New York Steph.

After she checked to make sure she had both sets of keys, one for her Bronco and the other for the shop, she stepped outside and secured the door. She could see in the glass Leo was leaning against what looked like a white… could that be a GTO with deep-red pinstripes down the sides, or was the reflection distorted? To quiet her nerves, she took a deep breath and focused on the man, not the machine. "Hello there."

He was casually dressed too, in dark-washed jeans and a black t-shirt which showed off his toned biceps and chest muscles. She'd bet there was a six-pack under the shirt. She smiled when she saw he was wearing black sneakers. So far, she had noticed he wore only work boots.

He straightened and smiled that cockeyed way that made her heart flip unexpectedly. "You look great."

"Thank you."

"I hope you're hungry. The diner serves huge portions." He walked her around the passenger side and held the door for her. She appreciated the sweet gesture.

"One thing about me: I'm always hungry."

He closed the door after her and came around the front. After he got in, he turned the ignition and the car started with a low rumble. She loved the sound of a finely tuned machine. But she wasn't about to say that; she still wasn't sure how much she wanted to reveal about herself. Over lunch, she'd decide if she wanted to share more.

"You're not a pick-at-a-salad kind of girl, are you?" He dropped the car in first gear and eased out of the lot. He moved through the gears as he picked up speed.

"Definitely not. Everyone eats; why pretend you don't?" She looked around the interior. "Nice wheels."

"Thanks. I restored this last year. I'm thinking of selling it since I just picked up another Mustang, a fastback."

"Do you only buy, restore, and sell, or do you keep anything just for you?"

"So far I haven't found one car I have to keep forever."

Again, she held back asking questions about the car, which she normally would. Part of her knew it was stupid, but the other side of her brain knew most men got weird when they found out she actually loved working on cars. Even though he had said he found a woman who could handle a wrench attractive, most men were intrigued only until they knew it was a reality. Taking a breath, she asked, "Do you eat at the diner often?"

"Every couple of months I like to stop in. The burgers are thick and juicy, and the French fries have just the right amount of crisp and salt. And they happen to be fresh cut on premises."

She cocked an eyebrow and laughed. "Sounds like the perfect addition to a frosty shake."

It didn't take long before Leo downshifted and eased into the gravel parking lot. The shiny metal-front diner was typical. The long, low-slung fifties-style facade had a bright-red neon sign centered over the entrance.

"I've never eaten here before but I've driven by a few times." Stephanie got out of the car and closed the door. "I thought this was only a breakfast place."

"It was, but about five years ago, it changed hands and the new owners reinvented the joint." Leo waited as she came around to the front of the car. They walked to the door, which he held for her.

"Thank you." She flashed him a smile. So far, the date wasn't exactly scintillating and if he suspected she was holding back, well, she needed to change things up.

The sign on the podium told them to take a seat. She pointed to an empty booth toward the back. "How's that?"

With a sweep of his arm, he said, "Lead the way."

Once they settled in, the waitress came over and took their order. Stephanie said, "It was nice meeting your sister the other day. She seems really nice."

"Liza's great. She's younger than me by about a minute."

"I didn't realize you were a twin."

"We're the youngest of six. Two older brothers and sisters, and then Liza and I rounded out the crew."

"I've met Tessa—and you have another sister?"

"Anna. She works at the winery and she's getting married in August. The wedding plans are in full swing. In fact, the Chevelle I'm working on is going to be their car for the day, a gift from the car's owner, who's a friend of my future brother-in-law, Colin."

"That's nice." This was when she missed having family. "How many nephews do you have?"

"Including the two monkeys you met, five. Well, with all these boys, we finally had our first two girls. My brother Don and his wife Kate gave us a set of twins, one of each, and Jack, our middle brother, and his wife Peyton had a baby girl, too and they also have the fifth boy."

His face softened. He really was a softie. "Must be hectic for holidays."

"And loud." The waitress approached the table with a large tray. She set a chocolate milkshake in front of Stephanie, and Leo had vanilla. When she placed two over-flowing platters in front of them, Stephanie gasped.

"When you said huge, you weren't kidding." She picked up the ketchup bottle and liberally coated the stack of fries, then added some on her burger and passed the bottle to Leo.

He grinned and followed suit. "Dig in."

O ver lunch, they talked about sports they had played in school and places they had traveled. He was thoroughly enjoying how she attacked her burger and how she laughed when its juices trailed down her arm. She was completely natural and easygoing. Her eyes sparkled with mischief as he teased her.

"I'm really glad you asked me to lunch. I haven't done much of anything since I came home."

He dipped his gaze. He felt like a jerk, reminding her of why she had to come back. "How long have you been home?" He wondered if she'd had the opportunity to see her father before he passed.

As if sensing his real question, she said, "We had some time together before he died. It was after that I asked for an extended leave from work."

He placed his hands over hers. "I really am sorry. I had the pleasure of meeting him a few times and he was a good man."

"He was." She gestured between the two of them. "He would be happy we were having lunch together."

He pushed the last of his fries to the side of the platter and dropped his napkin on the plate. "Do you mind if I ask you a question?"

"Sure." She toyed with a French fry and the ketchup.

"Did you rebuild the Bronco with your dad?"

"The model or the real thing?"

He folded his hands on the tabletop. "I already know about the model, but I would like to know about the real one."

"What makes you think I know the difference between a carburetor and a starter?"

"Just a hunch—you looked pretty comfortable at my shop."

She waited for a half beat. "Being an only child and motherless, I spent a lot of time following Dad around. It was only natural to learn from him. He certainly wasn't into sewing or shopping."

He grinned. A woman who was passionate about classic cars was rare; she appreciated more than just the look of them "I knew it."

She gave him a challenging smile. "How?"

"I saw how you held back when you laid eyes on my car today. You had a ton of questions you were dying to ask."

She leaned forward and a slow sexy grin slid over her face. "And now that you know the truth?"

He leaned closer to her. "Bring them on."

The waitress had brought pie and coffee and placed the check on the table. They continued to talk through the process of the detailing on the Chevelle when she came back.

"Excuse me." She was dressed in street clothes. "Would you mind cashing out? I'm at the end of my shift."

Stephanie looked at her watch. "Leo, it's almost five."

He pulled out his wallet and withdrew some bills. "Keep the change."

The waitress glanced at the cash and smiled. "Thank you. Come again."

Stephanie's cheeks were flushed pink. "I can't believe we've been here for hours."

"I can't remember the last time I sat and just talked." He slid from the booth and she got up. "Ready?"

"Any chance you're too tired to drive?"

He didn't give her ability to handle a stick a second thought. He pulled the keys out of his pocket and handed them to her. "Don't scratch the paint."

She winked. "If I do, I know a place that can fix it."

He had never ridden shotgun in one of his cars and suspected he was in for a treat.

She flashed him a saucy grin. "Buckle up."

She rolled her window down, turned the key, and revved the engine. The thrill of the power under her hands was heady. She was happy Leo trusted her to drive his car. The gears moved smoothly as she dropped it into first. If felt good but there was a flash of nostalgia. The last time she'd driven a muscle car, Dad had been sitting next to her. Kicking up a few stones, she pulled from the lot and then flew through the gears until they were cruising just over the speed limit down a little-traveled county road. The wind was teasing her hair as she drove. This felt good. She snuck a look at Leo from the corner of her eye. He was relaxed, his arm resting in the open window, sunglasses in place as if they had done this before.

He pointed to the left. "Turn here and you'll have a nice open stretch with little traffic."

She slowed to second and took the turn, the car hugging the curve. She opened it up and grinned. This was a great car and Leo was an amazing guy.

She made a few turns and found her way back to the shop. When she pulled up and parked, she wasn't ready for the date to end. She could ask him to have dinner with her. She turned the car off and left the keys dangling in the ignition.

"Thanks for letting me drive. I'd forgotten how much fun it is."

"You look pretty good over there. What did you say you did for a living?"

"Sales rep."

"Could have fooled me. You belong in this business. It's plain to see you love cars."

"I do but, well, I'm not sure what's going to happen next." She got out of the car, guessing he'd walk her to the door.

She withdrew her shop keys and put them in the lock. "I had a really good time today. Thank you."

He trailed his finger down her forearm and took her hand. "I did too. Any chance we can do it again?"

"I'd like that." She wondered how long before she could see him again.

"I was going to check out a swap meet tomorrow near Syracuse. If you're free, I'd like the company."

"I'd like that. What time?"

"I'll pick you up around nine. But we'll need to take the truck in case I find the parts I'm looking for."

She pulled out her phone. "I'll text you the house address and if you don't mind, you can pick me up there."

He took a step closer. "I'd really like to kiss you."

She leaned in closer. Standing on her tiptoes, she tilted her head to invite him in. "Then kiss me."

He lowered his mouth to hers.

10

The next day was sunny but cool and Stephanie dressed with care. She wore jeans and tennis shoes, a short-sleeved t-shirt, and added a lightweight pale-yellow jacket and, for an extra dash of flair, a cotton print scarf in a rainbow of colors. She pulled her hair off her face in a clip and added a final swish of mascara and lip gloss. She wanted to look pulled together but not out of place at the swap meet. She was excited to go; it had been years since she had been to one with her dad.

Satisfied with her reflection, she hurried into the kitchen and tossed a few pieces of fruit, some cookies, and a couple bottles of frozen water into a tote bag. Her run this morning had been short timewise but long in miles. She had really pushed herself, so the appetite would be revved up soon.

At the honk of a horn, she slung the tote over her shoulder and draped a small crossbody bag over the opposite shoulder. She opened the door just as Leo was ready to knock on it.

"Good morning."

"Hello." He leaned forward, tilted her face up, and

lightly kissed her. He caressed her cheek. "You look fantastic."

"Thanks." She patted the strap on the tote bag. "I brought snacks and some bottled water."

"You didn't need to do that. There's usually all kinds of food vendors."

"I know, but we might get hungry on the road." She gave him a sheepish grin. "I eat a lot."

His gaze roamed from her eyes to her toes. "Where do you put it?"

She pulled the door closed and double-checked to make sure it was locked. "I jog so I can hog."

He chuckled. "Cute." He took the bag from her and put it in the back.

Within minutes, they were cruising down the road. Leo opened the sunroof. "If that's too much, we can close it."

"No, it's good."

He clicked on the radio and turned the volume down.

"What are we looking for today?"

He pulled a list from his shirt pocket and passed it to her. "If I can find a few things, I'll be happy."

She scanned the list and pulled out her phone to take a picture.

He glanced her way. "What did you do that for?"

"If whatever you don't find is critical, I can check our sources for you." She passed it back to him. "Unless you'd rather I didn't."

He gave her a lopsided grin. "Well, that won't give me an excuse to ask you to other swap events."

She felt her smile grow. "Sounds promising. But remember we can always take a road trip to pick something up."

His head bobbed. "True."

He reached for her hand across the console and gave it a squeeze. "I'm glad you wanted to come with me today."

"Well, I'm glad you asked. Dad and I used to go when we could or if he was having trouble finding something specific." She pointed out the window at the cloudless bright-blue sky. "And the weather is perfect. Even with the breeze."

He released her hand and put his on the wheel. "Tell me more about what you do for work in Portland."

"I'm a sales manager for a pharmaceutical company and I have a team of twelve reps under me. I spend more time managing the business than I do making sales calls. You know, tracking sales projection, forecasts, and actual results."

"Sounds like a lot of desk work."

She nodded. "It is, and I interface with the drug companies and marketing department. It's different than the shop; there, I actually interact with people. I like that aspect of BRR. Now that I'm in management, I miss the personal contact with humans."

"Was it hard to get a leave of absence to come out here?"

"I had a lot of PTO built up. With our company, you can just keep rolling it over, so I had a lot of time banked."

"When do you have to go back?"

She looked out the window. "October. I need to get Dad's business on solid ground before I leave. We have some loyal employees and I'd hate to shut it down. I could sell, but what would a new owner do? Destroy the reputation Dad built, bring in his own employees? There are so many details to think about. And I really want to hang on to it." She looked out the window.

"You want to run it?" He glanced her way. "You have the knowledge of both sides of the business."

"That is another possibility. But I have a good life on the West Coast." She looked down at her hands clasped in her lap. Maybe if she had stayed, Dad would have taken better care of his health. "I have moments where I wish I never left Black River." She felt a lump rise in her throat. She wished she could turn back time and change things.

"You're here now and that's all that matters."

Stephanie turned and smiled at him. "Are you always this nice?"

"I make it my mission to be nice to pretty girls riding in my truck going to a swap meet."

She had to wonder how many times he had taken a girl on this same adventure. It didn't matter. This wasn't going to be a lifetime love affair. She would go home in a few months and Leo would find another pretty girl to take to the fairgrounds.

Stephanie grew quiet for the next few miles. Leo wondered what she was thinking about because she had just shared more than she realized—she was torn between staying and leaving. Maybe he could find a way to get her to stay if things seemed to work between them.

"Tell me how Tessa got into the wine business."

She had no idea that was a loaded question. Best to be transparent. "My family owns Crescent Lake Winery, and most of the family works in the business. Up until about three years ago, Tessa handled marketing for the winery. After Don moved back to town and took over the president's office, she made the decision to strike out on her own. Sand Creek was struggling and she took a leap of faith, bought the winery, met her husband, and together they've turned it around."

"Who else works in the family business?" She half turned in the seat. "You're that passionate about cars that you had to strike out on your own?"

It was better to explain that everyone else fit instead of answering her question directly. "The oldest, Don, is president, and his wife Kate owns and operates a bistro. Jack manages the fields and works with Anna; she's our enologist. Peyton, Jack's wife, is in charge of the tasting room, and Liza does event planning and although she doesn't work for the winery exclusively, she's had several weddings at the gazebo."

"Impressive, and you have a gazebo at the winery. That's different."

"A few years ago, someone wanted to get married at the winery, as they had their first date there. So Dad had one built, but it was to Mom's specifications."

Stephanie's eyes grew wide. "All because someone asked?"

He chuckled. "If you knew my mother, she is a romantic down to her toes. She'd do anything for love."

She placed a hand over her heart and smiled. "I think I'd like your mom. She sounds like she has a big heart."

He looked her way. "She'd like you too." Before Steph had to think about what he might mean, he was slowing the truck. "We're here." He pulled into a huge field that was bursting with cars, trucks, and even a few motorcycles.

"Looks like it's rocking." Her eyes were bright. "You should find something to bring home."

He backed the truck into a spot and grinned. "I'm just wondering what treasures you'll find."

"Oh, no worries. I don't have a wish list like you." She hopped out of the truck. "Let's go pokey."

This was going to be a fun day. He locked the truck after leaving the sunroof cracked and they strolled toward the entrance. As far as the eye could see, there were people selling car parts, t-shirts, hats, and of course all types of fair food.

"Doesn't it last four or five days?"

"It opened on Thursday and it will go until tomorrow." As they walked, their hands brushed and they interlaced fingers and continued to stroll. Leo liked the way her hand fit in his; her fingers were strong but soft at the same time. The gentle wind teased her hair as their steps crunched through the sun-dried field.

"Do you want to start on the right or left?" She gazed his way.

"You lead and I'll follow."

Her laugh was musical. She tugged him right down the middle lane. "Let's go this way." She stopped at the first vendor's table. She smiled and said hello. There wasn't much on display other than some newer vanity license plates. She smiled again and thanked him before they moved on.

She did this several more times before Leo said, "Are you going to stop at every vendor?"

"Does it bother you?" She gave him a sunny smile. "I don't need to."

"Just curious." He gave her hand a light squeeze. "You seem intent on looking for something. Care to share?"

"Dad always said you never really know if there is a hidden gem in plain sight at an event like this." With a one-shouldered shrug, she said, "I try to slow down and at least do a quick scan before moving on."

"I've always just breezed in to where I think I'll find what I need and move on." He looked down at her and lightly kissed her. "It's time to change things up."

They continued to stroll up and down row after row of vendors with more tchotchkes than treasures. Stephanie bought a t-shirt that had a picture of a Mustang on it, telling him she was going to wear it in support of his new project.

He slung his arm around her shoulders and steered her toward the food vendors. "Ready for some lunch?"

Just as they began to walk in that direction, Stephanie veered toward a large field filled with all makes and models of vintage cars and trucks.

"Come on," she urged. Her pace quickened.

"What did you see?"

She was on a mission. He lengthened his stride to keep up as she jogged in the direction of an old red pickup truck.

"Steph, what's going on?"

"I know that truck. Dad was working on it before he got sick and he told me he sold it to someone who really wanted it." She gave him an intense look. Her eyes snapped. "I want to know why they're selling it."

"How do you know it's the same one?"

She pointed to the *for sale* sign next to the truck. "That has our shop's logo on it."

How the heck she had seen that from where they had been just minutes before was beyond him.

She pulled away and walked up to a guy in his mid-twenties.

"Excuse me." She looked from the front to back of the truck. Her jaw was set and her mouth showed the bare hint of a smile. "What are you asking for it?"

"Well, hello there." He gave her a lazy grin, like a cat getting ready to lap up cream. He named a sum and she didn't blink.

"How long have you had it?"

"It's been kicking around for a while." He still hadn't figured out his potential customer wasn't being receptive to his charms.

Leo hung back. She could handle this bozo.

"Did you do the work yourself?"

He bobbed his head. "Yup."

She made him an offer that was half of his original price. He balked and said, "I can see you're out of your element here."

Before he could finish, she pointed to the sign. "That's my company's logo. My father sold this Chevy to a collector who just had to have it. I want to buy it back and I happen to know exactly what he was paid for it. So if you could be so kind as to agree to a fair price, I'll take it off your hands."

"Look, lady, I can get twice the price of what you're offering by waiting it out today."

"Maybe, or maybe not. But right now, I'm offering you a fair price. Heck, I'll even bump it by ten percent if you give me that sign and hand over the keys."

"No cash, no deal."

Leo stepped forward. She probably didn't have the cash on her, but he did. He always brought enough just in case there was a deal he couldn't pass up. "She's got the cash. Is it a deal or not?"

The seller stuck out his hand. "Lady, you got yourself an old truck."

Leo placed his hand on her shoulder and kissed her cheek. For her ears only, he said, "When you see what you want, you go after it."

She gave him a sideways glance. "You have no idea."

11

*L*eo knew one of the guys who ran the swap meet and arranged to have Steph's new old truck moved out of the field.

"Thanks for helping me out." Stephanie's grin was contagious. "I had forgotten about this truck until I saw it."

"Can I ask why you wanted it back?"

"Until Dad got sick, I always thought we had plenty of time to do one more project together. This will be it in a way." She hugged his arm to her body. "Want to help out from time to time?"

Those big eyes could get him to say yes to almost anything. "Yeah, sure. Let's head back and we can get the flatbed. Bring it home today and then you can start to look it over."

"Dad always made a project book for each vehicle he worked on. He would give one to the new owner and keep a duplicate. Including pictures, part lists—well, you know the drill. Everyone's proud of their books. I'd really like to find the one for this truck."

He steered her toward the exit by way of a burger stand. They placed their orders to go.

Stephanie said, "We should sit and enjoy a picnic. The truck can wait a few more minutes." She looked around. "Do you mind sitting on the ground under that tree over there? The tables are full."

"We can sit wherever you'd like." His admiration grew for her with each passing hour. First the truck and now sitting on a little scrap of well-trodden grass, and she liked to eat.

He handed her their sodas and took the cardboard tray with their burgers and fries. A table opened up but she made a beeline for the trees and dropped to the ground.

Leo did the same and stretched his legs out in front of him and placed the little tray on them. Much better than inviting ants to their picnic.

As they devoured everything, Steph said, "Who do you get your paint supplies from?"

"Westwood Auto." He tossed the paper wrapper into the bag. "Why? Are you thinking of a new supplier?"

"That's who we use." She wiped her fingers on a paper napkin. "Have you noticed any problems with shipments lately?"

"Like what specifically?" His curiosity was piqued.

"Well, either my team isn't logging what they're using correctly or I've been overcharged. I've been reviewing the books since I've been back and things just aren't matching up. Dad's business was always very profitable. And now..."

The comment hung in the air. Maybe it was sloppy inventory control or she had an employee problem.

"Do you see other discrepancies?"

"Nothing significant at this point, but I've only started to really dig into the accounts."

"How can I help?" He sat up a little straighter. If someone was skimming, he didn't want it to go on any longer than it may have already.

"There's nothing yet. I just need to review and cross-check. I'm not saying anything to the office manager or the guys in the shop at this point. At least until I know more."

"What's your next step?"

She hopped up and brushed off her backside and held out her hand to him. "Our next step is to get your flatbed and pick up my new wheels." She jiggled the key ring. "Maybe some night, you want to come over and take a closer look at my new hot rod?"

He slung his arm over her shoulders and pulled her close. "That sounds like a date. You let me know the night and I'll pick up a pizza and beer."

Looking at him, she said, "How about Thursday, and you can bring wine too. I'd love to taste something from your family's winery. After all, I need to compare it to Tessa's, right?'

She certainly had a way of being direct. His family would like her; she was a lot like Tessa. With a chuckle, he said, "I think I can get a bottle or two. White or red?"

"Your choice." She looped her arm around his waist and they walked.

"Cabernet it is. I'm not a huge fan of whites."

*A*fter staring at invoices for two more days, Steph decided to dive into the office supplies inventory. It certainly had to be easier than reconciling the project logs and parts. Why Dad hadn't gone to an inventory control system on the computer was beyond her. Once she had this sorted out, that was next on the list.

She got up and stretched before grabbing a pad and pen. She literally ran into Val coming around the corner to her office and reached out to steady the older woman. "Val. You seem to be on a mission."

She held up several pieces of paper. "I have those corrected invoices from Westwood. Just a minor glitch."

Steph took them and gave them a cursory glance. "That's a relief. I didn't want to think they were over-charging us." She handed them back. "If you've doubled-checked, go ahead and file them. I can move on to other things on my list."

Val leaned against the doorjamb. "Like that truck you bought over the weekend."

She grinned. "Yup. I'm looking forward to working on it."

"What about the handsome guy I saw delivering it earlier today?"

"Leo? We're just friends." She was, after all, going back to Portland and the last thing she wanted to do was break his heart, or hers—although maybe having a lot of people know about it was worse.

"If I were you, I'd think about making him more than a friend. He's cute."

"Val." She pretended to be shocked and then dropped her voice. "Actually, he's coming over tonight and we're going to have a quick dinner and take a gander under the hood."

"I hope you brought other clothes. It'd be a shame to ruin that silk blouse and slacks." She gave her an exaggerated wink. "I'll bet he'd be willing to look under the hood."

Stephanie turned Val and pointed her back to the front desk. "Stop. You're incorrigible. And for the record, I need to pick up a couple more pair of jeans and t-shirts for work." She waved over her front. "This was as casual as I had for today."

"You look great and you can't blame a newly single gal for living vicariously," Val called over her shoulder with a grin.

She was glad Dad had had someone with such a fun-loving spirit like Val in his life. With a wave of her hand, Steph smiled. "We both have work to do." She pushed open the storage room door and closed it behind her with a chuckle. And Val was good for her too. She didn't feel as lonely at the shop, unlike at home, where she was surrounded by memories and regrets.

She glanced around the space. The room needed to be organized and then a full inventory. At the moment, she wished she was wearing jeans and a t-shirt. Before she started, she needed to change.

A persistent knocking on the lobby door interrupted Stephanie's count. Why was someone knocking?

"Val?" She stepped into the lobby and saw Leo through the glass with a pizza box in one hand and a bag in the other. Then she noticed the time. It was after six.

She pushed open the door. "Hey, have you been out here long?"

"No, but I was getting concerned when you didn't answer." He stepped in and looked around. "Where should I put the pizza?"

"How about the conference room? Around the corner and to the right."

She flipped the lock and shut off the overhead lights before following him to the other room.

She looked at her hands, covered with a thick layer of dust. Holding them up, she said, "I need to wash up."

"Take your time."

When she came back, he had paper plates and napkins laid out beside two plastic wineglasses, along with an open bottle of Cabernet. She picked up the bottle to examine the label.

"You did bring something from your family's winery." She gave him a smile. "Thank you."

"You said you wanted to try it." He poured and then handed her a glass. "Cheers."

She took a sip and smiled over the rim. "This is good."

"It's my favorite. I'm a Cab guy." He pulled out a chair and, with a twinkle in his eye, said, "Care to join me for dinner?"

She looked under the cardboard lid. "The works. Good choice."

Over pizza, they talked about the Chevelle he was finishing up. He was very thorough and detailed, and she realized she had missed this with her dad. They didn't talk about pharmaceutical sales, and even if they could have, she hadn't wanted to. Her dad's life was cars, and she had loved meeting him on his turf. It hurt she wouldn't be able to do that again and she wanted to kick herself for not making more time for him.

"How goes the business investigation?"

She frowned. The whole thing tainted her dad's reputation and was a slap in the face to the family environment he had worked so hard to build over the years. "Val was able to get Westwood to fix their mistake, so that's good, but I cleaned up the office storage room today and did inventory. There were a lot of boxes that at first glance, you would have thought were full. But the boxes are actually empty and in reality, we're low on a lot of things."

"Could it be people are just lazy about throwing empty boxes into the recycle bin?"

"I'd like to think so. Tomorrow, I'm going to compare recent invoices to what I have on hand. I really don't like to think of anyone taking coffee and other items." She snapped her fingers as inspiration struck and she rushed from the room.

Leo followed her. "Stephanie, what's wrong?"

She looked over her shoulder. "I want to check something." She flung open the storeroom door. It banged against the wall.

Leo held it open and watched as she strode down the back row. She pushed on a large cardboard box, giving it a good shake. "Are you freaking kidding me?"

"What's wrong?" He stepped into the room.

She fumed. "There were three chairs. I have one and this box is empty." She shoved the other box. It didn't move. "At least the third one is here."

She began to pace. "I'll be right back." She hurried from the room.

*L*eo went over to the box that she had said contained the third chair. He gave it a closer look. It had been opened. He pulled back the flaps. The packing material was intact. When he lifted off the insert, he discovered there wasn't a chair inside but a couple small cinderblocks to give the box weight. Stephanie was not going to like this news and he hated to be the one to tell her.

She stormed through the door leading into the shop. Hands on hips, her lips were in a thin, firm line. "I don't see a new chair anywhere in this building."

"You're not going to like what I just discovered."

She dropped her hands and her shoulders sagged. "What now?"

This was just one more weight on her shoulders and he wanted to prop her up in any way he could, but she needed to know. "The box you thought contained a chair actually has a couple of cement blocks in the packing."

"I have two brand-new chairs missing."

A gleam came into her eyes and Leo knew her mind was

whirling. He was glad he wasn't on the other side of her burgeoning plan. "What are you going to do?"

"I'm all about facts. Before I let on that I know someone is stealing from me, I'm going to gather all the details and do a lot more investigation. When I'm ready to confront the perp, that person is going down." Then her face fell. "I can't believe anyone would steal from my father. He would give anyone the shirt off his back if they had asked."

"People steal for a few reasons—need, want, or the thrill."

"Well, if someone is doing this for the thrill, I'm going to bring their fun to a screeching halt."

He wanted to be supportive, but how low could someone be to do this since Eddie had died? This person was heartless.

"Stephanie, you're not alone. I'll help track down whoever it is."

She gave him a tender smile. "I really appreciate that." She stepped forward and he folded her into his arms.

$\mathcal{A}$ couple of weeks after Leo had delivered the old Chevy pickup to Black River Restoration, Steph was tinkering with the engine. She adjusted the droplight to get a better look at the fan belt. Just knowing Dad had worked on this truck a few months before gave her pause. It was a tiny connection to him. The back door banged and she glanced up as Leo strolled in. She'd lent him a swipe card just in case she was up to her elbows in grease. Her heart skipped. He looked damn good crossing her shop floor.

"Hey there. Did you find your dad's project binder?"

"I did." She leaned on the fender as she flashed him a smile. "It's been a long time since I've held any tools of the trade."

"Is there much to do to the engine, or just body work?"

"For now, I think I'll focus on some custom exterior touches and see how she runs before tinkering with it." She pulled the light off the hood and said, "Careful."

Leo took a step back and she firmly closed the hood.

She walked around the truck. "I'd like to add a red oak

wood bed with stainless-steel strips, maybe with a low gloss finish. Make it pop and add a stainless-steel gas tank."

"Do you want a new paint job first?" He ran his hand down the back rail of the bed. "The wood and stainless will look sharp."

Using a bright light, she was examining the paint one square foot at a time. "Yeah, there are some dings. Not my dad's doing, from the looks of it. More like careless parking." She turned off the light and smiled.

"I did some research last night and this burgundy was an official color in the fifty-two, but I saw a gorgeous shade, moonlight cream. I'm thinking of repainting the exterior, adding some burgundy pinstripe, and then having the interior redone in camel-colored leather and, of course, white wall tires."

He gave a low whistle. "Now that would make this truck your own."

She thrust up her chin, proud to have found it. In a small way, it would be her and Dad's last project. "Dad's engine and my exterior, the perfect combination."

"A nice legacy." He touched her arm. "Does this mean we're on the lookout for a model to match your new truck?"

She couldn't hold back a laugh. It was amusing that he already had that little idiosyncrasy figured out. "It's tradition to have a model of all the cars and trucks Dad and I worked on and I think it's something I'll continue." She thought about what she had just said. There would be more restoration projects in her future.

"I'm curious. What do you drive when you're in Portland?"

She felt the heat rush to her cheeks. She grew up on muscle cars and now it was easier to be seen as the successful businesswoman in an expensive vehicle. "An import and something for daily use that's a little more practical." She shrugged her shoulder.

"That's a little vague." He took a step closer. "Why, Ms. James, you drive a fancy import; now that is very interesting."

She heard the inflection on the word *fancy*. "If you must know, yes, and on top of that, it has a hard-top convertible option."

He tapped his chin with his index finger. His eyes danced and she held her breath, afraid of what he was about to suggest. "A Benz?"

"Yes, but in my defense"—she held up her hand to stop his teasing—"Dad picked it up for a song and restored it, and it's from the eighties. It was for my thirtieth birthday. And because I know you're going to ask, it's black with red interior."

He took another step forward. "I've often told people the car they drive reflects their personality."

A shiver raced down her arms as he came closer. "What do my choices say about me?"

"You're complex, have an appreciation for classics, and are someone I find absolutely fascinating."

With his last word, he pulled her into his arms and kissed her until she was breathless.

"What do your cars say about you?" Her voice was soft to her ears.

"I have an appreciation for nothing but the best in my life. I love the thrill of discovering what lies underneath the hood, exposing all the secrets of the ride."

Was that a double entendre for her as well as a car?

He brushed her hair back from her face and tucked it behind her ear. His eyes searched hers, as if asking a question.

"Do you have secrets too?"

He traced the line of her jaw with the tip of his finger. "Do you?"

"Maybe."

"Intriguing. Shall I look closer?"

"Come home with me." She couldn't believe that came out of her mouth. She grabbed his hand, stilling it mid-caress. "We can watch a movie and get to know each other." If she were being honest, a movie wasn't what she originally had in mind when she opened her mouth, but then she wondered if she was ready to slip between the sheets and was thankful the queen bed she had purchased had been delivered.

"We have all the time in the world for everything." He brushed his lips to hers. "A movie sounds nice."

He continued to hold her close, gazing into her eyes. Waiting for what, she wasn't sure. "Follow me home."

At this very moment, Leo knew that he'd follow her anywhere. But to say that would be downright stupid on his part. He needed to take it easy, move at a slower pace, and uncover each layer of Steph, bit by bit. She was not one to open up easily, but in time she might. He wished time would slow, but October would come quickly.

"I'll help you lock up for the night." He slipped his hand down her arm and interlaced their fingers. "But nothing too sappy, okay?"

She wrinkled her brow.

"The movie. Let's watch a comedy or action flick."

She smiled. "Tell you what, you can pick."

"I like the sound of that." Leo knew he'd pick out a rom-com. If nothing else, his sisters had taught him how to choose just the right movie when on a date.

*L*eo parked in the driveway of her bungalow-style childhood home. The yard was well maintained, and vibrant flowers lined the brick walkway leading up to the bright-blue front door. It was complete with a white picket fence and looked like a nice place to grow up.

He jogged up the walk, carrying a hastily picked bunch of wildflowers he had seen on the drive over. Before he could knock, the door swung open and he hid the flowers behind his back.

Steph greeted him with a welcoming smile. "Where did you go? One minute you were there and then the next"—she flicked her fingers away from the palms of her hands—"poof."

He leaned in and kissed her cheek and presented her with the flowers. "I stopped for these."

Her smile widened and her hand covered her heart. "That is so sweet." She took the flowers and stepped to one side. "Come in."

His eyes swept the interior. Light drifted from the hall into the living room. A newspaper was tossed on the sofa cushion, but otherwise everything was tidy.

"Nice place."

"Thanks. When I was in college, Dad let me pick out a new living room set. The other had seen better days and other than the recliner, I don't think anyone ever sat on it." She turned on a lamp and the room was bathed in a soft glow.

"Wine, beer, or a soft drink?"

"Surprise me." He looked at his boots. "Can I leave these by the door? They might have some grease on them."

"Sure. Make yourself comfortable."

She walked to the kitchen. Her sock-clad feet didn't

make a sound on the gleaming wood floor. He could see a long counter and a row of cabinets when she flicked the light on. The sound of a cabinet door opening and closing drifted to him, and then the water turned on.

Was Stephanie at all nervous having him here? He was going to play it cool. It had been a long time since he had been this close to a woman, especially one who had captivated him with her quiet strength, intelligence, and yes, even her beauty. But he had never given much stock to an exterior. It was like looking at an old car in need of restoration. He gave a snort. There wasn't a woman on Earth who'd want to be compared to an old car.

He sat down on the couch and picked up the paper. It was a few days old.

Stephanie walked into the room and set the vase of flowers, which were now artfully arranged, on the coffee table. "I'll be right back." Within moments, she walked in with a beer and a glass of white wine.

"I hope this is okay. I thought a beer might hit the spot for you."

He sipped. It was icy cold. "Thanks."

She tossed the paper aside and sat down facing him, tucking her feet under her. She licked her lips and sipped her wine. The liquid seemed to vibrate in her glass.

She was nervous. Damn, was it like *what the heck am I doing* or excited nervous?

"Tell me about your place in Oregon. Do you own a house or condo?"

She visibly relaxed and gave him a grateful smile. "A town house actually, which overlooks a park."

She lowered her glass after taking another sip. Did he sense her jitters? He was acting as if they had sat together in her house many times and wasn't contemplating the next big step, like getting horizontal. Her town house was a safe topic.

"A few years ago, I got tired of apartment living. There was a complex that had just been renovated and, on a whim, I stopped in for an open house. That was all it took. I bought a spacious two-bedroom that overlooks the park."

"But you still have neighbors like an apartment. You don't mind that someone is literally on the other side of your wall?"

"No. I never gave it any thought." She glanced around the room. Would it make a difference now? After adjusting to the solitude that living in a house brought, was it something she had sorely missed?

"What about you? Do you own a house?"

"Yeah, my brothers and sisters and I tend to buy a home that needs a lot of TLC. We get sucked into the nostalgia of what it once was and what it could be. I'm actually on my second house. This time, I bought an expanded ranch."

"That's a lot of house for a single guy."

"When I'm done, it'll make a great family home. I'll sell it and pick up something else."

"Did you ever want to settle into one spot?"

"Someday." He looked deep into her eyes. "Do you miss home?"

He touched a raw nerve. She missed knowing someone loved her unconditionally. She was a woman without a family and he didn't know how lucky he was to have grown up surrounded by people who loved him. Missing home was unexpected, but being alone was worse. She dropped her voice. "I didn't realize how much until I came back."

He scooched closer to her and cupped her cheek in the palm of his hand. Her heart quickened. She wanted to be kissed, and she leaned into him. "I'm very glad you're here." He searched her eyes as if trying to read her mind. Tilting her chin up, he tentatively kissed her.

Steph leaned into the kiss, deepening it and reveling in the connection with Leo. Of all the people she never thought she'd connect with, another car mechanic made sense. She could be a saleswoman all she wanted, but at heart, she was her father's daughter.

His hand slid around her waist, warming the small of her back. Heat began to build in her blood. She set the wine aside and, in one smooth movement, wrapped her arms around his waist. His tightened around her, holding her against his chest.

They made out like teenagers but without the rush of pulling at clothes. There was no curfew or parent who would interrupt them.

As she kissed him, the cold band of loneliness that had encircled her heart for a very long time released its grip. She took a literal and figurative breath while his lips trailed down her neck and nuzzled behind her ear. She wanted his hands on her body, but she wasn't on birth control and didn't have any protection in the house. She had to hit the brake and put this on hold. For tonight anyway.

"Leo." The huskiness of her voice surprised her.

"Hmm." He made his way back to her lips.

She placed her fingers on his. "We need to slow down."

He pulled back and looked deep into her eyes. "Our pace, fast or slow, is totally in your hands."

"It's not that I don't want to," she began. "But I'm not on birth control and…"

He pecked her lips. "I have protection, but if this moves beyond where we are right now, that is your choice."

She slid her hand around his neck and pulled him in. "If you're prepared, then—" She traced the outline of his mouth and whispered, "Stay with me tonight." If she were a starry-eyed girl, she'd think they were meant to be together but she wanted him, and tonight was right.

He said the one word she longed to hear.

"Yes."

13

———————

Stephanie took Leo's hand and eased him up from the couch, bobbing her head toward the hall. He pulled her to him and looked deep into her eyes, brushing her hair back from her upturned face. When he hesitated, she decided to take matters into her own hands. Standing on tiptoes, she kissed him hard, then slipped her hands under his t-shirt and, in one motion, pulled it off over his head and dropped it on the floor.

Walking backward, she drew him down the hall to her bedroom, clothing discarded as they went. His body was long, lean, and muscular, his skin warm under her touch. Despite the lack of her clothing, which had disappeared with each step until she was in nothing more than scraps of lace and satin, she didn't feel exposed. Without turning on the light, she kept her hand in his.

"I want you."

Leo's voice was husky. "I need you."

His heart hammered in his chest. Stephanie was stunning. Her confidence was sexy as hell;

she wasn't a woman who shied away from what she wanted. And in this moment, she wanted him. She lay back on the sheets and the bed gave under his weight as he knelt over her.

With a laugh, she pulled him closer.

"I don't want to crush you."

"As long as I can breathe, we're fine. Now stop talking and kiss me."

She ran her hand down the length of his backside and nibbled his lower lip. He didn't hesitate another moment and crushed her mouth, demanding, urging her to explore his body. His hands trailed over her curves, relieving her of the last bits of lingerie until there was nothing between them. A trail of goosebumps appeared and when he ran his hand over her skin, she trembled under his touch.

He could feel her heartbeat in her kiss. Taking it slow, he let his lips follow where his fingers had trailed.

In time, she whispered, "More."

He rolled off her and grabbed the small square packet from his wallet. She took it from him and ripped it open, and then she eased him back. It was clear what she wanted from him.

He groaned and allowed her full control over their pleasure.

When they were both spent, she lay on top of him. A shiver raced through her, so Leo drew a blanket over them. He held her tight in his arms, his long legs wrapped over hers. His slow, rhythmic breathing lulled her into a deep, dreamless sleep.

*T*he first glimmer of the burnt orange sunrise slipped through Stephanie's bedroom window. She could feel a slow, satisfied smile creep across her face. She wasn't alone. Leo's face was softened by sleep. She wanted to reach out and follow his jawline but instead she was content to watch him.

She was losing her heart to him. But she had to go back home—well, to Portland. Her heart sank a little at the idea of their time ending, so she pushed the thought aside.

Leo stirred and tightened his arms around her. With heavy lids, he gave her a sexy smile and kissed the top of her head.

"Good morning, beautiful. Sleep well?"

"I did. And you?"

"Like a baby."

"It's early." She tried to sit up but he pulled her to his chest.

"Too early to get up."

Stephanie sighed as her blood began to hum. "You're right. It's much too early."

Leo and Steph lingered over coffee. The remnants of eggs and toast sat forgotten on plates.

He stretched his legs out in front of him. He liked looking at her across the breakfast table. "What are your plans for the day?"

"I need to get into the shop. See if I can track down the missing chairs and anything else I might uncover."

"And your truck?"

Her smile widened and her eyes sparkled. He could sense her excitement. If she was like him, she could envision what the truck looked like finished, down to the last detail.

"I'm going to reach out to the company we use for upholstery and check on lead times."

"I could help you do that."

She seemed surprised. "Make the call or redo the seats?"

"Whatever you need." He took her hand.

"I appreciate that, but I'm going to strip the interior and send them out, if they can fit me in. If they can't, I'll figure that out later. I'd like to get the truck done before I head to Portland."

He kept his face neutral. He didn't like it when she talked about leaving, but he had to face the truth—whatever they were doing had an end date.

"I'll help you pull everything."

"That sounds like fun, but don't you have your own project car?"

"I've got all the time in the world to finish it, but you're on a timeline." And it would give him more time with her. Jeez, that sounded self-serving to his ears.

She gave his hand a squeeze. "I'd like that. How about this weekend?"

"It's a date." He liked that they were making longer-term plans.

She picked up their plates and set them in the sink before she leaned against the counter and smiled at him. "What are you doing tonight after work?"

"That depends. I was going to ask you to have dinner with me. Like, we get out of jeans and do the whole table-cloth and candlelight kind of date." He held his breath. His stomach clenched until she smiled. Relief coursed through him.

"What time?"

She gave him a slow, sexy smile that had him rethink going to work. "Six. If that works for you." He'd have to put those thoughts on pause until later.

He closed the short distance between them to pull her into his arms and hold her lightly as he kissed her.

"Bring a change of clothes if you want to spend the night."

"I won't say no." He kissed her again. She could tempt him to forget about time, but he had a few things he had to get done before tonight. "I'm going to run home and get cleaned up for the day. I'll see you later?"

"Sounds like a plan."

Stephanie watched Leo walk out the door and close it firmly behind him. She twirled in the kitchen with her arms wide. Shoot; did she have something to wear for a dinner date? She hurried into her bedroom and flung open the closet door. She flicked through the clothes until her eyes landed on a soft floral sundress with a matching shrug. With the right hair and makeup, she could make this work, especially with a pair of high-heeled sandals. She hung the dress on the back of the bathroom door before getting ready to head to work.

When she looked around her bedroom in the daylight, she realized having Leo spend the night here was awkward. At least she bought the new bed, but still—this was her dad's house. But she was a grown woman and technically it was her house now. She pushed the thought away. It was too much to deal with right now and she needed to get to work.

When she sailed through the front door, Val was sitting behind the desk.

"Morning." She felt the silly grin on her face. To Val's credit, if she wondered what was going on, she didn't ask but gave Steph a return smile.

"Good morning, boss lady. Ready to attack the day?"

"I sure am." She turned and walked backward. "I'm expecting a guy from Computer Connection. Let me know when he gets here."

"Sure. Is there something wrong with your PC?"

"No. I want to check out some new software for inventory and project management, something I had asked Dad to do for the last few years. It'll help me get this place up to speed for the twenty-first century."

Val leaned on the counter. "I'm happy to help in any way I can."

"Thanks. I appreciate that."

Steph had begun to turn when Val said, "For the record, I encouraged Eddie to enhance the systems, but he liked to keep track of things the old-school way."

"I know he didn't like change." She gave the older woman a smile. "I need more robust processes if I have a chance to successfully run this business from Oregon."

"That's still your plan?"

She thought of Leo asleep in her bed this morning and her heart thumped in her chest. With a sharp nod, she said, "That's the plan." She took a step down the hall. "Val, when Gary gets in, can you let me know, please?"

Val gave her an unreadable look. "You got it, boss."

Stephanie walked into her office and wondered why it irked her that Val referred to her as *boss lady*. Had she called Dad *boss man*? Sadly, she couldn't ask her dad. That was a battle for a different day. She had to figure out how she was going to ask Gary some pointed questions without pissing him off.

A knock on her open door caused her to look up. Gary filled the doorway. He was a big guy who had been with Dad for as long as she could remember, and he was a trusted family friend too.

"Hey, Steph. Val said you wanted to see me."

"Come in and take a seat."

She waited while he got settled. "I wanted to check in and see how things were going in the shop. Any problems or concerns?"

"I've been doing as you asked. Keeping an eye on how things flow in the shop. Everyone seems to be working steady. Zira is still learning, but she's damn good. Chuck keeps a tight control on the schedule, staying on top of us all so we keep everything running smoothly."

"Good." She nodded and tapped a pen on the pad in front of her. At least something was on track and Gary was doing a good job managing it all. It made dealing with the theft easier and kept it from overshadowing everything. But until she figured out what was going on with it, there was a cloud over all they did. "I'm considering installing an additional security system with cameras inside in addition to the exterior cameras we have in the lots. We have a lot of blind spots." She watched as his eyes opened a little wider before returning to their normal size. "It's not to spy on anyone but—"

He held up his hand and met her gaze before she could finish her sentence. "Stephanie, this is your business and if it's what you want to do, then do it. I would suggest you explain to everyone why; you don't want to lose their trust. Spin it that it's more for their security and our customers."

She pushed back from the desk and closed her office door. She hesitated, uncertain if she should confide in Gary. Then again, he had been a good friend to her father and she needed to trust her instincts.

"I would like to tell you something and ask for you to keep it strictly confidential."

He clasped his hands and leaned forward. "You can count on me."

She perched on the edge of her desk. "We have a theft problem."

"You can't be serious. Who would steal from you?" Then it dawned on him. "That's why you want the cameras. Not for during the day, but after hours."

"Yeah." She made another decision. "Keep your eyes open for me and if you see something off with inventory or whatever, will you let me know?"

"Will do." He got out of the chair. "I'm really sorry

about this."

"Me too. Can you ask Chuck to come in? I have a computer company coming in today and I'd like to have his input on what we need for the shop floor."

"He's a solid guy."

"I know his background and his time in prison for hacking, so don't start worrying."

He gave her a grin. "You're a lot like your dad."

Her smile slid from one side of her face to the other. "That's the nicest thing you could have said to me."

She waited for Chuck to come in. She had read everyone's files and wasn't surprised there were a few people who'd had some run-ins with the law. Chuck was one of them. Dad had hired him almost six years ago and, based on the performance review notes in his personnel file, he had learned a lot and always showed up on time and only took time off for his two-week vacation.

Steph had thought about the possibility he was the thief, but she couldn't believe someone went from hacker to stealing office supplies. Besides, he wouldn't have access to all the keys to the kingdom, and she needed someone on site who was good with computers. Who knew? Maybe he would pick up on something as time went by, seeing patterns and such.

The thump of boots coming down the hall slowed when they reached her door. A sharp rap on the doorjamb sounded before Chuck stuck his head in. "Hi, Stephanie. Gary said you had something you wanted to talk to me about?"

"Chuck, would you like to help me select a new computer system for inventory and project management?"

"Finally, we can get rid of the logbooks." His face split into a grin. "What can I do to help?"

"Pull up a chair. We need a must have, nice to have, and our dream list in less than thirty minutes."

14

As Steph made the short trip to her house, she was satisfied with the progress she had made, even if it had been three weeks and she still hadn't solved the mystery of missing chairs and supply inventory. She simply ran out of hours in her day. Chuck was on board with learning the new computer system, and they should be able to get it installed as soon as she purchased three desktop workstations. She was going to put two in the shop, with Chuck and Gary both being the main data entry people. Of course, Val would get an upgrade to her computer too. Steph would be able to track the office supplies and be backup for the guys as needed.

She hated the idea of cameras inside her business. For now, she'd put the guilt on the back burner. If something didn't jibe soon, she'd have to install them. She couldn't afford, nor could her employees, to allow the stealing to go on. It could force her to close the doors if things got worse.

She parked the Bronco and hurried into the house, not that she needed to. Leo wouldn't be picking her up for another hour. And even though she didn't know where they were going, where didn't matter as long as she was with him.

A sharp rap on the door caused Steph to glance at the clock. It was too early for Leo to be picking her up. She padded to the front door in bare feet. A delivery truck was pulling away from the curb and a small brown box sat on the brick step. She hadn't ordered anything. She took it to the kitchen and slit the packing tape, folding back the flaps.

Tucked inside was Styrofoam secured around a smaller box. She carefully lifted it out to discover it was a model of the truck she had just bought. She smiled. Leo. It was a sweet gesture.

She placed the model in the middle of the table and cleared away the shipping box and packing materials. He was going to be pulling in soon and she wanted to be ready.

*L*eo glanced at the small duffel bag resting on the passenger seat. Two nights in a row wasn't a record for him, but the pre-planning and packing a bag definitely was a change of pace. He was a little nervous about his dinner plans. Thank heavens he could always count on his family. In this case, Liza and Kate had come through like rock stars.

When he got to Stephanie's, he tossed the bag in the back seat. He didn't want to appear like he was pushing her into something, especially if she'd changed her mind about him spending the night. Getting out of the car, he noted that the air was still warm. That was fine; he wasn't worried about the temperature. He had that covered too. He took a deep breath and knocked on the front door. When he heard her call for him to come in, he stepped inside. "Hi. I'm here."

She poked her head out of the bedroom and flashed him

a smile. "I'll be finished in a minute." She pointed to the phone in her hand. "Take a look in the kitchen."

He walked into the brightly lit space, pleased to see the replica model in the middle of the table. He hadn't bought the paint, as she hadn't decided on a color when he'd placed the order. But he had another surprise in store for her. When she did, he'd paint the model and add the right color for the interior.

Arms slid around his waist from behind and she kissed his back. "Sorry about that. My best friend, Maggie, called and we were catching up."

"Nice. You'll have to tell me all about her later." He turned and pulled her close, kissing her warm, inviting lips.

"You look gorgeous and your perfume is intoxicating." His mouth trailed down her neck and he kissed the hollow of her throat.

She tipped her head back, giving him full access, and sighed with pure pleasure.

As much as he would have loved to continue this, he had promised her dinner. There would be plenty of time afterward to pick up where he stopped. "Are you ready to go?"

"I'll just get a sweater." She walked into her bedroom and looked back over her shoulder. "Did you bring a bag?"

"It's in the car." She did want him to stay. Good to know.

She picked up a small handbag that didn't look like it would hold much of anything and draped a sweater over her arm.

"Where are we having dinner?"

"It's a surprise." He pulled open the front door and asked, "Do you have your keys?"

She held them up. "I do."

Once she locked the door, they strolled to the car and she smiled up at him. "Would you like me to drive?"

"Call me old-fashioned, but tonight I'd like to be a bit more traditional."

She hugged his arm close to her body. "That sounds nice."

He held open the car door and waited while she tucked her dress inside before closing it. Once they were on their way, he said, "I should have asked, but do you have any food allergies, like to seafood?"

"None. I can eat pretty much anything as long as it's not moving." She gave him a sidelong look. "Are you planning on taking me someplace where they have an eclectic menu?"

"No, but I did preorder our meal." He glanced at her. "I hope that's okay."

She leaned back against the seat and gave him a sexy smile. "I'm not going to worry about a thing. Whatever you've planned will be wonderful."

If she noticed they were headed to Crescent Lake, she didn't say anything. He figured it did make sense that he would know that area better than restaurants near Black River.

As he drove, they chatted about books they liked and action movies and which ones had the best car scenes. She perked up when she saw the land surrounding them on both sides had become acre after acre of vines.

"I'm guessing there will be wine involved?"

He chuckled. "So much for not being curious."

"I never said that." She laughed. "I'm always open to new things, but the landscape does pique my interest."

"We're almost there."

Up ahead, the sign for Crescent Lake Winery came into view. Actually, it couldn't be missed. It was a large white sign with deep burgundy lettering that seemed to shimmer in the growing twilight.

"We're having dinner at the winery?"

"Not exactly." He clasped her hand. "Trust me." At least she hadn't zeroed in on the gazebo.

She chewed on the inside of her cheek, a habit he had discovered she did when her mind was racing with possibilities.

He pulled up to the warehouse door and parked. "Are you ready?"

Her eyes sparkled. "Sure."

They entered a shadow-filled room only lit with emergency lights. She asked, "We're having dinner here? It's not my idea for a romantic dinner unless you're into creepy dates."

He tucked her hand into the crook of her arm. "Not exactly."

They entered a larger room with small tables scattered around and crossed to an interior set of French doors that led to the bistro. He escorted her to another set of glass doors; she saw the gazebo and the round table set with pale-pink linens.

Her eyes grew wide. "Is that where we're having dinner?"

He gave her a kiss on the cheek and held open the door. She sucked in a breath, and by the sparkle in her eyes, he could tell she liked it. He began to relax. He wasn't a dud at romance after all.

Gas torches added additional warmth around them. Pale-pink and white roses filled a low bowl in the middle of the table, surrounded by fat white candles. Two bottles of wine were uncorked. Next to the dining table was another covered with chafing dishes.

She threw her arms around his neck and pulled him into a kiss. "This is so romantic."

"I'm glad you like it."

She kissed him again. "I love it. But how did you do all of this?"

He held out a chair for her. He was thrilled he'd been able to pull this off, and her kiss had said it all.

"Liza set the scene and Kate did the cooking and wine selection. We have a full five-course meal prepared by a top chef."

"Fancy."

Leo poured her a glass of white wine and a glass of red for himself. "I'd like to make a toast."

She picked up her glass. A small smile played across her lips.

"To what I hope will be many dinners I share with you." They clinked glasses and she kept her eyes locked on his over the rim.

"And breakfast and lunches too?"

He gave a hearty chuckle. "I do love a woman who speaks her mind. As many meals as you'd like."

***

On their way back to her place, Steph was relaxed and genuinely happy. The meal Leo had arranged was delicious, from the tomato crostini to the salad, the seafood alfredo, and the very decadent flourless chocolate cake with berries, complimented with sparkling wine. And finally, an excellent cup of coffee. She had to admit his sister-in-law was an extraordinary chef.

"Hey, you okay over there? You've been quiet since we left the winery."

"I'm wonderful." She smiled and took his hand, interlacing their fingers after she ran hers over the top of his with a light caress. "I've never had a night like this before and your family was so sweet to do this for us."

"Are you kidding? My family couldn't wait to help me plan our night." He brought their hands to his lips and placed a kiss on the underside of her wrist. "At some point, I'd like for you to meet them."

She gave him a sharp look. "I don't know. We agreed to keep this simple, and adding family complicates things."

"I know, but I'd like for them to meet the woman responsible for this smile on my face. You're special to me."

Meeting his family, any of them on purpose, was a big deal, but she was curious about them. She was torn between what to do, but if they kept it simple, it wouldn't be too bad. "How about drinks? Keep it low-key and just your parents. I can't do a big family gathering."

He applied light pressure to her hand. "Drinks with my folks. Got it. I think you'll like them and I know they'll like you."

She hoped this wasn't something she'd regret later. A shiver raced over her skin as his touch warmed it and her breath quickened with anticipation of what would happen after they got home.

"We should have cleaned up and not left everything a mess."

"I was assured that I wasn't to worry about a thing. And there will come a day when someone will need help and I'll jump in with both feet. It's what my family does." He released her hand so he could downshift. "Are you sure you want me to stay tonight? I won't be upset if you've changed your mind."

"I'd really like to see you across the breakfast table tomorrow."

She had never met a man like Leo. The other men she dated were always more concerned with their needs, which is why they never lasted. He was still giving her the opportunity to change her mind about the direction and speed at which things were going.

She half turned in her seat. "Can I ask you something?"

The semi-darkness of the car provided enough light so she could see his expression.

"Anything."

"So far, I've found you to be sweet, kind, thoughtful, and generous. So why hasn't some girl snapped you up by now?"

If he was caught off guard at the direct question, it didn't show on his face. "It's you."

"What do you mean by that?" Was he trying to evade her question?

His lips quirked upward. "You bring out the best in me."

"Are you saying you're a Jekyll and Hyde kind of guy?" She half held her breath. How on earth did she expect him to answer that?

His laughter was like velvet to her ears. There was no way he wasn't exactly who she thought.

"I'm not in a committed relationship because I never wanted to settle. I've dated some very nice women, a couple longer than others, but ultimately we just didn't have the same interests and goals for the long term."

"Oh." That was not what she had expected. Should she remind him she had to go back to Portland? Why ruin a perfectly lovely evening? Now was not the time to do that.

"For the record, I really like spending time with you, and you're easy to be with." He parked in her driveway. "Steph, I know you're leaving, but I'd rather have the next few months with you than miss out altogether." He leaned over and caressed her cheek. "I hope you feel the same."

Without hesitation, she said, "We should get inside." She gave him a playful but passionate kiss, reassured that he knew their time was limited. "I don't want to waste a single minute with you."

15

June morphed into July and Steph and Leo had settled into a nice routine. Most nights, they had dinner together and stayed at her place. It was time to invite her to his house even if she felt more comfortable at hers. Little by little, he had noticed she had been making changes so that the house reflected her style and less of her childhood. It gave him hope she might be sticking around. Now it was time she got to see another layer of who he was. First, he was going to stop by his parents' to get caught up on what had been going on with the family while he had been absorbed in Stephanie.

Taking the front steps two at a time, Leo walked into the house. It really hadn't changed much since he was a kid: collage photos of the family covered the walls, from school pictures to holidays; fresh flowers were in every room; and there was always something fresh baked on the counter if you were hungry. The only change was now grandkid drawings were on the corkboard in the kitchen.

He rounded the corner of the kitchen and could see Mom and Dad sitting on the back deck. He couldn't help but smile. A couple of years ago, his father had open heart surgery and thankfully continued to thrive. It had put a scare into the entire clan, but he finally retired and now only dropped into the winery occasionally—well, except for the crush season.

Leo slid open the screen door. "Hi, guys."

"Hi, son," Dad said. "What brings you by?"

He bent and kissed Mom's cheek. "Just checking in. It's been a couple of weeks since I stopped over."

Mom's face split into a wide grin. "I hear you've been spending time with a new girl. Is it serious?"

He flopped into a deck chair and shook his head. His mom wouldn't be content until all her children were in happy relationships. "Still trying to get me hitched?"

"I just want my baby to be happy." She pretended to pout. "Is that a crime?"

He waited for what came next.

"Sherry, when he's ready, he'll know. Stop pushing."

Before the conversation could go any further, Leo said, "Have you heard anything from Anna and Colin?"

"I talked with her before they took off for a long weekend at his parents'. She is getting excited for their wedding."

"That's good." He laced his fingers together in his lap and relaxed. "What else is going on?"

"Jack said we're having a good growing season and Don said Peyton is selling every bottle she can."

"I expected nothing less." Leo was proud of his older brothers. They had taken to the family business like ducks to water, and they worked in harmony with each other, as well. Jack was happiest in the fields and Don loved the wheeling and dealing required of the man in charge. He was glad they had stepped up for the family business so he was able to pursue his dream of working with cars. If things had been different, he might be tethered to a job he didn't love.

"There's a board meeting next week, don't forget." Dad gave him a hard look. "I reminded Liza and Tessa already."

"I'm sure you did." He had agreed to sit on the board only to keep Dad happy. Anxious to change the subject, he asked, "Do you think Anna would mind if I brought a plus one to the wedding?"

Mom clapped her hands together as she beamed. "Is this the lady you've been seeing?"

"I'm sure someone has filled you in on a few of the details, but yes, her name is Stephanie James and she's the woman I've been dating."

Mom was nodding. Leo had figured out a long time ago when she pursed her lips like that, she couldn't control the questions about to escape. He had about thirty seconds to take control of the situation.

"Before you hammer me with twenty questions, would you like to meet her?"

Mom looked at Dad but didn't wait for him to answer. She blurted out, "Come for dinner tonight. I can let everyone know."

He shook his head and arched his brow. "No. I will not have the entire family drilling her with questions. If you and Dad would like to meet her, how's tomorrow instead of tonight? We can come by and have some wine and appetizers and if, and only if, you haven't smothered her, we'll stay for dinner."

Her mouth hung open. "I don't smother anyone." She didn't look hurt but amused.

"In all seriousness, Mom, Dad. She doesn't have any family. Her father died a few months ago and she lost her mom when she was little. Our family can be a little overwhelming if you're not used to huge gatherings."

"Leo, of course we can keep it small, just the four of us. I had no idea about her father. That is so sad."

"Thanks, Mom. Let me ask her if tomorrow night's

good." He got up and went into the kitchen for some privacy.

Stephanie answered on the first ring. "Hey, hand-some. I wasn't expecting to hear from you already." Her laugh was soft, almost as if she didn't want anyone to hear her. "It's only nine. Missing me already?"

"Seems like it's been days." He chuckled. "But I'm not calling to have you tease me."

"Is this a business call?"

"It's about our plans for tomorrow." He hoped she wouldn't say no; one of the changes he'd been noticing in her was that she seemed increasingly curious about his family. Even though she was leaving, he wanted her to learn more about him. Like peeling the layers from an onion. A thought did cross his mind. Would it be tough since she had just lost her dad? He'd never do anything to cause her heartache.

"What did you have in mind? Chinese or something?"

"How would you feel about coming with me to my parents'? We'll have some wine. They'd like to meet you."

She grew quiet.

"Steph?"

"I'm here." He could hear her sigh.

"We can do it another night and get takeout tomorrow instead."

"Leo, it's not that. I'd love to meet them. What time should I be ready?"

"Are you sure?"

"Yes. Really. It just struck me that I don't have anyone for you to meet."

He could hear the melancholy in her voice and his heart clenched. What could he do to put salve on her battered heart? "What about your friend back home? I'll bet she would love to interrogate me."

She laughed. "Yes, Maggie would be thrilled to grill you. Maybe we can do it through video chat or something."

"Can you sneak out a little early tomorrow? I can pick you up by five and then make the drive back. And—" In a rush, he said, "Do you want to stay at my place?"

"I'll be ready by four thirty and I'd love to spend the night. I've been wondering when you'd ask."

Her voice was light and breezy. Relief washed over him. It was going to be fine.

"And once we're at my parents', anytime you want to leave, just say *jinx* and we'll take off."

"Jinx? That might be hard to work into a conversation."

"Trust me, it's always best to have a code word. Just in case."

"What should I wear?"

"Just be casual. My parents are jeans kind of people."

"See you later, sweet cheeks." She disconnected before he could respond.

He stepped out on the deck. "We'll be over after five tomorrow." He pointed to his parents. "Best behavior. No questions about our future, okay?"

"Stop worrying. We've met people before." Mom smiled.

Leo grinned. "I just needed to go on record."

S tephanie glanced at Leo and gave him a nervous smile. "What?"

"You've smoothed the front of your top three times. You need to relax a little. My parents are going to think you're terrific."

She didn't know why she was nervous. Leo's parents were just people. But they were his parents and it mattered that they liked her. There was a tiny part of her that wished she had a future with him and in her daydreams, they welcomed her into the family so she wasn't so alone anymore.

"I hope they like the chocolates." She rambled on, "I couldn't bring a bottle of wine to people who own a winery, and if I baked something, it would never be as good as your sister-in-law, and there are always flowers. But doesn't everyone bring flowers when they don't know what to get? But truffles"—she held up her index finger—"now, that is the perfect hostess gift." She flashed him a smile. "Don't you think?"

"I had no idea so much thought went into a simple evening."

"It's far from simple." When she looked at him and the way his eyes twinkled, she discovered he was teasing her. "You're such a jerk." She gave him a playful poke.

He slowed the truck and pulled over to the side of the road and parked.

"I appreciate that you have a case of butterflies about meeting my parents, but it won't matter if they don't like you. The most important thing for you to remember is they're just people and it's just drinks. I have fun with you and enjoy spending time with you, and no matter how long or short we have together, it's just, well, completely unexpected."

"In a good way, I hope." She wiped her moist palms on her floral skirt.

He took her hand, turned it over, and placed a kiss in the center of her palm. She felt a thrill race through her. These little gestures were so damn romantic. They slayed her every time and made her long for things she couldn't have, but her real life was waiting for her in Portland.

"I'm crazy about you too." She leaned toward him and tenderly brushed her lips to his.

"Are you ready?"

"Yes, I am. But our code word is still jinx, right?"

He grinned. "Yes, but since it's just Mom and Dad, I suspect you won't need it. Now, on the other hand, if the entire family was there, you might."

"Thanks for keeping this simple."

"I had to remind Mom to not get the family phone tree going."

"She wanted to invite everyone?" A tremor rippled in her stomach and she reined in her flight response.

"She's a firm believer in just diving in, but I convinced her otherwise and Dad, to his credit, backed me up."

"Tell me about them so I can get a better idea of who they are."

Leo pulled the truck back onto the road and said, "They've been married for over forty years. Mom worked with Dad for a while at the winery, keeping the books, but once they had a few kids, she stepped away and kept the home running smoothly. She had an iron fist in a velvet glove. Dad grew up in the wine business and he loves it. He's had two heart attacks and finally got the message to slow down. He's solid as they come."

She smiled. He must get that from his father.

"They've done a bit of traveling, but they're happiest when they're surrounded by family."

"They sound like great people." His life was the total opposite of what she'd experienced but had always wished for.

"How about we do a short driving tour of the winery before heading to the house?"

"That sounds interesting."

"On the left and right of us is our land."

All she could see were rows and rows of grapevines. In the distance sat a cluster of buildings. She knew they were part of the winery since they were on Price land. It was impressive, and she had no idea the business was this extensive. "How far are we from your parents' house?"

"A couple more miles. All of this surrounds the main house."

"All these vines are yours?"

He laughed. "Not mine, but they do belong to the winery. My great-grandfather settled here when he was a young man and planted the first vines."

"I always thought Napa Valley was the best place for grapes to grow."

"When the glaciers moved through this valley, they left in their wake ground which was excellent for grapes. They don't grow all the varieties used for wine, but they do all right."

She could see his eyes sparkle and hear the pride in his voice. Despite his proclamation that his only love was the business of restoring cars, he had one foot in the vineyard. As much as he proclaimed this wasn't his business, wine was still flowing through his veins; it was a part of his heritage. What did she have? The restoration business she planned to manage from long distance? No, she was a very successful manager at a pharmaceutical company, well paid, had a beautiful home, and lived the best her life could provide. It wouldn't be long before she'd be back in her old routine. Even though she had thought briefly about what it would be like to be a part of Leo's family, Portland Stephanie had a predictable life where no one had any expectations of her except to be a damn good executive.

16

Leo pulled into a long driveway lined with old maple trees that eventually gave way to rows of vines. He bore left at the fork but pointed to the right. "That's the way to the house, but this will take us to the winery."

She marveled at how the landscape seemed alive. The greenery from the leaves glistened with early dew, and clusters of grapes were deep green. "How long does it take for the fruit to ripen?"

"About two weeks. But we're still a couple of months from that. Picking begins in mid-September, and then we'll have the crush."

"What's that?"

"After the harvest, grapes will be pressed into juice before it can be made into wine. My parents make it this big event, open to the public."

"Do you go?"

"Everyone lends a hand. It's a huge undertaking and there isn't a lot of time to get it done before the grapes will rot. I've been a part of the crush my whole life. The only one who stays away is Liza. She's allergic to bees."

"Bees?"

"They love the nectar, so they're everywhere. We always have EpiPens on hand just in case Liza stops over."

"So her boys miss out on the excitement?"

"No, I'll pick them up. They love it. Both of them are falling under the spell of growing and winemaking. It's a part of them, but George does have a love of cars too."

"It's in your blood."

With a shake of his head, he said, "Once I was old enough to get a job someplace else, I stopped working at the winery. Don't get me wrong. If I need to help, I'm always ready to jump in, but I love motors and the thrill of restoration."

He pulled up to one of the warehouses. "The offices and tasting room are to the right."

"The gazebo is there," Steph said, pointing as she recognized where they were. "But I didn't see these other buildings when we were here for dinner. I guess I wasn't paying attention." She smiled and tilted her head toward Leo. "Distracted would be a better way to describe it."

"This isn't exactly exciting, just big metal warehouses." He pointed out what each building was used for and answered her questions before he eased down the road leading toward the office.

"Where does that road go?" She gestured out the side window.

"To the house." He glanced at his watch. "Mom's going to wonder if we got lost."

"I'm glad you showed me all of this." She was awestruck. Every building was pristine and the operation seemed to be huge. Four generations had worked this land, and they were gearing up for a fifth. It was obvious they were doing something right. If she channeled her energy into Black River Restoration, could she achieve something even more than what it was now? She had been wondering how she was going to manage her career and the garage without shirking her responsibilities for either. She owed it to the staff at Black River to do more than juggle the business, didn't she?

"Dad may talk about the business, so I've found it's better to have a point of reference."

"Will he grill me about wine?"

Leo chuckled. "No, but he will ask you what your favorite one is and for tonight, I'd skip telling him that you've fallen head over heels in love with Fuse."

"Is your sister's winery a sore spot?"

"Not at all. Dad thrives on helping any other winery grow. But he does have a bit of an ego, so I'm hoping they serve something you'll like."

"I'll fake it."

He laughed even harder. "Don't do that because if you come back, he'll make sure he has it on hand."

Did he wonder if there might be a repeat visit? Deep down, she wanted to keep things simple so it wouldn't be hard to leave in the fall. "I'm sure to enjoy at least one of the wines."

Leo stopped in front of a two-story house. The late-day sun bathed the house in a golden glow. From Stephanie's vantage point, she wondered how eight people had lived there without falling all over each other. The large wrap-around porch had been decorated with hanging baskets and lots of chairs arranged for relaxing. Beyond that, she saw a screened-in area which she assumed had granted access into the home.

He took her hand. "Are you ready?"

Before Steph could answer, a tall, sturdily built man who strongly resembled Leo was coming down the front steps, holding hands with a woman of average height, dark-blond hair, and a welcoming smile.

"I'm ready." She withdrew her hand and remembered to grab the box of truffles from the console.

Once out of the car, Leo took her hand and led her to the steps. "Mom, Dad, this is Stephanie James. And Steph, these are my parents, Sherry and Sam."

She extended her hand and put on her salesperson smile, which always put everyone at ease. "Very nice to meet you, Mrs. Price." She shook Sam's hand. "Mr. Price."

"It's lovely to meet you, Stephanie, and please. We're Sam and Sherry." Leo's mom slipped her arm through Steph's and guided her up the stairs to the front porch.

Sherry was attempting to put her at ease and Steph realized it was just part of her demeanor. Warm and welcoming, much like Tessa was the first time they met. It actually settled the butterflies in her stomach. She could just enjoy the evening, no pressure from Sherry.

"I thought we'd have our wine and appetizers out here tonight. It's such a nice evening."

"You have a lovely home." She glanced over her shoulder to see Leo and Sam right behind them. There was a love seat and a couple of chairs with floral cushions and a wicker coffee table that was set with four wineglasses and a tray of appetizers. Fresh flowers sat on several surfaces as well.

Sherry gestured to a chair. "Sam, you can sit next to me and Leo and Stephanie can have the love seat."

She was glad when Leo slid his arm around the back of the small sofa. It was sweet that he was so close. She wished they had come up with a code word for *everything's fine.*

"Sam and I were very sorry to hear about your father." Sherry's hazel eyes were warm and her smile was so much like Leo's that Steph knew where he got his sweet side.

She wouldn't let tears well up. Not tonight. "Thank you. It's the hardest thing I've ever been through. I'm sure Leo has told you I've been spending my time getting the shop running smoothly before I head home."

Sam opened a bottle of wine. "Do you have family in Oregon?"

"No, it's just me." She looked down, suddenly feeling very alone in the world. She noticed the abundance of pictures on the wall—happy smiling people—and Leo was in most of them. Different moments captured from holidays as a reminder of the connection they had with each other. A basket of children's toys peeked out from behind a chair—grandchildren's toys. She thought of Dad's house. Her parents' wedding photo, one of her and Dad after the Bronco was finished, her college graduation picture, and finally one of her and Maggie on her dresser. Nothing ever out of place. It wasn't a home, just a house, not like this place. She met his brown eyes. "I have some very good friends who are like family."

"Friends are important too." He looked away as if he didn't know what to say next.

"Dad, what wines did you grab for us to try? Steph had the Cab and Cayuga White and Tessa's sparkling wine when we had our dinner at the gazebo."

Sam perked up. "Tell me, what did you think of them? They are both the foundation of our winery."

"They were excellent. I tend to be partial to whites, but Leo has introduced me to a couple of reds that I've enjoyed. I am especially fond of Fuse." Inwardly, she cringed. She had already forgotten that Leo had suggested she shouldn't mention that particular wine.

Sam's eyes bugged out, and then he gave a hearty chuckle. Nodding, he said, "You have very good taste." He winked. "But I never said that."

He pulled a bottle from the chiller. "I selected an interesting bottle that Anna created as a picnic wine. It's a sweeter red." He showed her the label. "Would you like to try it? I also have a Pinot Grigio if you prefer."

"The picnic wine sounds interesting." She turned to Leo. "Are you having some?"

"No, I'll have the Cab Franc."

"What's that like?"

Sam cocked his eyebrow and waited for Leo to answer. There was a pregnant pause.

"It's a dry red but has a soft mouth feel with a peppery, fruit-forward spice."

Sam beamed with pride as he handed her a glass and then poured a deep red wine and passed it to Leo. "Sherry, what will you have?"

"I'll have what Stephanie is having."

Sam handed her a glass, and then he poured a white for himself.

Leo held his glass to his nose and extended it for Steph. "What do you smell?"

She closed her eyes and blocked out everything but the aroma in his glass.

He said softly, "Take your time."

"Berries, earthy and"—she inhaled deeply—"pepper-corn." She opened her eyes to discover Leo grinning.

"Would you like to taste it?"

She took the glass and as Tessa had her do, she held it in her mouth for a few moments before swallowing. She tilted her head from side to side. "You're right. It is a very soft feel in my mouth, almost velvety." She felt a blush rise in her cheeks as she became aware of Sam studying her. "But I'm certainly not an expert."

Sam leaned forward. "Did you like it?"

Nodding, she said, "It was very good."

He slapped a hand on his leg. "She's a keeper, son. She knows her way around a good vintage."

"No. I wouldn't say that, Mr. Price." Damn, he was direct. It was nice that she was making a good impression, but there was no need to start looking at them as a long-term couple.

"It's Sam, and not everyone can pick up on the subtle notes of a wine."

"Alright, Sam. Enough putting Stephanie on the hot seat with a wine tasting." Sherry held up the appetizer platter. "Help yourself."

Steph selected endive stuffed with soft cheese and sun-dried tomato. "This looks delicious." She nibbled on the end as Sherry turned to Leo.

"How is your latest job coming along?"

"The Chevelle? Really good, but it's taken longer than expected; there was a delay with the paint. Steph's guys are doing the job next week, and then I can deliver it to Drew." He bumped her shoulder. "But before she agreed to do the job, she had to inspect the quality of my work."

Sherry laughed. "Good for you. Keep him on his toes."

"In my defense, I've been out of the business for quite some time. Was I supposed to take his word that the body work was up to my standards?"

With a hoot, Sam clapped his hands. "Good for you. A business reputation can be damaged with one misstep, and Leo, you should know that."

"I do. It's just fun to tease her about it."

After hearing Sam and Sherry laughing with Leo, she couldn't help but relax. His parents were down-to-earth, and as her dad would have said, they were good people. The pang of regret was swift and sharp; Dad would have loved Leo and his parents, and he was a lot like Sherry when it came to welcoming people into the fold. Just look at what he had built with the folks at the garage, an eclectic family.

• • •

*L*eo was having a lot of fun watching Steph open up to his parents. He hadn't had a moment's hesitation about getting together with them. She was easy to love.

He sat up straight on the cushion. Love? Did he love her? His gaze slid to her face. He had never seen her this animated before. It was as if hanging out with an older generation eased her heart. But did it make her miss her own parents more? He was filled with questions as the minutes passed.

Steph gave him a sweet smile. "Would you like more wine?"

"I think we should get going so we can pick up dinner."

"If you want, I happen to have a lasagna in the oven." Sherry looked from Leo to Stephanie and back to Leo. "You're welcome to stay."

Steph clasped his hand. "I'd love to have dinner with your parents if that's okay with you."

Mom gave him a quick look and a smile tugged at the corner of her lips. Once again, he'd been outmaneuvered. In his experience, no one ever turned down homemade lasagna.

"Sure. We can stay."

"What can I do to help?" Steph looked at the table and said, "Oh. I almost forgot to give you this." She handed Sherry the box of truffles.

"Dear, you didn't need to bring us something." She accepted the box and noticed the logo. Her eyes lit up. "Are these truffles?"

"They are."

She held up the box for Sam to see. "They're our favorites. Thank you."

"I'm glad."

Sherry stood up. "Let's go inside and the guys can help us get dinner on the table."

Relieved that his mom seemed to really like Steph, Leo picked up the open bottles of wine. "I'm starved. Steph, you will not be disappointed. My mom is the best Italian chef who doesn't have a drop of Italian blood in her veins."

"Leo, stop." Mom laughed. "Stephanie, don't listen to him. He'd eat burnt toast if I served it to him."

He opened the door and let the ladies and Dad walk into the house. It made his heart smile as he overheard his mother chattering a mile a minute. Yeah, Stephanie was the perfect fit.

17

*S*teph felt wrapped in contentment on the drive to Leo's place. It had been a long time since she'd had dinner with a man's parents. Sherry was lovely and Sam was a big teddy bear. But she could see where he would have been a demanding parent when Leo was growing up. Occasionally Sam had reminded him about the upcoming board meeting and that Leo's presence was needed. He even invited Steph to come around to the tasting room and see firsthand how the process worked. But her time in New York was growing short. Even though she still had a few months left, her boss had called earlier to see when she was going back to work. She missed her job and Maggie, but she couldn't leave until she discovered who was stealing from the family business.

"Hey, you're pretty quiet over there. Is everything okay?"

She looked into his deep-brown eyes. "I had fun tonight. I like your parents."

"I do too." He gave her a smile. "They really liked you."

"You're just saying that."

He slowed and turned right. "No, I'm not. Dad would

never have asked you to come around if he didn't like you."

"What about the crush? Is it a big party and everyone's welcome?"

"There are separate events. One's geared toward the public and the other is a family thing. Dad mentioned that if you're here, he'd love to have you come to the closed event." He gave her a long look. "Is that what's troubling you?"

Could he read her mind? "I'm not sure what you mean."

"Didn't you say you had a six-month leave? That will be around the time the crush begins."

He had an excellent memory. "My boss called today and asked me when I was going back to Portland." She couldn't say home. It didn't feel like it anymore. A wave of sadness washed over her. There was so much she wanted to tell Leo, but the words were like dust in her mouth.

"What did you say?"

The question hung in the air. She wasn't sure how to answer him.

He clicked on his blinker and turned into a tree-lined driveway that gave way to open lawn on either side after about twenty yards. His headlights were on high, probably to illuminate the low-slung ranch that was his home.

Before she got out of the car, she wanted to talk and then leave it alone for the rest of the night. It became real that nights with Leo were limited.

"I reminded him the plan was October. I get the feeling he might want me back sooner." She looked at her hand-bag. "There is the issue of someone stealing. I need to get all the systems online and Zira needs some mentoring. I'll feel better when I know she has more confidence in her skills." She grasped his hand. "I want to enjoy all the time we can together."

He squeezed her hand. "We will." He inclined his head toward the door. "Ready to take the tour?"

She gave him a grin. "Lead the way."

They paused by the front door while he toed off his shoes and she left her sandals. He tried to see the room through her eyes as he ushered her into the kitchen: a large, open floor plan between the kitchen, dining area, and living room, with oversized windows in the front and a wall of sliding doors leading to the backyard. An island dominated the space, but Steph made note of the small sink, the countertop stove, and two ovens on the far wall. The floors were maple and they gleamed under the lights.

She did a slow three-sixty turn. "Do you like to cook?"

"Yeah, and kitchens are a huge selling point, so I'm planning a high-end kitchen before I flip."

"You're going to sell it?'

"After I finish the landscaping and the family room in the basement, it will go on the market."

"How many have you flipped?" She walked behind the island, her fingers trailing over the granite countertop.

"This is my second."

Nodding, she said, "Right, I think you mentioned that before. I'm impressed. It will make a nice family home."

He held out his hand. "Want to see the rest?"

She placed her hand in his. "How many more rooms are there?"

"Four bedrooms, including the master, and two and a half bathrooms."

They walked down the hallway and paused at each bedroom so she could look. The rooms were spacious and the main bath had white tiles and a tub with a standalone shower.

"Very nice."

Leo steered her to the right. "I added on the master suite to really make this house attractive to a family."

When he pushed open the door, she gasped. "This is amazing." The windows on the back wall had a large window seat. "You could get nice and cozy with a book and watch it snow."

Going deeper into the room, he noticed she wiggled her toes in the plush silver carpeting. Along one wall was a row of doors.

He opened the first set and then the next. "A walk-in closet with built-in drawers."

With her eyes wide, she asked sweetly, "Did you put in a closet for the man's clothes?"

He cocked his head. "I think this is big enough to share." He waited half a beat and laughed. "But maybe I should add on to the house so there's more closet space."

She bobbed her head from one side to the other. "Maybe." She pointed to a door. "The bathroom?"

"I can't wait to hear what you think about this room. Strictly from the female point of view."

He flicked a light switch. To the left was a double sink vanity with excellent lighting and a small mirror that pulled out from the wall. He pointed to it. "Makeup mirror."

"I see that. You get an extra point." She took a few steps and examined the large pane of glass. "Isn't that window a little too revealing for a bathroom?"

"I try to add a little something different in each house. This window happens to be special. From the inside, you can see out during the day and it lets in the natural sun. At night, it blocks the view, but the special feature is day or night, you can never see in this window from the outside."

"Very impressive. And a dual-headed shower."

He smirked. "It's big enough for two."

"I can see that. Maybe we should try it out sometime."

He pulled her into his arms, something he had wanted to do since they walked in. He searched her eyes. "Do you like the house?"

"It's much larger than it appeared from the driveway. Each room is spacious and you're right; it will make a nice family very happy."

She tilted her head back and seemed to invite him to kiss her. He bent low, happy to oblige. A slow, tender kiss was on his mind, but she surprised him with a deep, sensual kiss in return.

She pulled back, her eyes sparkling. "I'm suddenly not interested in the rest of the tour. Can it wait until morning?"

In one smooth motion, he scooped her into his arms and strode into the bedroom, placing her in the center of the snowy-white down comforter.

Her dirty-blond hair fanned out, giving her a halo look.

"You are so beautiful." He could hear the huskiness in his voice.

Her gray eyes glowed with desire as she pulled him closer. "I want you. Show me that you want me too."

He lowered his body over hers and claimed her mouth. All thoughts of continuing their earlier conversation about her leaving were forgotten. They had tonight.

The smell of coffee brewing pulled Stephanie from her sleepy fog. She dragged the covers over her head and rubbed the sleep from her eyes. She wasn't ready to face the day so, groaning, she turned over to look out the window. Pots of shrubs and piles of dirt were scattered throughout the backyard.

The bed dipped and she half turned and placed a hand

on Leo's cheek. She liked seeing him first thing in the morning.

"Good morning, sleepyhead." He handed her a mug of coffee. "Cream, one sugar."

She pushed herself to a half-sitting position. "Thank you." He was the sweetest guy she had ever dated. He actually remembered how she took her coffee. Why couldn't she have met him in Portland?

"What time do you need to get to the shop?"

She took a sip and glanced at the clock on the side table. "At this rate, I won't get there on time." She liked to be there by eight, but it was after seven. "And you're going to be late too."

"My boss is easygoing." He leaned against the pillows and stretched his jean-clad legs out in front of him.

As much as she would have liked to run her fingers through his thick blond hair and then follow the trail down his body, she had responsibilities, and the task of tracking down her thief roared its ugly head.

He was watching her closely. "Why the frown?"

"I don't know how to find out who is stealing from me. I thought about installing cameras inside, but that seems a little creepy."

"I've been giving this some thought, and I came up with kind of a crazy idea."

She sat up straighter and crossed her legs underneath her. "I'm listening."

"What if you told everyone you were installing cameras inside the shop and lobby and they would only be activated if there was a break-in? Reassure them that they wouldn't record during regular hours unless someone pushed a panic button."

"Kind of like a bank alarm?" She picked at a fuzz on the blanket. "I don't think anyone would buy that."

"They would if you linked it to a silent alarm. You

wouldn't have to make sure they were actively monitored. I'll give you the number for my guy if you want."

She took another sip of her coffee, letting the idea gel. "It could work. I could say besides the button in the shop and front desk, the alarm could be linked to sensors attached to the doors and windows, so if someone broke in, the real alarm would go off and the cameras would start recording." She could see it did have possibilities. "I'll call your security company from home and ask if I can meet them somewhere to discuss it. I don't want anyone over-hearing our conversation."

"I'm happy to be with you when you meet them if you want."

She placed a hand on his arm. It was warm, and that brought more comfort than the actual idea did. "I'm going to take you up on that offer. In this case, two heads are better than one." Without spilling her coffee, she leaned into him and pressed her lips to his neck. "As your payment, I'm going to cook dinner for you. Whatever you'd like."

He set his coffee aside and did the same with her mug. With a wicked gleam in his eye, he said, "I know of another way you can repay me."

With a laugh, she placed a hand on his chest and gave him a playful shove. "Later, handsome. Work first and play-time after dinner."

"Do you want to stay here tonight? The fridge is stocked. I can pick up a couple of steaks and we could have a fire in the backyard. Just the two of us."

She pecked his lips. "It's a date." She hopped off the bed and rethought his invitation. "How about a quick shower?"

His brow arched. "For two?"

Standing with her hands on her hips, she gave him her best saucy smile. "I could use help washing my back."

"You do realize we're going to be late."

She turned to walk into the bathroom, feeling his eyes on her. "Time's a-wasting, Price."

His jeans flew through the air and dropped next to her.

"You don't have to ask me twice."

He grabbed two large fluffy gray towels from the rack on the back of the door and then stepped around her and turned on the showerheads. Steam began to fill the space.

"How much time do I have to wash your back?"

She stepped under the warm water. With a low laugh, she said, "All the time you need."

18

*L*ater that day, Leo listened to his voicemail. There was one from Drew Cameron, checking on his Chevy, and the other was from Stephanie. She had set up an appointment with the security company for tomorrow at nine and asked if he could meet them. But only if he had time, since she knew he was on a deadline for the Chevelle. As he returned her call, waiting for her to pick up, he looked over the punch list for Drew's car. Everything was right on schedule now that the delays with the paint were behind him.

He could hear the smile in her voice when she answered.

"Hi," he responded. "I got your voicemail and I will be there, but you need to tell me where we're going to meet."

"Well, I wanted to ask a favor. Would you mind if we met at your garage? This way, no one can overhear us."

"Sure. How's everything else going over there?"

"Like clockwork."

"Good. This afternoon, I was going to work on the restoration book for the Chevelle."

"What's your next project?"

"I have a sixty-seven Camaro coming in next week, so I'm going to tinker with the Mustang."

"Well," she drawled, "I was hoping you'd take a look at the truck. There's a skip in the engine."

"You have an excellent mechanic on staff. Maybe you should give Zira a crack at it." He twirled a pencil in his hand after closing the project book. "Or I could work with her here if you think that would help? You shouldn't bring me into your shop. I wouldn't want anyone to get the wrong idea."

"I agree. I'd love to work with her but with everything going on, I just don't have the time." There was a pregnant pause. "I called my boss today and confirmed I will be back in October unless things aren't resolved by then."

He felt his heart drop. Her tone of voice was different, and it hit him that she really was going to leave. All he could think to say was, "Oh."

"Leo."

"Hey, we both knew you'd be headed back. Let's agree to enjoy the rest of our time together." His heart hammered in his chest. How the hell was he going to let her go? He forced his voice to be light. "I'll leave it to you to pick up wine for dinner."

"Are you sure?"

Was she asking about wine or his acknowledgement of her plans? He smiled into the phone. "I trust you to pick a good vintage."

"Hey, what's with you and vintage? Wine and cars?"

"I prefer to enjoy life with depth of character. Good wine, a classic car, and even the people in my life. Real, honest, original, and a degree of intensity." He wasn't sure that conveyed what he wanted to say.

Steph's voice brought him back to the moment. "I know exactly what you mean. I feel the same way."

He knew they were kindred souls, but it didn't seem to

matter. Soon, the woman he wanted as his partner for life was going to leave and take his heart with her.

"What time will you be over?"

"That depends on you."

He could hear the smirk she now had plastered across her face. He double-checked the time. It was almost ten. "I'll be home by four. Come whenever you're ready." Did he need to ask her to plan on staying the night?

She seemed to hesitate. "Would it be okay if I brought some shampoo and a few other essentials to leave at your place?"

Relief coursed through him. It might not seem like a big deal on the surface, but she was feeling comfortable at his house. As far as he was concerned, she could bring everything and stay permanently, but that wasn't an option. "Whatever you need; make yourself at home."

"Alrighty then. I'll see you later."

He waited until he heard the line go dead before he placed the phone on the desk and hung his head. He could use some advice. Liza was his best bet in matters of his heart.

She answered on the third ring and sounded out of breath.

"Hey, sis. Am I interrupting something?"

"I just got back from a run."

"You hate running." It was one of the many things they agreed on, but he also knew they both did it for good heart health, trying to beat that bad gene they might have inherited from Dad.

"Today was a killer."

He heard a glass clink against the phone and waited while he guessed she drank water.

"Okay, I'm back. I heard Mom and Dad met Stephanie, and Mom said she is really nice."

"Dinner went well. Dad even asked her to come to the crush with me."

"Wow. He's turning into quite the softie. He wouldn't let any of us bring someone we had just started dating until it was serious." She paused again. "Is it serious?"

"That's why I'm calling. Are you going to be home after two? I could use some advice."

"I have to pick the boys up at three, so come anytime before or after that."

"Drew's stopping over around one and when I'm done, I'll be over."

"That's Colin's buddy, right?"

"Yeah. He's a good guy. He's letting Colin use the car instead of a limo for the wedding."

"That's nice of him. It's hard to believe the wedding is in a few weeks. I'm sure Mom is planning a bash next week for the happy couple."

With a snort, Leo said, "That'll be the start of the wedding festivities."

"And we have a shower planned too. Should we invite Steph? You are bringing her to the wedding, aren't you?"

"That's an awful lot of family compressed into a few weeks." Not that he didn't want to have her with him for all the parties, but it might really send her running back to Portland. "And it's kind of what I wanted to talk to you about."

"Like I said, come whenever."

"Okay, catch you on the flip side."

Leo locked the shop after Drew left. He was another satisfied customer and a potential referral too. He looked around the front of the shop, proud of what he had built here. Could he pick up and move three thousand miles away if Stephanie would want to continue their relationship? It was just one idea swirling in his brain. The other was to ask if she'd want to continue to run Black River Restoration and stay here. The worst alternative was that it was over and she was gone from his life permanently and he would have to pick up the pieces.

It was sunny out, but too bad the weather didn't match his mood. In a few long strides, he was in the truck and headed toward his twin's house.

Her van was parked near the back door and the hatch was open, revealing bags of groceries waiting to be carried in. He scooped up four and walked through the open door. He set them on the counter. Liza was putting things in the freezer.

"I'll grab the rest of the bags."

"Thanks." She began to unload the next one, setting cereal boxes and bottles on the counter.

When he finished carrying the last of the bags inside, he helped her put everything away, as familiar with her kitchen as with his own. When they were done, she poured him a glass of soda with ice and pointed to the patio.

"We should sit outside. It's too nice to be indoors."

Once they were comfortable, she gave him a pointed look. "Out with it."

"I'm in love with Stephanie." Now that he said it out loud, it didn't sound quite as scary as it once had.

She grinned from ear to ear. "That's great news." Her smiled faded as she watched him. "It's not good news?"

"When her dad got sick, she came home a couple of weeks before he passed. Since then, she's been working to get the business to where she can handle it remotely. Well, at least until she decides if she wants to sell it. Her boss called and asked when she was coming back. I think he's getting anxious to have her back in the office."

"Oh." Liza sipped her soda. "Is she in love with you?"

"I think so, but we've never said as much to each other."

Her eyes grew round. "You haven't told her how you feel?"

"No. You're the first person to know."

"Leo, she should be the first and I should be the second." She was half serious and half teasing. "A lady needs to hear these things, you know."

"I'm not sure if I should tell her. If I do and she leaves, it won't make a difference. If I tell her and she stays and something awful happens between us, she'll have imploded her career for nothing."

"There is another option." She leaned forward and touched his arm. "She tells you she loves you too and you live happily ever after."

"I'm thinking about asking if I could go to Portland for a visit and while I'm there, check out the area to see if I could move my business there."

She leaned back in the chair. "You'd move to the West Coast and start over? Really?"

"Sis. I've never felt about a woman the way I feel about Stephanie. I've been waiting for her my entire life. Someone who I can have fun with, who shares my passion for cars, who feels right when I hold her. I don't want to lose that."

Liza smiled. "You're in love." She clasped her hand over his. "Tell her how you feel. Everything else will fall into place."

"If I decide to make the move, how do you think the family will take the news?"

"You'll be missed, but more than anything in this world, you know every member of our family will be thrilled for your happiness." Tears sprang to her eyes. "I'll be the happiest and I'll miss you the most."

"You know I'm never more than a phone call away." It hit him like a gut punch. Who would help Liza with the boys? Especially as they approached the preteen and teenage years. He'd have to talk to his brothers and brothers-in-law and make sure they spent time with George and Johnny. They would need a strong guiding hand in the coming years.

"I know you're thinking about me and the boys, and stop it. We will be fine."

"I know but…"

"We're not your responsibility. There are lots of single mothers with sons. Maybe I've relied on you too much over the past few years."

"You're my sister and time spent with the boys is something I've always enjoyed. That will never change." No matter where he lived, he'd stay connected to them.

"Changing the subject." Her brow arched. "You're going to ask Stephanie to be your plus one for all the upcoming events, right?"

"Definitely, but I'm not going to pressure her either. I don't want to miss any time with her or the family, and once everyone meets her, they'll see why she is so special to me."

"In that case, let's have a barbeque here; we can make it just the family. You just name the day. I'll invite the entire family if that's okay. I know with just losing her dad, family gatherings might be tough for her."

Leo stood up and kissed her cheek. "It sounds like fun and I'll let you know what she says. I'm gonna take off. I need to pick up a few things before Steph gets to my place."

Liza looked at him. Her hazel eyes twinkled. "Tell her how you feel. You'll be glad you did."

"I hope you're right."

19

Steph pulled up in front of Leo's house. She finally felt like she belonged in New York, but her heart was heavy. Things were going well at the garage despite the ongoing theft issue, but that would be resolved soon. Business was solid and ideas for expansion were bubbling, but they wouldn't work if she wasn't here, and she had finally rediscovered the thrill of hot rods. She hadn't worked on enough cars yet but was slowly finding her old groove.

Dating Leo was amazing and given more time, she'd look up some of her old high school friends. But how could she leave her job after her boss had been gracious to give her a leave of absence? She needed to go back and work her butt off, if for no other reason than to show her appreciation to the company since they had been supportive of her during Dad's illness and death. And if she was gone much longer, maybe they'd discover they didn't need her. After all, everyone could be replaced even if she had turned the territory around.

She looked at the house and a lump lodged in her throat. After giving it a great deal of thought, she was going to tell Leo that she was in love with him. This was an unexpected turn of events, but since Dad had told her he was sick, everything had been upside down.

The garage door began to rumble upward and Leo, her very own browned-eyed blond guy, poked his head around the doorjamb.

With a wave, he said, "Pull in."

She pointed up and he called out. "No worries; you've got plenty of room."

After she parked inside and the garage door had closed, he pulled open the driver's door, kissing her before her feet hit the concrete.

With a laugh, she said, "Can I get out first before you get my motor running?"

"I've missed you." He looked into her eyes as if he were seeing her for the first time. Her heart skipped a beat. Dear heavens, she loved this man.

"I have beverages and sweet treats."

He held her tight. "I've got all the sweetness I need right in my arms."

"Leo." She looked around. "Nice garage, but is there any reason why we're just standing here?"

He gave her a lingering peck. "Nope. Just happy to see you. I'll get the stuff; you can carry in your tote bag." He had glanced at the oversized canvas bag on the seat. "Just one?"

"This time." She laughed. Her heart hammered in her chest. Was he suggesting she bring over more of her things? And what would be the point? She wasn't going to be here that much longer even though as each day passed, the idea held more appeal.

He scooped up the wine and beer she'd brought along with a bakery box and held it up to his nose. With an exaggerated sniff, he said, "Yum. Cardboard. My favorite."

She grabbed her bag and shut the Bronco's door. "I knew that." She followed Leo into the house but when she stepped inside, her mouth dropped open. "What the heck did you do?"

Vases of wildflowers seemed to be on every available surface. Soft jazz piano played in the background, and the table on the back deck was set for two, complete with candles. White twinkle lights added the finishing touch.

Tears filled her eyes. She was overcome with joy. "You did all of this for me?"

Leo set the bags and box on the counter. Then he took her tote bag, set it down, and slid his arms around her waist.

"Stephanie, I wanted tonight to be special. I love you and I wanted you to always remember the moment I told you." He turned her in his arms so she could look around the room again. His breath tickled her ear. "I love you."

He hugged her close. She wiggled around to face him and took his face in her hands and pulled him close. "I'm so glad you told me. I was going to tell you tonight too."

"Tell me what?" He tipped his head. "Can you be more specific?"

"I love you, Leo Price, from the tips of my toes to the top of my head and to infinity."

She couldn't help but sigh as he claimed her mouth, sealing their love with a kiss.

They sat in the glow of candle and twinkle lights, but Leo leaned back in his chair. He needed to bring up the family events and hoped Steph would want to go with him.

"Dinner was great. The steak was delicious and cooked perfectly." She smiled across the table.

It warmed his heart to see her there, although it was going to be hard when they had to say goodbye. Instead, he'd treasure these moments. "I'm just happy you agree with me regarding how a porterhouse should be cooked. There's nothing worse than getting a good cut of meat and turning it into shoe leather."

She grinned. "In full disclosure, Dad taught me how to grill. Everything I know, I can attribute to him."

"Grilling is an art form." He sipped his beer. "I saw my sister Liza today and she asked us to come for a barbeque sometime soon."

Her face lit up. "Your entire family?"

"Well, yeah." He shrugged and gave her a small grin that he hoped came off as irresistible and that she'd say yes.

"Oh. How many people are we talking?" She toyed with her glass while avoiding his eyes.

"Nineteen, including all the kids. Twenty-one if you count us."

She lifted her eyes. They were unreadable. "I've met six so far."

The idea of meeting his family might be daunting, but he wanted her to get to know everyone. They were an important part of who he was. "I get it. I just thought I'd ask." His shoulders dropped. It was a disappointment, but he understood. It was a lot of new people.

"I didn't say I didn't want to go. I just need to know how many names I'll have to remember." Her smile slowly appeared. "When?"

"Liza suggested next week. Not to rush things, but what about Sunday?"

"Okay, just ask what we should bring. Family potlucks can be fun and I'm sure based on your mom's cooking and Kate's bistro, the food must be outstanding."

He beamed. "I'll text her later." He decided to push his luck a bit further. He wiped his damp palms over his jeans and took a deep breath. *Here goes nothing.*

"If this goes well, would you consider going to Anna's wedding with me? It's before you go back."

She laughed. The musical sound lightened his heart and it took the edge off his anxiety.

"I would love to go with you to your sister's wedding. Tell me the date and time. Besides, it'll give me an excuse to go shopping for a dress and shoes." Her eyes narrowed but they were filled with laughter. "Let me guess. There will be a few more family events leading up to the wedding."

"Maybe." He grinned. "She's getting married at the end of next month."

"If you ask me very sweetly, I'm sure you can convince me to be your date for them all."

"I can be sweet like fine milk chocolate."

With a throaty laugh, she replied, "My favorite."

"How about we pick up the dishes and I can make a fire? It's a nice night and the stars are just peeking out."

"That's something I miss in the city; there are no peepers or the gentle hoot of an owl, and the stars. They're endless here."

"Is that a yes?"

"Most definitely."

She pushed back from the table and picked up the dinner plates. Leo slid open the door and grabbed the rest, stacking them on the counter. He left the door open and started the fire while inside, he could hear running water and dishes clattering as she loaded the dishwasher. This was what couples did when they lived together, and for all intents and purposes, they were, as they had spent every night together for weeks.

It was only recently that she had started to stay here. Her house was small, with one bathroom, and it just wasn't as comfortable as here. He'd like to make an official statement that they were living together, but that was wishful thinking. Besides, it might add undue pressure to the time they had left.

"Hey, what are you doing out there? Stargazing?"

Caught daydreaming, he could feel a flash of warmth slide up his neck. What would she think knowing he was wishing they could do this every night for a long time to come? "They're just starting to make their appearance. Are you coming out?"

She wiped her hands on a towel. "I'm going to change into pants and grab a fleece."

"Good idea." He flicked a match into the pit. "Even with me by your side, you might get chilled."

Stephanie walked down the hall to the master bedroom, glad that she had thought to leave a few extra articles of clothing here. Without turning on the light, she stepped out of her shorts and pulled on pants and a pair of socks. With the days growing shorter, some nights had a nip in the air, even in July. She pulled on a deep maroon fleece and zipped up the front. Now all she needed was her clogs and she was ready. Before she left the room, the scent of flowers caught her attention. She turned on the lights and discovered Leo had put a large vase of flowers on her side of the bed. He needed a proper thank-you for setting a very romantic mood.

She closed the door behind her and walked slowly to the deck. Her breath caught. He was placing a few small logs onto the flickering flames. The glow from the firelight lit up his strong features. He was a very handsome man physically, but his true appeal was his heart. He wore it well and for anyone to see.

She hurried down to the dew-damp grass, glad she had chosen to wear shoes. "This is nice."

He held his arm out and slipped it around her waist. "Warm enough?"

"I am now." She snuggled in close and inhaled his soap, clean with a hint of musk. It wasn't the fire she was referring to, either. How was she going to leave all of this? She could have a good life here, a simpler life than in Portland, but small-town living contained a richness that she hadn't found over the last ten years in Portland. Could she come home again?

"I brought the wine out, but do you want some coffee with dessert?"

"No." She began to pull away. "I'll go in and get the tart."

"No need." He pointed to a small table off to one side. "I even cut it and there are plates too." He kissed her temple and then his lips found hers.

Contentment like she had never known blanketed her. She pushed all thoughts about the future to the recesses of her mind.

"I don't want this night to end."

"Sweetheart, night gives way to a new day, and we have to seize it and savor each moment."

"And treasure them," she murmured against his lips, thinking he had said it all there.

Time seemed to stand still as they kissed under the stars, warm from the fire in their hearts.

20

The next morning at nine, Leo opened the door to his office. A white panel van with small letters stating *security* was in the lot, and Steph pulled in seconds later. She gave him a wave and parked.

"Sorry I'm running behind. Tiny crisis at the shop." *Tiny, my foot!* This time, she had discovered a computer monitor box was empty. The timing could haven't been worse since she needed to poke around and find out if someone had installed it in a workstation without giving her a heads-up.

He held open the door and she hurried in. A whiff of her floral shampoo teased his nose. The man from the van was right behind her.

He stuck out his hand. "Hi, Artie. Thanks for coming."

"Hey, Leo. Good to see you again." He scanned the space. "How are the cameras working out? No problems?"

"All good, thanks."

Artie nodded. "If you ever want to upgrade, give me a call."

He was a bit pushy for Leo's taste but he got the job done. That was all that mattered.

"Thanks. I'll keep that in mind." He gestured to a small round table with four chairs. "I thought we could talk about Stephanie's shop."

She said, "I'm going to put my bag in your office."

While they waited, Leo said, "I know you're aware Stephanie is trying to make sure her employees don't feel like they're being spied on, but she needs to stop this steady stream of stealing."

"That's what I do best. One rotten apple in the barrel creates a nasty smell."

Leo nodded. "Interesting analogy." He was relieved when Steph rejoined them. Hopefully Artie could get the job done quickly, before any more stuff came up missing.

"And this is a similar layout to Black River Restoration?" Artie glanced around and made notes on his clipboard.

Stephanie looked at Artie. "Yes. We have a large paint booth area, but I'm not concerned about that space. It is really the two supply rooms and back doors. I wanted to meet here so I could speak freely."

"Steph, you should also be thinking about the front door," Leo said. "Whoever is doing this may not have an issue about taking something right out the front. Remember, the chair box was empty."

She frowned. "I know you're right. I just hate thinking this person is so bold, thinking he's entitled."

Artie held up the clipboard. "Let's sit down, sketch out the layout, and I'll show you what I'm thinking."

After a few moments of working on a generic floor plan, Artie turned the clipboard so Stephanie could see it clearly. "Overall, I think it will be easy to install the cameras and tuck them into the existing lighting so they would be hard to see unless you were really looking for them." He pointed to several X's on the rough sketch. "Put them here, here, and here." He flipped over the paper. "Going into the lobby, we can add cameras so they point to the front door and to the storage room, along with two that will cover the hallway leading out to the other door. Of course, this will depend on what I find when I actually see your shop."

Stephanie studied the paper. A heavy feeling in the pit of her stomach caused her temper to rise. It was awful that she had to do this. "Should we put one inside the storage room, the one nearest to the lobby?"

"Might not be a bad idea." Artie jotted a note. "Depending on the size of your place and inventory from my supplier, I can get everything installed and up and running by the weekend." He glanced at Leo. "Is it okay if I share the cost of your job to give her a ballpark number?"

He nodded. "Sure."

"BRR is twice the size of Leo's place and I have a few more areas that should be looked at."

Artie gave her the figure and said, "It could be double this cost, but I won't know until I see the shop."

She had prepared herself for a large quote and was surprised to see it was almost half of what she had projected. That was if his rough estimate was even close. "I'll want a written estimate and a contract."

"It's the only way I work." Artie picked up his clip-board. "Give me a call when I can do a walk-through and my guys can work at night, after you close up for the day."

Stephanie stood and extended her hand in one motion. "Thanks for meeting me here."

"Not a problem. You'd be surprised how many times I meet a client away from the job site. When you're having an issue, it can make the situation worse if people know someone is on to them."

After Artie left the shop, Steph sat down and dropped her head into her hands. Leo sat quietly by her side.

"Am I doing the right thing?"

He placed his hand over hers and she closed her eyes briefly, drawing strength from him. She opened her eyes and met his. "I feel like a heel, sneaking around behind peoples' backs just so I can spy on them."

He sat up straight and tilted her chin up. "Look at me."

She pulled herself up.

"Someone has broken your trust. Not the other way around. You have every right, for yourself and for all of your honest employees, to find out who is stealing, not just from you but from them too. Theft impacts your bottom line."

She tapped her head. "I know it here." Then she tapped the middle of her chest. "But here is a different story."

"Do you have any idea who you think it is?"

"It's got to be one of the newer guys."

"Will you prosecute?"

She wrung her hands together and looked across the room, not making eye contact. "Probably not. I'll just fire them and move on."

He waited for her to continue.

She dropped her eyes to the floor and scuffed the toe of her boot. "I mean, I could file a complaint with the police, but what would that really do except cost me more money for a lawyer to take him to court? I just want this to be behind me."

He tugged at her hand and pulled her into his lap.

She relished the comfort he provided and enjoyed the feel of his arms around her, pulling her close.

"I want to talk about something else besides my thief. Should we bring something on Sunday to your sister's place?"

"I usually bring chips and ice."

She pulled away from his chest and wrinkled her nose.

"That is spoken like a bachelor. I happen to know you're a pretty good cook."

"When it comes to get-togethers, there are some amazing cooks in our family. Mom, Kate, Peyton, and Liza. Anna, not as much; she can cook but isn't a fan. And Tessa. She can but is happy to have Max do all their cooking. He's the better of the two."

"You're not scaring me, you know. I want us to contribute more than ice and potato chips. Would you call Liza and ask her what she'd like us to bring?"

He toyed with her fingers. "You might be opening a can of worms. Once you offer and actually make something, you'll be on the hook every time."

"I'm good with that." She pointed to his phone.

With a chuckle, he picked it up and called his sister.

"Hi, Liza. I'm here with Stephanie and you're on speaker."

"Hi, Stephanie."

Her voice was warm and Steph could picture her sunny smile.

"We were just talking about Sunday. What do you need us to bring?" Leo gave her a smile.

"The usual is fine."

Liza sounded as if she was holding back a laugh.

"What would you like in addition to Leo's usual?" Steph asked.

He opened his mouth to speak but she placed a finger over his lips and shook her head with a grin. "Do you need dessert or an appetizer?"

Now Liza did laugh softly. "I'll tell you what. Surprise me. Food at family events never goes to waste. All I ask is if you make something that isn't kid-friendly, tell me before it goes on the buffet table."

"You've got it." She gave Leo a playful poke in his chest and mouthed, *I told ya.*

"You should come by around noon. The boys are already talking about a whiffle ball game before we eat."

"You got it, sis. See ya later."

"Looking forward to seeing you both on Sunday."

"Bye, Liza." Stephanie jumped in before Leo could disconnect.

He tossed the phone on the desk. "Like I said, now you've done it. Unless you make something that is completely inedible."

"It just so happens I make the most decadent fudgy brownies, so good they'll make you never want to eat anyone else's brownies again."

He chuckled. "That's a very bold statement."

She grinned. "I'll be honest. It's the only thing I can bake, so I've worked to perfect them."

"Maybe you should whip up a batch for me to taste before the barbeque."

She slid from his arms. "You can wait."

His pout was epic, she thought. "Is there anything I can do to change your mind?".

"Nope," she said, bending down to peck his lips. She straightened and took a step toward the office, but he grabbed her hand.

"What are you going to do about Artie?"

"I'm going to hire him and see if he can start the install on Friday night and hopefully he'll finish on Saturday."

"I'm going to guess this means we'll be at the shop too."

"I should be there and would like the company."

He said, "Sure, I'll be there for you."

"Thanks, and besides, we have plans on Sunday." He was a sweet guy, but she was more than capable of managing BRR just as he managed Vintage. It was amazing she had met him on the worst day of her life. Whether he knew it or not, Leo had helped her get through many dark moments. His never-ending kindness and that heart-melting smile lifted her up when she needed it most. She was going to miss that when she returned to Portland.

"Hey, what's wrong?" He was standing in front of her and put his arms around her. "You just looked like this whole thing overwhelmed you."

"I'm okay. It's just, so much has happened in the last few months and I am very thankful you and the boys came into the shop that day."

"Ah. I see." He kissed her forehead. "I'll be here whenever you need me."

She drank in his handsome face and cupped his cheek. "You are the sweetest man I've ever met."

He leaned in close and searched her eyes. Was he trying to see beyond the surface and into her heart?

"You bring out the best in me."

She pushed aside the thought that surfaced. She was not going to think about a future she couldn't have with him. It wasn't possible. She had to go back to her old life. People were counting on her.

"Will you come back from time to time?"

And there it was. How often would she be able to come back and still maintain her career?

"I have the business to run, so of course I'll be back." Her stomach tightened. She hoped that was the truth.

"Steph, if you asked me to check out Portland, I would."

She was taken aback. "Like open your business three thousand miles away just so that we can be us?"

His deep-brown eyes and expression were solemn. "I'm willing to explore options."

She stood on her tiptoes. With a slow, lingering kiss, she felt her heart open. "That is something we can think about." She kissed him again. "But not right now. I just want to spend the next few days enjoying what we have. I love you even more in this moment than I did."

"I'm serious." His eyes never left hers. "I've never felt like this in my life, and I like the man I am with you."

"Leo."

He claimed her lips, tender at first, and then the kiss deepened as if he were branding her with his love and ruining her for anyone else.

Steph closed her eyes and sank into the kiss. She knew in her heart that she never wanted to be without this man by her side. But there was no way she would ask him to give up his life to follow her west.

Her head was swimming when he stepped back. Her eyes fluttered open. "You sure do know how to kiss."

"You need to get back to work or I'm going to take you home and keep you there until tomorrow morning."

"As tempting as that sounds, you're right. I have things to get done." She gave him a saucy wink. "Can we pick this up tonight?"

"I'll grab Chinese and we'll have dinner and see where the night takes us."

He kissed her and turned to ease her out the door.

"See you at home." His home did feel like it was her safe haven. Something she hadn't expected to find was a man who cared for her and how seamlessly they fit into each other's lives.

21

Stephanie was stacking brownies on a blue-and-white-checked plate for the barbeque at Liza's when hands slid around her waist and pulled her back against a hard, warm chest. She laid her head back and gave a small laugh.

"Good morning."

Leo nuzzled her neck. "What time did you get up?"

"A couple of hours ago. I wanted to get these made, and because you spent so much time at the shop this weekend helping me take inventory again, I made you breakfast as a little thank you."

She turned in his arms and marveled how a man could look this handsome and be so kindhearted and be holding her in his arms on a Sunday morning.

"No need to work so hard. You were exhausted last night; you probably should have slept in."

With a shake of her head, she slipped from his arms and crossed to the coffee pot to pour him a mug. "I had a few things to do." She gestured to her laptop. "I finished cross-checking Chuck's inventory, so I know we are accurate as of tomorrow when we open up."

He took the mug from her after she added a splash of cream. "What about the office supply closet?"

"I need to finish that up before the end of the morning."

He pulled out a chair at the breakfast bar and sat down while Steph moved around the kitchen, heating up the griddle and pouring pancake batter.

"Tomorrow, I'm going to get to work at seven so I'm there when everyone comes in. We'll go over the new computer system and I'll tell them about the cameras."

"Do you think that's a good idea? Maybe it would be better to not mention them but talk about the need for accurate inventory."

Steph flipped the pancakes and then set a pitcher of maple syrup in front of Leo. "Do you think that's being dishonest?" She bit her bottom lip. The cameras were recording twenty-four seven.

"You have no reason to let on there is an issue and since you're prepping to go back to Portland, it makes sense to talk about inventory and the new software package, but keep the cameras on a need-to-know basis. The whole point is to identify who the thief is, not tip them off."

She set a stack of steaming pancakes in front of him and then filled another plate for herself and joined him. "What do I do if this hasn't been resolved by then?"

He poured a liberal amount of syrup over his stack and handed her the bottle. "Whoever has been doing this is confident they won't get caught. It will be resolved in a few weeks." He cut into the stack and grinned. "These are going to be good." His gaze slid to the platter of brownies. "Can I have one for dessert?"

With a laugh, she said, "They're for the party. You can't wait that long?"

"With all those kids zooming around, I might not get one." He gave her a sad, puppy dog smile and waited.

"I put two aside for us and picked up a quart of ice

cream from Licks and Drips, and we can have them either tonight or tomorrow night."

"I do like how you think." He attacked the pancakes with gusto.

"Leo, can you tell me a little more about your family so I will know who's who before I meet everyone?"

"You know you have nothing to worry about. They're going to think you're terrific."

"Please." Meeting large family groups was way out of her comfort zone, even though meeting strangers was part of her job. This was personal and therefore it was very different but she'd fake it until it got comfortable for her.

Between bites, he said, "Well, you know Mom and Dad. Who, by the way, are happy you're coming."

She smiled. "I'm glad I met them before so there will be a couple of friendly faces in the group."

"You have nothing to worry about. Everyone is nice. But then there is Don and Kate, with their three kids. Ben is almost five and they have twins, Spencer and Madison; they're going on two."

Steph leaned back in her chair. "That's quite the handful."

"Between the kids and the bistro, Kate is amazing. Don's a huge help, a real hands-on dad. They make a good team."

She watched as his face softened as he talked. She had never been around kids before, but it was obvious how much he loved his nieces and nephews. He was going to make a good dad. She felt a stab to her heart because it wouldn't be with her. "You're really close to them, aren't you?"

"My brothers and sisters are my best friends." He pushed his plate away and continued. "There's Jack and Peyton. They have two kids. Owen's eight and Hannah's one. You already met George and Johnny, and fair warning,

Owen and Ben have that same high energy and the knack for getting into mischief, and the three little ones are so stinking cute."

"You told me a little about Anna and Colin."

"She's the quiet one in the group, and Colin is over the moon about her. He took a leave of absence from his job at the hospital so he could be with her in France."

"Wow. Now that's what I call love." It was similar to what Leo had talked about doing just a couple of days ago—moving to be with her. She didn't want to go down that road, at least not at the moment. "I met Tessa at the winery but I don't think I've met her husband yet. Do you like him?"

"Max is a stand-up kind of guy. His sister Stella will probably be with them."

"How will I ever keep them straight?"

With a laugh, he said, "No one is going to expect you to. As long as you know the parents and me, you're golden. At least for today. The next time you see everyone, there might be a quiz."

She felt her mouth drop open. "Please tell me you're joking."

"Relax." He gave her a quick kiss and stood up to clear away breakfast. "I'm going to take a shower after I finish kitchen duty." He pointed to her laptop. "Finish up and then we'll take off. I still want to grab ice and chips." He gave a smirk. "Can't break with tradition. I have a reputation to maintain."

there were cars, trucks, and a minivan parked in Liza's driveway as Leo pulled in. He gave Steph's hand an encouraging squeeze. When he thought about meeting all these people from her perspective, it was overwhelming. He should have made a point of introducing her to them in smaller groups, like one family at a time.

"If you get overwhelmed and want to leave, just use our code word and we'll take off."

With a nervous laugh, she said, "I'll be fine. I'm looking forward to meeting everyone. And besides, I want to ask Liza what she's wearing to the wedding. All of my good dresses are in Portland, so I'll need to go shopping."

"Darling, you'll be beautiful no matter what you wear." He tucked a strand of hair behind her ear. "Ready?"

She pushed open her car door and heard the boys calling to her and Leo as they raced across the driveway. They skidded to a stop in front of them.

"Hi, Uncle Leo. Hi, Stephie." Johnny smiled up at her.

"What's with the nickname?" Steph asked.

Johnny tipped his head and squinted one eye as he looked at her. "It just fits now. Is it okay?"

"Yeah, I guess so." She looked at Leo, who frowned at the boy. Was this Johnny's way of saying he accepted her into his circle?

Johnny looked up at his uncle. "See, Uncle Leo? She likes it."

George grinned. "Can I carry the ice?"

Johnny piped up. "What kind of chips did you buy? The sour cream ones?" He grinned at Steph. "They're my favorite and Uncle Leo brings them sometimes."

"Johnny, the bags are in the back. George, I put the ice in a cooler, but I could use your help in carrying it." He pointed to the back seat of the truck. "John, take the chips to the house."

"Okay." He took the two plastic bags by the handles and dashed off.

George grinned. "I'm ready to carry the ice."

Leo held back a grin of his own. He could have easily

carried the cooler, but it was good for the boys to help. He pretended to struggle a bit as he picked up the large cooler out of the back of the pickup. He made a good show of grunting and even let it hit the ground.

George was very serious. "Don't worry, Uncle Leo. I've got one side." He flexed his biceps. "See."

Leo poked the muscle. "You're getting strong." He took one handle and George picked up the other.

Steph closed the tailgate and then walked alongside George. "Do you like brownies?"

"Yup." He eyed the platter she was carrying. "Is that what's under the foil?"

"It is."

"Can I have two?" His deep-brown eyes never left hers.

With a laugh, Leo said, "Start with one and don't forget to share with everyone else."

He didn't answer. "Mom said we should take the ice out back to the deck."

They changed course to go around the garage instead of through the house.

"And she told me just where to put it." He looked at Steph, squinting in the bright sun. "I'll show you where to put the brownies too, and then Mom said I should introduce you to everyone."

"Well, thank you, George."

"Buddy, you can go play with your cousins. I'll take care of the introductions."

"Mom told me to do it."

"Would it be okay if I go with you?" He looked at Steph over George's head and gave her a smile.

"Well, yeah. She's your girlfriend."

Leo was dying to laugh, but he smothered it. George was very serious.

As they entered the backyard, he noticed Steph's smile didn't relax. There were people everywhere. Peyton's parents were there, along with Colin's family and his buddy Drew.

George telling him where they had to put the cooler interrupted his train of thought. This was a lot more people than he had thought would be here. Stephanie was the only new face in the group.

"Is this your entire family?"

George piped up. "Yup. Aunt Anna and Colin are gonna get married pretty soon, so this is Mom's way of kicking off the big event." He looked up at Steph. "At least that's what she said to Mimi."

"Good to know."

Leo had no idea the party had grown. He caught her eye and mouthed, *I'm sorry.*

She flashed him a smile. "I should have made a double batch of brownies."

He relaxed. "Maybe even triple." Thank heavens she didn't seem to be mad. But he was going to have a little chat with his sister. It would have been nice to have a heads-up.

Speak of the devil. Liza was coming across the backyard with a smile on her face. "Stephanie, welcome." She gave her a warm hug. "It's nice to see you again."

Steph handed her the plate. "I didn't bake enough brownies."

Liza took the plate. "Are you kidding? There is enough food out there to feed an army."

"It kind of looks like one arrived."

Liza grinned at Leo and then at Steph. "You're going to fit right in."

22

Steph gave Liza a warm smile. Leo's sister gestured to her backyard. "Things kinda got out of hand once I started inviting people."

"I see that. I should have suspected it would grow." Leo took Steph's hand and gave it a reassuring squeeze. This was not what she had in mind when she'd agreed to come. The last time she was with this many people was at a company picnic, and at least there, she didn't have to talk to anyone, just eat, make sure the boss knew she had shown up, and then slip away. That would not be an option today.

Liza returned Steph's smile. "Make yourself at home." She pointed to a table under a large oak tree. "Anna and Colin are over there with Mom and Dad. Leo, you should take Steph over before everyone clamors for the happy couple's time."

"I wouldn't want to take up your sister's attention since she's the bride-to-be."

Liza snorted. "You're the main attraction today, not Anna."

She stammered, "What?" She looked to Leo for support or at least an explanation.

"Darlin', everyone wants to meet you," he said. "But don't worry; this is still about my sister and Colin. Once everyone meets you, well, you'll be just one of the gang." He slung an arm around her shoulders and kissed her head. "Might as well get it over with, and then we'll just relax."

Liza leaned in and, for Steph's ears alone, said, "Don't worry about anyone. You've put a perpetual smile on my twin's face. No one is happier about that than this family."

She had to wonder if Leo had been lonely or, worse, didn't date before she came along.

George tugged on her hand. "Stephie. Come on."

Once she was moving, he dropped her hand. They crossed the lush grass and she was relieved when Sherry gave her a welcoming wave.

"Hi, Stephanie. Leo."

He leaned in and kissed his mom's cheek. "Hey, Mom."

A tall woman with dark-auburn hair swept off to the side stood up and pulled her into a hug. "I'm Anna and I'm glad you came today. I've heard a lot about you. I feel like we're already friends."

Surprised at the gesture, Steph hugged her back. This was not something she'd been prepared for, total strangers hugging her.

"Hi. Welcome home and congratulations on your upcoming wedding."

Anna took a step back and gestured to a tall man with kind hazel eyes. "Thank you. This is my future husband, Colin."

"It's a pleasure to meet you." Steph shook his hand.

"Welcome to the chaos." His hazel eyes twinkled.

With a nervous laugh, her eyes widened and she looked at Leo. She really needed an escape plan now.

Sam gave a hearty chuckle. "Stephanie, we bark but we don't bite."

"Poppi"—George looked between his grandparents—"I like Stephie."

Sam stopped laughing and grew serious. "We do too." He looked at her. "Seems you have a champion in my grandson."

"Stephie, do you want to see our fort? Uncle Leo built it for us with my other uncles."

"That sounds like fun."

Anna asked. "George, can I come too?"

"Sure." He ran ahead, calling for the other boys to come with them.

Steph walked next to Anna as Leo hung behind. She was pretty sure Anna was looking to have a few minutes alone with her. Hopefully the grilling would be reserved for the burgers later.

They walked behind the boys, who raced along the lightly wooded path. She figured it would be best to break the ice.

"How was France?"

"Beautiful, amazing, and romantic, but I missed home."

"Colin was with you. Did that help?"

"It did, but there's nothing like being able to hang out with my sisters, stop in at my parents' whenever, and see Colin's family."

"You're lucky." She knew Anna didn't mean anything, but suddenly she felt very alone. She had no family. Before Dad died, when she felt isolated, all she had to do was call and hear his voice and instantly she knew someone had her back. Being surrounded by Leo's family, it was easy to see they were connected and she was the outsider.

"I hear through the grapevine that you're running your dad's car restoration business."

"I want to keep it afloat. There are a lot of families that depend on those jobs. It's the right thing to do."

"It's more than that, Stephanie. It is really nice that

you're working to keep the business going. Do you think you can run it from the other side of the country?"

Jeez, Anna was blunt. "I have some good people who will take care of different aspects of the business. I'll come back every few months to check on things in person."

Anna gave her a side-glance filled with doubt. "And Leo? How does he fit into the picture?" Anna stopped walking. "I'm sorry if you think I'm out of line or meddling, but I know my little brother. All it took was one look to see he's given you his heart." She started walking again. "I saw that same look in Colin's face when I was getting ready to go to France."

"We haven't figured that out yet."

"Your feelings or the future?"

Stephanie rolled her shoulders back. Part of her bristled at Anna asking these questions, but the other part of her understood. If she were in Anna's shoes, she would be asking too—but maybe not on the first meeting.

She might as well be honest. "I love Leo, and he feels the same way. As far as our future goes, we're just not ready to make any big decisions."

"Do you want to leave?"

"I made a commitment to my boss. If he gave me a six-month leave of absence, I'd come back."

"And do you want to leave Leo?"

Softly she said, "No."

"Trust me when I tell you this will work itself out." Anna gave her a knowing smile. "I've been in your shoes."

She wasn't sure if she should ask but did anyway. "I'd appreciate it if you'd keep our conversation between us. We need time to figure this out."

"If you need someone to talk to, I'm here for you."

Anna's smile was so much like Leo's that Steph did have the sense everything would be okay. "Thank you."

"Now, let's go look at this fort."

Steph fell in step next to Anna. This family was not a shy bunch. If she were being honest, a part of her appreciated that they really cared about each other, but on the other side of the coin, it was intimidating to have someone challenge her way of thinking. She was used to following her own path and being accountable to no one in her personal life.

*L*eo watched his sister and Stephanie stop and talk on the short walk to the boys' fort. What was that all about? Anna had better not be trying to sway Steph about anything. The last thing he wanted was for her to bolt from too much family pressure, no matter how well-intentioned the conversation. He wanted to go over and interrupt them.

"Leo." Mom's quiet, authoritative voice told him to turn and face her. "Sit down and stop staring at them."

Dad got up. "I'll let you talk to Mom." He moved away.

Leo sat down next to her. "Tell me. How do you do that?"

With a bemused smile, she asked, "Do what?"

"Know what I'm thinking at the moment I'm thinking it." His gaze drifted back to the ladies, who were now trailing after his nephews.

"Years of practice. It starts the first time you hold your baby and you learn their facial expressions, moods, and reactions."

"Do you know Steph has agreed to come to all the parties leading up to Anna and Colin's wedding?"

"I'm not surprised. She cares for you very much." Mom touched his arm and he looked at her. "Did you tell her that you love her?"

"I did, and the feeling is mutual."

"Then why the long face?"

"She's going to Portland." He laced his fingers together as he leaned forward and studied the ground.

"She might change her mind." Mom exhaled a heavy sigh. "You're going to Portland, aren't you?"

"If she lets me, yes."

"I've never heard you say you'd follow a woman anywhere. You need to go where your heart takes you."

He raised his head and watched Steph across the yard. "Thanks, Mom."

He strolled with purpose across the yard in time to hear George telling Steph how he and Johnny found the wasp nest and it was so big, even Uncle Leo was afraid to take it down. Then he went on to say they had to make sure to get rid of it because his mom was allergic.

"Hey, guys." Leo stuck his hands in his pockets.

Steph gave him a smile. "This is quite the fort. I've never seen one this elaborate with windows, a wooden ladder, and built-in furniture."

"In my defense, when the boys started talking about it, Don, Jack, and I built what we wanted as kids. It took on a life of its own."

"I see that."

George stepped between them. "Come on, Stephie. We have more people to meet."

Grinning, she gave Leo a little wave and followed George, with Johnny running alongside them.

Anna shoulder bumped him. "I like her."

"Did you go the twenty questions route?"

"No, about five. The most important ones."

"I'm not even going to ask." He said, "Tell me. Was living in France all you hoped?"

"I'm glad Dad encouraged me to take the job. I learned as much from Henri as I taught his daughter."

"How did Colin like living in France?" They walked to the cooler and he pulled out two beers and handed one to Anna. He was curious if Colin had any regrets about making the move.

"He loved it, but I know he missed his work, although it brought us closer together."

That was something to think about. She didn't say he'd missed family and if Leo made the move, he'd have his career, even though he would have to rebuild it from the ground up. "Have you decided whose house you're keeping?"

"Yes, we're keeping mine. We both love the country setting and it will be better when we have kids. His place is in a development and doesn't have much of a yard." She took a pull on her beer. "Liza tells me your house is just about finished. Are you going to put it on the market or hold on to this one? From what she said, it'll make a great home for a family."

"I'm not making any plans at the moment."

"Maybe you should."

He took a pull on his own beer. "I'm working on it." He pointed to a guy walking around the corner. "I didn't know you asked Drew Cameron to come today."

"Colin invited him. I also heard he hired you to restore his car."

"The Chevelle. Sweet ride." He lifted his beer in greeting as Drew approached them with a potted flower of some kind.

"Hey, Drew. Glad you could make it." Anna smiled.

"Hi. This is quite the party." He looked around.

"You didn't need to bring me a plant." She stretched out her hands.

"Actually, this is for your sister for inviting me."

She withdrew her hands and gave him a knowing smile.

"That's very nice of you. Come on. She's around here somewhere."

Leo's gaze followed Steph and the boys as they made the rounds. George didn't give her any time for conversation; he was all about brief introductions. He'd make sure Steph got to talk to everyone before the end of the day. She was smiling and seemed to be totally relaxed with the kids. George was talking a mile a minute and she threw her head back with a hearty laugh. He had to wonder what was said. This had to be a little overwhelming, all this family and their friends who were like family. Thankfully everyone was welcoming, but he still needed to reclaim his love. He jogged over to her. "How's everything going?"

George said, "Don't worry, Uncle Leo. Stephie is now friends with our entire family." He gave a little wave. "See ya."

"So, are you ready to run as far and fast as you can? You've been questioned by Anna, spent time with my nephews, and you haven't been given anything to drink or eat."

She brushed his lips with hers. "Relax. I'm having a good time." She slipped her arm through his. "But now that you mention it, I'm a little dry."

"Then come with me. It just so happens I know where you can obtain an adult beverage if that suits you."

"You talked me into it."

Liza was waving at them.

"Looks like you're needed." She steered Leo in her direction.

"I forgot. I'm on grill duty."

She squeezed his arm with her hand. "I'll help."

He gave her a sidelong look. "How are your grilling skills with burgers? I know you can cook steak, but this group all likes them cooked to order."

"Okay, not mooing for everyone." With a chuckle, she said, "You can be on cheese duty."

With a snort, he grinned. "First brownies and now you're going to man the grill? You just downgraded my very important role at a family barbeque." He kissed her cheek. "My family is never going to let you go."

She murmured, "Well, that's something to think about."

23

*E*arly Monday morning, Stephanie was sitting at her desk, sipping coffee as the sun brightened her office. She looked at the picture of Dad on her desk as she thought about the picnic at Liza's. After meeting and talking with everyone, her head was spinning, but in a good way. She felt welcomed, and more than that, she had a sense of belonging that she hadn't experienced before. This was only making it harder to leave.

The sound of a door banging made her sit up straight and pretend to be working instead of daydreaming. She glanced at the clock. Seven fifteen.

Val poked her head in the office door. "Hey, boss lady. You're here pretty early."

"I wanted to get a jump on the day. You know, with the new inventory system and project planning. Also, I bought a new laptop I want to get on the network." She flashed Val a smile. "I'm hoping a dedicated computer will help me stay organized—you know, keep my business separate from my personal life." Not that she needed to explain herself, but it was better that Val thought she was working hard to keep everything running smoothly.

Val's smile was tight. Did she seem annoyed? Steph brushed it off that she was just on edge. "I'll be going home in a few weeks and need to be prepared."

"You can count on me. I'll keep things running smoothly and check in daily if you'd like."

That made her feel better, knowing she had a set of eyes here. "Thanks, Val. I'd like to set up reviews for everyone in four weeks. Could you put together a schedule and allot thirty minutes per review?"

She brightened. "Your dad was never that formal, but I think it's a great idea. If you want, I'll set up some folders on the computer and you can store your notes in there."

"Already done."

"Oh, sure," Val smiled. "Of course you would have already gotten started. You have people you manage at your real job." She gestured to Stephanie's mug. "Do you need more coffee before I open up?"

"No, I'm good. But spread the word as people come in that I want everyone to gather in the main bay at eight. I have a couple of announcements to make." She watched as zero emotion registered on Val's face. It was odd that she didn't show the least bit of curiosity and was maybe a little bit too solicitous, from setting up meetings to even getting coffee. It was something Steph would talk to her about during her review.

"You got it, boss."

The heels of her shoes made loud clicking sounds on the tiles as Val went to her desk.

Steph pulled up the camera on her new laptop. The images were crystal clear and she could see Val talking to each person as they came in. Too bad there wasn't sound, as there seemed to be more conversation than just passing along information the way Val did with her. She guessed that was to be expected. Things were very different now that she was the boss.

She leaned back in her chair and closed her eyes.

Dad, I hope you know I'm doing my best to make you proud of me. These last few months have been the hardest of my life. I'm pretty sure you're keeping an eye on me, and you know I met Leo. He's a lot like you in so many ways. Sometimes it makes me miss you even more. I'm gonna make sure this business stays afloat. I promise I won't let you down. Miss you, Dad, and say hi to Mom for me.

This wasn't the first one-sided conversation she'd had with her dad and it wouldn't be the last. But she needed it before she faced her team.

*S*tephanie stood in front of the group. They were looking at her with curious stares, patiently waiting for her to talk.

"Good morning, everyone. I know we all have a busy day ahead of us and I will make this brief. I have a couple of announcements. The most important is that I left donuts and bagels in the breakroom, so help yourself."

Smiles encouraged her to keep going.

"As you know, I'll be headed back to Portland in October, but I am going to keep the shop running. I have no intention of closing."

She could swear she heard a collective sigh of relief. Hopefully her next announcements would be met with the same smiles and nods around the room.

"In just about a month, I'll be doing one-on-one reviews with each of you. At that time, we'll discuss raises and what I expect moving forward. I've already decided on a few changes, and I want to make them official. Val will continue to run the office. Chuck is going to manage inventory and project planning. He alone will be responsible for doing the project book for each client. Gary will quote all new projects and create a timeline. Before I go, I will appoint a shop manager who will report to me and act as my representative. If anyone would like to throw their hat in the ring for the job, come see me."

A few grins appeared and Steph guessed she'd have some visitors today. It was good to see their response, and she felt better knowing everyone was eager to keep things rolling along. Of course, this was tempered with unearthing her thief, but that was a matter of time.

"The last item of business is about our security. I've installed a system in the building. How it works is that if at any time we are broken into, an alarm will sound here and at the police station and the camera will record activity. This way, we'll have evidence needed to prosecute the intruder."

Gary crossed his arms over his chest. "Does that mean you're keeping an eye on us all the time?"

She hadn't expected him to ask that. "Good question. I have no intention of monitoring your work. If I had any doubt in your skills, you wouldn't be working for me. This is in the event of theft or vandalism."

Zira asked, "Is the alarm silent like a bank or will it be loud?" She grinned. "Just wondering. I think it sounds like a great idea."

"As I said a moment ago, it's loud, so if someone does decide to attempt a break-in, the noise might scare them away, but the camera on the exterior doors and windows will have already been activated and we'll catch them anyway."

Val stepped forward. "I think it's about time we stepped up security. It's good for all of us. If you need me to do anything, just ask."

A murmur of agreement from everyone bolstered Steph's confidence that she had done the right thing. But she didn't get a sense anyone in this room was apprehensive about a security system. Could it have been someone from outside the company finding their way in to steal? No. This had to be an inside job and the cameras would uncover the guilty party, and then she could move forward with the best team.

"Thanks, everyone, for the support. As I said, this business will continue and I hope to grow it. If anyone has any ideas, please feel free to share them. And don't forget about the donuts and bagels. Work safe."

The group broke up, everyone going to their areas, but Zira followed her into the lobby.

"Stephanie, do you have a minute?"

"Come on in the office and we can talk." Once inside, Steph closed the door. "Have a seat." She sat in her chair behind the desk. "What's on your mind?"

"It was really great that you were so open with everyone today and I think it's good to have cameras in case of an emergency, but maybe they should be on all the time." She looked down at her hands.

"Is there something you want to talk about?"

She shook her head. "I don't know anything specific, but I'm pretty sure someone has taken cash out of my backpack a couple of different times."

A shiver ran down Stephanie's back. "When did this happen?"

"There have been a few times when I've gone to the ATM at lunch to get cash. I like to have sixty dollars in my wallet. But at the end of the day, I might have twenty bucks. The first time it happened, I thought I must have dropped it, but now that it's happened a few times, I know I wasn't being careless."

"Why didn't you tell me before this?" Stephanie clasped her hands together to keep her temper in check. Someone was targeting an employee. Or was it more than one person?

"I like working here and I didn't want to be perceived as a problem."

"Never hesitate to talk to me, okay?" She pushed back from the desk and sat on the edge. "Where do you leave your backpack?"

"In my locker."

"Does it have a lock on it?"

She shook her head. "No. Nobody uses them. I got the impression that everyone could be trusted. Everybody has been so nice."

"How much in total have you lost?"

"About one-eighty."

Damn, this was getting worse by the minute. Stephanie withdrew her wallet from her bag and handed her four fifty-dollar bills. "Take this, with my sincere apologies."

She shook her head and pushed the bills back to Steph. "No, I can't take your money. That isn't why I told you. I just thought you should know, that's all." She stood up and stuck her hands in the pockets of her jeans. She took a step toward the door but stopped almost immediately. "I don't want to get anyone in trouble, but if someone is that desperate to take money from me, who knows what they might do with the cash you have on hand."

"I appreciate you telling me."

Zira opened the door.

"Before you go," Steph said, "I wanted to ask you if you'd be interested in taking a course or two for advanced skills. I have some ideas, but it will be some of your personal time and you'd be out of the shop a few hours a week. If you decide it's what you want to do, we can choose courses together."

"Wouldn't that upset the guys? I don't want special treatment."

"Zira, I'm going to be offering different types of training to everyone. If I want to expand the business, we all need to be the best at everything we do. I am a firm believer that working with top-notch people helps us grow."

She brightened and Steph relaxed. She knew it was hard being the only woman in a male-dominated job. "In that case," Zira said, "I'd love to. Just tell me when and where and you can count on me." She quivered, her hands held down at her sides balled into excited fists.

Steph held out her arms and Zira all but leapt into them for a hard hug. "Thanks for the talk. I'm so glad I work here."

"Keep up the good work." She pressed the bills in Zira's hand and closed it. The girl shouldn't have to suffer because a random act of theft happened under her roof.

"Thanks." With the door wide open, she looked back over her shoulder. "You can count on it."

When she was alone, Steph sat down and looked out the window and stared at nothing in particular. Trying to button up BRR to run without her here every day was hard and she wished she could be in two places at once.

Hearing someone clear their throat, she looked up. Chuck was standing in the doorway.

"Got a second?"

"Absolutely."

He stepped inside and ducked his head. "Did you have a chance to look over the inventory? I wanted to make sure I did it right." His cheeks flamed red. Did he have a guilty conscience or was he uncomfortable with the new responsibility?

"I did and it looked just as I expected. Did you have any trouble with the software?"

"Not at all. I was wondering how often you want me to do a full inventory."

"Since you'll be tracking what is used daily, run a report once a week to check the min and max, and then I think you should do a full physical inventory once a month."

He never flinched or seemed concerned.

"I'd like for you to put the report where the accountant and I can both access it. I'll set something up on the new system for you."

Chuck looked at the floor. "I really appreciate what you're doing for me."

He shifted from one foot to the other while the silence continued. As much as she wanted him to talk to her, Stephanie sat quietly and waited for him. Chuck needed to know he could talk with her about anything that was on his mind.

"I know you're aware I have a record."

"Everyone makes mistakes. I read your job application and my dad left me some notes. He was a good judge of character and he made the decision to give you an opportunity to start over. Why wouldn't we continue down that same path?"

"Well, I appreciate your vote of confidence. Thanks."

He hurried out the door. Before she could fire up the laptop, Val popped around the corner.

"Busy morning. Need anything?"

"Thanks, Val. All I need is to get some work done. But if anyone else feels the need to chat, can you let me know right away? I need for everyone to know my door is open."

"Sure thing. I'm going to order lunch out. Let me know if you want something. I think I'm doing the deli today."

"Why don't you ask everyone? It's on me." She gave Val a half smile. Hopefully she'd stop feeling bad about installing cameras everywhere, but now she had another reason to stop this thief. He was stealing from other employees. That just wasn't right. Not at all.

24

$\mathcal{A}$t the end of a long and exhausting day, Steph walked through Leo's garage and into the kitchen with her new laptop backpack dangling from her fingers and called out to him.

From somewhere down the hall, she heard a muffled response. Dropping her bag and stepping out of her clogs, she went in search of a welcome home kiss. She entered the master bedroom and while she could hear him, she didn't see him. He poked his head out of the walk-in closet.

"Hey, beautiful." He took a step toward her and pulled her close. Kissing her thoroughly, he smiled. "Guess what I'm doing?"

"Cleaning your closet?"

"Well, sort of. I'm organizing and making space just in case you want to leave more clothes here." He cocked his head to the side. "But no pressure."

"Leo, are you sure you want to go down this path?" Was he trying to show her how well they lived together? It had crossed her mind that if she moved more stuff to his place, it would be even harder to leave when it was time to go back to Portland.

Taking her hand, he crossed the room with her and they sat on the bed together.

"Steph. Every day that passes brings us one day closer to the day you get on that plane. I don't want to waste a single minute that we could spend together. I want to be with you."

"But Leo—" Her heart was full of love.

He placed a finger across her lips, preventing her from saying anything more. "Do you love me?"

She nodded.

"Do you want to spend as much time as we can together?"

"Yes," she mumbled.

"So why not?"

She wanted to be with Leo and he had a point. Why waste any of the precious time that they had? "Are you sure you want me to stay with you?"

"Hey, I wouldn't clean out my closet for just anyone."

She moved so she was facing him. "Have you ever lived with a woman before?"

"No. I've never wanted to share my home with anyone. Until you."

She gave him a smile. "For the record, I've never lived with anyone either."

He smacked the middle of his forehead. "I'm a jerk. Would you prefer if we stayed at your place? I just assumed since my house is bigger and more centrally located between our two shops, it was the logical choice."

She ran a finger down his cheek and lightly kissed him. "I love your house, and being here is a fresh start for us." She dropped her eyes. "Sometimes it's hard being home. I keep expecting Dad to walk in the back door and tell me what he's fixing for dinner." Tears constricted her throat like a vise. "When I remember it's just me, I find myself crying and can't stop."

He wrapped his arms around her as the tears fell. This time it wasn't that raw, unbearable, gut-wrenching grief, but the acceptance that she wasn't going to see Dad again. It was a different kind of grief. He held her, murmuring soothing words of comfort while she cried. But the comfort came because he was steadfast and gentle. He loved her.

She wiped her cheeks dry and pulled away and smiled through her sadness. He was everything she had always wanted in a partner and there was a date this would end. "Maybe we could run over to the house tonight. I want to clean out the refrigerator and pick up a few more things." She looked at him without blinking. "But only if you're one hundred percent sure."

"I'm sure."

"And you have to promise me"—she squared his face to hers—"if at any point you need your space, just give me the word and I'll go back to my house."

"That won't happen." He gave her a wide smile. "Trust me."

With a sidelong look, she said, "You have to promise me."

"Okay, I promise." He pecked her lips. "Now kiss me like you're sealing it with one."

"I can do better than that." She eased him back on the bed and let her lips and hands ignite the smoldering fire between them.

After getting back from her house, Steph put the food, her clothes, and toiletries away and sat at the breakfast bar and opened the laptop. Leo had gone to take a shower. She wanted to see what the camera views looked like after dark. Did they really show what was going on or —what she really hoped—what wasn't? She logged in with her username and password. The cameras came up in a grid. The lobby lights were on. Had Val forgotten to shut them off at the end of the day? Within minutes, Gary strode through the shop door into the lobby and looked around. He moved down the hallway toward Steph's office. The camera at the end of the hallway picked him up as he opened the storage room door. He disappeared from view for a moment, and then he returned and continued down the hall, looking in each office and the conference room. He paused at the end of the hall, shook his head, and went back to the lobby, snapped off the lights, and walked back into the shop. Only then did the light that had been spilling through the small window go dark.

She watched the screen for a few more minutes, but nothing changed.

Leo padded down the hall, shirtless, with low-slung jeans and bare feet. His hair was combed back from his face. She glanced his way and frowned.

"What?" He got a glass of water and sat down. He pointed to the laptop. "Did it work?"

She nodded. "It's the strangest thing. When I logged in, I saw Gary walking through the offices, checking out the storage and conference room. Very methodical."

"Then what happened?"

"He left and the camera that covers the back lot shows he got in his truck and left."

"Did he have anything with him?" He drained the glass.

"His lunch box, but nothing else." She rubbed the back of her neck and rolled her head from side to side.

"Headache?"

"Could Gary be our guy? He's been Dad's friend for as long as I can remember."

Leo got up and began to massage her shoulders. He worked his hands up to the base of her head.

She groaned. "That feels so good."

He continued to ease the tension from her shoulders. Her eyes closed and her thoughts began to spin. "Why do you think someone steals from their boss?"

"They either need money, think they're underpaid and deserve more, or maybe for the thrill of it."

He was now making a circular motion with his fingertips on her temples.

"Why would Gary do this to me?"

"Don't jump to conclusions. It might be completely innocent. He might have been working late and noticed the lights were left on."

"You have no idea how much I hope it's not him." She did a shoulder roll. "I'm ready to whip up something for dinner."

"I'll help."

She closed the lid of the laptop and tapped it. Tomorrow she'd have to find a way to discover what Gary was doing without saying she was watching the cameras.

They moved about the kitchen like a well-practiced routine. Leo poured her a glass of wine.

"I forgot to tell you I talked with Zira about taking a course." She set the glass aside and chopped the broccoli for the stir fry they were making.

"How did she react?" He picked up a piece and popped it in his mouth.

"She's really excited."

Leo scraped the cubed chicken into the hot wok. "That's great."

She handed him the cutting board with a rainbow of cut veggies. "She also told me someone stole almost two hundred dollars from her."

"You're joking, aren't you?" Leo pushed around the cubed chicken while the oil sizzled. "Can you whisk together a sauce?" He pointed to the pantry closet. "The cornstarch is up toward the top."

"Sadly, she was serious. I gave her the money back but what kind of person am I dealing with?" Steph leaned against the counter and shook her head. "I can't solve it tonight, so let's focus on us. Like, we're being a normal couple making dinner and chatting about our day."

His grin filled his face. "I have to be honest. I like this. But we can talk about what's happening."

"No. We should talk about what comes next for us." Why on earth did she bring this topic up now when all she wanted to do was forget her departure was looming?

"This comes off the gas in two minutes. Why don't we talk over dinner?"

He was still bare-chested. "Do me one favor. Put on a shirt. Your current look is very distracting."

"Well, that's a boost to my ego." He turned off the burner. "You take care of the sauce and I'll get dressed."

"T-shirt, skip the buttons," she called after him with a laugh.

She thought about the day he'd said he was willing to move to Portland, although she had never paid attention to the classic car market there, but if he'd consider making the change, she'd do everything she could to help.

When Leo came back to the kitchen, he was wearing a dark turtleneck.

She clapped her hands together and laughed hard. He held up his hands. "How's this? Less of a distraction?"

"Not really; it's molded to your body. But I do like the look."

He gave a mock bow. "You asked."

"Dinner's ready." She handed Leo their plates and her mouth formed a large O. "When did you have time to light candles?" He pulled out her chair and she looked into his eyes. "You are so sweet."

"Candlelight, wine, and you add up to a romantic evening." He set the plates down and held her chair.

She squirmed. "I want to ask you to come visit me in Portland." It might seem crazy to him, but she wanted and needed to be with him.

"I can take some time and come out."

He seemed guarded in his answer. Should she ask him if he really wanted to make the trip?

"Why do you have to go back?" he continued. "You have a good business here and you're good at it."

She could feel her back bristle. "If you don't want to come with me, just say so."

"All I'm asking is if you've looked at all the options."

She carefully placed her napkin across her lap. "I took a leave of absence; I didn't resign. People are depending on me."

"You have people who are depending on you here too."

"I'm doing my best. That's what the last few months have been about. My boss knows I'm coming back. I gave my word."

"Stephanie, what do *you* want?" He reached across the table and took her hands. His voice was thick with love and even sadness.

She took a deep breath. Even though she had never been good at being completely open with anyone, now was the time. "I wish I had a choice to make but I have to go back to my career, the town house, and friends, like Maggie."

In her heart, she knew what she'd have—half a life, one devoid of the man she loved. Could she go back to the way things were? She wanted to ask him to move, to be with her, but that was a pipe dream and she couldn't be selfish. His business and his family were in Crescent Lake. The words died on her lips.

25

*A*fter stewing for a week, Steph strode into the shop attempting to look casual and not at all like she was on a mission. But she most certainly was. How was she going to get Gary to tell her what had happened without coming right out and asking him?

She smiled at Chuck, who looked up from his computer with a grin. She had to talk to Zira; that was her excuse. She walked in that direction, noticing that Gary was documenting the progress on the Corvette he had been working on. She would check in with him in a few minutes.

"Morning, Zira. How are things going?" She couldn't help but notice she looked more like Rosie the Riveter today than a car mechanic, with her shirt sleeves folded back, carpenter jeans, and a red bandana covering her short, dark hair.

"Hi, Stephanie." She stepped back from the GTO. She had a wrench in one hand and a grease-covered rag in the other. Her grin filled her face. It was easy to see she was in her element. She knew exactly how Zira felt, getting under the hood and working on an engine. There was nothing like it. Add the added benefit that she and Zira were breaking glass boundaries, and it all felt really good.

"I have some exciting news for you."

"Cool."

She handed her a paper. "I have that list of courses we should take a look at and see what you're interested in learning."

Her eyes darted to Gary. "Are you sure? I haven't heard any of the guys talking about going to any classes."

Steph wondered if he was giving her a tough time, but he had always been a good teacher when she was younger.

"Think of it this way. You're a part of my pilot program." Dad had hired her, but she was still green and needed training. Sadly, Dad hadn't had time to properly mentor her and with the clock ticking, Steph didn't have time to put on a set of coveralls and guide her either. No matter how much she'd like to.

Zira glanced at the paper. "Can I have until tomorrow to look this over?"

Steph couldn't help but smile. "Yeah, of course, and really think about how you see your future here." Before she moved on, she said, "I'll see you in the morning?"

"Absolutely." She pointed to the GTO. "I'd better get busy, and thanks for the vote of confidence. I won't let you down." She turned back to the car and focused on the task at hand.

Steph was the same way when she was working on a car, but when she was making a sales call, it was so routine, she could do it in her sleep. In the beginning, it had been a challenge but the list of meds she promoted never seemed to change.

She made the circuit, checking in with some of the other guys around the shop. She waved through the window to the clean room at Eric, who looked to be experimenting with some colors. He gave her a thumbs-up. He was a good paint guy and created some amazing custom colors. They were lucky to have him.

Her heart rate increased as she approached Gary. Stupid yes, but still she was nervous.

"Hi, Gary. The 'Vette is looking good."

He handed her the camera he had been using. "Take a look. The book is going to be a nice touch for the owners."

She scrolled through the pictures and marveled at how quickly the car had come along. "When do you plan on making the delivery?"

"Friday. I'll be ready before that, but they can't get here until after lunch." He took the camera and set it on his workbench.

"So, any feedback on the changes?" Did she sound easy and breezy or uptight?

He dropped his voice. "Frankly, I wish you had enhanced the security system even more."

Now that was a surprise. "Why's that?"

Gary looked around. "Can we talk outside?"

This certainly was unexpected. "We could go to my office."

"No. I don't want to take the chance of having anyone eavesdrop."

Steph walked to the back door with Gary by her side. He didn't look right or left and his mood was somber.

The door closed firmly behind them and even then, Gary took a few more steps away from the building.

"Something is going on around here," he began. "The other night, I came back to the shop. I'd left my phone on the bench. When I got here, there were a few lights on in the offices. At first I thought the cleaners were there, but I didn't see the van out front."

Stephanie crossed her arms over her chest. Her heart thudded so loudly, she wondered if he could hear it.

"I thought maybe you were here and that Leo had dropped you off or something."

"I wasn't aware you knew we're dating."

He gave her a strained smile. "I'm glad you met someone. He's a good man." He pointed to the door. "But to get back to this, I know the lights were off when I left. I try to be the last one to lock up. That started when your dad got sick."

"I appreciate you helping him. It eased his mind to know you had his back here."

"He's my best friend."

She couldn't help but notice he used the present tense. She got that. It felt like he was still here every day.

"Steph, I checked out the place and nobody was here, but something's not right. Someone who has access to this place was here and I think they were up to no good." He ended with a curt nod.

"Was anything missing?"

"Not this time, but there have been brand-new tools that disappeared. Like we'll get a shipment in of something that needs replacing; you know how your dad was a stickler for safety."

She nodded and smiled. "He always said everyone needed to go home the same way they walked in the door."

"Exactly. I've put stuff on the shelves myself, only to find it gone the next morning." He did the poof gesture, like a magician.

"How long has this been going on?" Now she was very interested. Missing chairs in boxes that looked intact. Missing cash. And numbers in the books that were alarming. Was it all part of the same problem?

"Right after Eddie told me he was sick."

"What did Dad say when you told him?"

Gary dropped his head. "I never did. I was trying to

find out what was going on, and then you came home, and I hoped it would stop."

Softly she said, "But it hasn't?"

"It did for a while. Like when you first got here, but now I notice things a few times per week." He looked her in the eye. "Put the cameras on all the time. You need to stop whoever is doing this."

"Gary, I appreciate you bringing this to my attention. But do me one favor: Keep this between us while I figure out what to do next."

"Sure thing. And I'm going to keep my eyes open and I'll let you know when something else comes up missing."

"One last favor? Can you put together a list of items that you can remember and the cost to replace them? It'll help me in the long run."

"I already started."

"Go back inside and again, keep this between us. I'm going to hang out here for a bit."

"You got it."

She watched as Gary walked inside as if unburdened. She believed him and was relieved he wasn't stealing from her. So who and why? Was it related to Zira's missing cash, or was that a separate issue? Was there any chance the incorrect invoices from Westwood were somehow part of this?

How many thieves did she have, and what were they after? And more importantly, how could she stop them?

She walked around the building and in the front door. Val greeted her with a bright smile. "I thought you were in the shop."

"I was but I stepped outside for a few minutes to get some air."

She had headed toward her office when Val called after her. "If you need something, let me know."

"Thanks, Val."

• • •

*L*eo poked his head in Steph's office. He watched as her face went from serious and focused to warm and welcoming. He appreciated her work ethic; it was another thing they had in common. He couldn't help but wonder if they combined their talents, what kind of business could they have?

"Hey, you. I didn't expect to see you today. Well, not at work anyway."

He leaned across the desk and kissed her. "I had to get some parts in Buffalo and thought I'd swing by on my way home to see if you want takeout tonight, or Mom invited us over too."

She tapped her chin with the pen she was holding. "Takeout or home cooking. Decisions, decisions." She flashed him a sunny smile. "Your choice."

He'd known she was going to toss it back into his court. "Mom's making a roast chicken on the grill with baby potatoes and carrots."

With a laugh, she said, "You sold it."

"Great." He sat on the corner of the desk. "How was the day?"

She seemed to hesitate and looked toward the hall, then tipped her head to listen. Now he understood there were things she wanted to say but she couldn't talk about, at least not until they were alone. He could be patient until they were able to head out.

"What time can you leave?"

She looked at the clock on the wall. "About fifteen minutes. Do you want to wait, or should I meet you at your parents'?"

"I'll hang out. Maybe I could walk around in the shop?" He was hesitant to assume she'd want him back there. "I'd love to see what everyone's working on and I promise I won't pick up any tool. Strictly a bystander."

"You could introduce yourself to Zira and maybe stop and say hello to Gary."

That was an interesting suggestion. "Can I just walk out there?"

"I'll go with you and introduce you to a few key people, and then you can talk with whomever you want."

As they walked down the hall, they kept their conversation light. Val's eyes widened and her computer screen went dark as soon as they entered the lobby. "Hello."

"Val, you remember my friend Leo Price."

She gave him a generous smile when he shook her hand.

"It's nice to see you again, Val. Stephanie has said you keep things humming around here."

She winked at Steph. "I haven't heard much about you."

"Leo is going out into the shop while I'm finishing up, and then I'm going to leave a little early tonight."

"You should go and have fun." She flipped her gaze to Leo. "If you need anything, don't hesitate to ask."

"Thank you." He opened the shop door for Stephanie and looked back over his shoulder to see that Val hadn't returned to work yet. His thoughts were diverted as Steph introduced him to Gary and Zira before she went back to her office.

"Good to see you again, Gary."

The older gentleman was exactly as Leo remembered, with a firm handshake and grease under his fingernails. He always liked to see that; to him, it meant a man was immersed in his work. He turned to Zira. She was not what he expected. Petite and cute with a ready smile was the best way to describe the girl. He liked her the moment she pumped his hand.

"I've heard a lot about your shop. Rumor has it you do good work."

He smiled and gestured to the car. "Thanks. GTOs are

fun cars to work on."

"Yeah." She pumped his hand again. "It was great to meet you."

She turned her attention back to the car she was working on, leaving him to seek out Gary. He was taking pictures of a Corvette and even though Steph couldn't tell him what she had learned, he wanted to get a better impression of the guy.

Gary gave him a wary smile. "Since Eddie isn't here, I'm going to ask you straight up. Do you plan to hurt Stephanie?"

Just the opening he needed. "Not any more than you do."

A grin spread from ear to ear. Gary clapped him on his shoulder. "I like you."

Instinctively, Leo knew Gary was not their guy.

---

26

*L*eo and Steph walked hand in hand up the steps to his parents' house. It was warm and welcoming, just like the first time he had brought her here. The door swung open and Sherry came out with Sam right behind her as if they had been waiting for them to arrive.

"I'm so happy you decided to come for dinner." She kissed them both on the cheek. "I just hate cooking for two."

"Mom, you say that all the time but admit it. You love cooking and it's a good excuse to invite your kids over for dinner." He winked at Steph. "We're onto her game."

Sherry whipped the towel from her shoulder and, with a playful flick of the wrist, snapped it against his backside.

He chuckled. "Didn't hurt, you know."

Sam eased around his wife and welcomed Stephanie. "I picked up a new white wine for dinner I thought you might like to try."

She was touched Sam remembered her preference, and so like her dad. He'd had a memory like an elephant. "Thank you. That was nice of you."

He jerked his head toward his wife and son. "Come with me while they have their mother-son fun."

Steph followed Sam through the house to the back deck.

"It's not overly humid tonight, so I thought it would be nice to relax out here. Sherry fixed us something to munch on until dinner's ready."

"She didn't need to go to so much trouble." Steph took a seat next to Sam, who was already pouring the wine.

"Don't say that to Sherry. It's her life's passion to fuss over family."

She didn't want to correct him and say that she wasn't a part of the Price clan, so she left it alone and took the glass he offered. She lowered her eyes and knew he hadn't meant that to be a prick to her heart. For the moment, the Price clan was the closest thing she had to family, even if she was living vicariously.

"What are we drinking tonight?" She held the glass to her nose and inhaled. She and Maggie had been watching an online master class to get a better grasp on how to appreciate wine.

"This is a Chenin Blanc." Sam also swirled the glass and then inhaled. "What do you think of the aroma?"

She swirled again. "Fruity, with a light floral smell too?" She questioned her nose but Sam beamed.

"Excellent." He held up his glass. "Let it sit on your tongue briefly."

She watched as he seemed to swirl it around in his mouth before he swallowed, but she just let it sit as he asked. She let the flavor of the wine be her focus. "It's on the sweeter side," she said when she let it slide down her throat. "Do I taste apple and pear?"

He beamed as if she were passing a test.

Leo and Sherry joined them and he poured them each a glass.

"Sam, are you subjecting Stephanie to a taste test?"

He held a finger to his lips. "Shh. I really want to know what she thinks. It's important." He focused on Steph again. "Do you like it?"

"Sam, I'm hardly a wine connoisseur, but yes. It's very good."

He held up the bottle and added a bit more to her glass.

"I don't think I've ever heard of this kind before."

Leo drank some. "I'm not surprised. We're the only vineyard growing these grapes. Jack would tell you they're temperamental and Anna won't let us sell any yet. She wants to make sure we can be consistent for a few years before we officially launch it."

She was surprised Leo really was more involved than he let on. Sam gave him an appraising look and nodded with pride.

"There's a man worthy of being on the Crescent Lake Winery board."

He swirled the glass of wine in his hand. "I am on the board, so I should be in the know on some things."

Steph could hear the edge in Leo's tone. She didn't want the evening to become contentious between father and son. "I do like it and I think others would too."

Sam sat back in his chair and stretched his legs out in front of him. "Steph"—he paused— "Wine is about enjoyment. It doesn't have to be fussy or win awards. Don't get me wrong; those are great, but for Crescent Lake Winery, it has always been about the person holding the glass. If they like it, then it's a winner in my book. And of course, as long as sales are robust."

"That's similar to how Dad felt about car restoration. For him, it was all about the love of cars. Well," with a chuckle, she said, "looks and speed count too. His shop started much like Leo's—small and building the clientele by word of mouth. Soon he was taking on more customers and started to hire people in the area he knew were good."

She sipped her wine. "People who want a car customized are willing to spend the money to get the car of their dreams and I want to keep that alive."

"How are things at your shop, Steph? Is business still steady?"

"We're busy." She gave Leo a glancing smile. "In fact, my newest mechanic is going to take some advanced classes. She didn't go to tech school and is self-taught, which is fine, but I see she has talent and I'd like to hone her skills. My dad hired her shortly before he passed away and I've been out of the garage long enough to be rusty, so I think some courses are best for her. Most of my mechanics have been with the business a number of years and some aren't as welcoming as I'd like, and of course, being that she's female, well, it's something they need to adjust to."

"You have a woman mechanic? That's interesting." Sherry crossed her legs. "Is it hard to be in a male-dominated industry?"

She thought of all the times a client came into the shop to ask a question and when she tried to help, they'd ask to speak with someone else, a real mechanic. It was only after she had one of the guys, or Dad, stand next to her for support that the customer did recognize her ability and from there, her reputation began to grow. It had taught her how to deal with all kinds of people, and that related to working in her current job.

"There are definitely biases, but Dad said all he had to do was wait until another qualified woman answered the help wanted ad and he'd hire her. He feels"—she blinked hard to make sure she didn't well up—"*felt* that my passion for car restoration was an edge the guys didn't have and he hoped to find that in another woman."

"If your father hired her, he must have had a good reason," Sam said.

"I firmly believe with some additional training, she'll blossom."

"I'm glad she works for you. It sounds like a perfect solution for you both."

Leo gave her a smile that warmed her to her toes. "Steph's an amazing businesswoman."

The timer went off in the kitchen and Sherry stood up.

Steph got up to follow her. "What can I do?"

"Not a thing. Sit and relax." Sherry slid the screen door shut, effectively leaving Steph with the men. Not that it bothered her, she had grown up in the garage and, by default, around men.

Sam grinned at her. "She runs the show here, so you might as well relax. If she needs help, she's not shy."

Stephanie sat down. She didn't remember what it was like to have a mom taking care of everything. She was young when her mom had died.

"Leo tells us you've been having some trouble at your place. Anything I can do to help?"

She shot Leo a sharp look.

He touched her arm and dropped his eyes before connecting with hers. "Dad has been running a business with a lot of employees for a lot longer than I have. He's good to bounce ideas off of."

It made sense but she was still miffed. "I wish you had asked me first." She could hear the frostiness in her voice.

"Stephanie," Sam said, "it's not like I'm going to gossip about you. Besides, I hate any kind of stealing. If someone is hard up, ask for help. But this is something else entirely."

She looked at him, wondering if he was being sincere.

With a satisfied nod, Leo said, "In fact, Dad said he didn't have any suggestions and you have it under control."

"Well then, thanks, Sam. It just really ticks me off to think about someone deliberately taking things."

"Have you thought about how you'll handle it when you learn the truth?"

"You mean when I actually know who's behind this?" She picked up her glass. "I'm going to ask them why."

"Do you plan to prosecute?" Sam's words had a strength behind them while he looked her square in the eye.

"Do you think I should?" Now, this part of the conversation piqued her interest.

"Do you know how much money you've lost?"

She thought for a minute. "Just shy of ten k."

He jerked his head back. "In what time period?"

"From what I can tell, somewhere around the time Dad was diagnosed with cancer. My suspicion is that when he started to not have an eagle eye on everything, it was easy to make things just disappear." She sipped her wine in an attempt to cool her anger.

"That's a big hit to the bottom line, for any business."

"It is." She swirled the wine in her glass. "Do you think I should just fire their ass or prosecute them and have my day in court?"

"Contact your lawyer. The cameras will give you proof, but it will be emotionally difficult."

She looked at Leo. "You've never said what you would do."

"I'm conflicted. I can see the benefit of firing them and moving on. I also think they need to pay restitution to avoid being prosecuted."

She wrestled with the idea of contacting the authorities. "Do you think I should make the decision now?"

Sherry came outside and looked at each person in turn. "It seems I've interrupted a serious conversation."

Over the rim of her glass, Steph asked Leo, "Did you tell your mom?"

"No, but I'm gonna bet Dad did."

Sherry perched on the arm of Sam's chair and slipped

her arm around his shoulders, a familiar gesture so relaxed, Steph could tell she had been doing it for many years. Had her parents been connected like them? It was something that until today she had never really thought about, but Dad had never dated, to her knowledge, so he must have not gotten over Mom's death. She thought of all the moments that were stolen from her. Maybe if she had seen her parents' loving relationship, she would have longed to have found it sooner. She glanced at Leo. It was something she'd found with him, however fleeting.

"Dear, don't be upset with Sam or Leo. They want to help, and so do I. But please don't worry. We haven't discussed it with anyone else, nor would we."

That gave Steph some small measure of comfort. At the moment, she was feeling outnumbered and a little over-whelmed.

"Would you like my opinion?" Sherry pushed a lock of blond hair from her compassion-filled eyes.

Stephanie recognized that Leo's parents really did want to be helpful and supportive. He probably didn't even realize how amazing his parents were. What she wouldn't give for just one day like this with her parents.

"Actually, yes."

"It might be best to find out why they did and then make your decision."

"That's what I was thinking, but what would be a good reason someone stole? It's just wrong, no matter which way you look at it."

Sherry nodded. "I agree. But in one extreme, if it is some sort of revenge, prosecute. On the other end of the spec-trum, you could have someone who was desperately trying to care for a sick child and thought what was taken wouldn't be missed. I'm not saying it's not wrong, but to know what motivated someone would help me decide how to handle it."

"Valid points. I never really thought someone might be in dire straits and since Dad was away from the shop with his own health issue, this person couldn't have gone to him and asked for help, and they probably don't know me from the next person. This isn't something anyone would talk with a coworker about either, but if it had been, Gary or Val were the logical choice, but they've never said anything either."

Sherry was right. To make a unilateral decision on how to handle this wasn't the right course of action.

"I'm going to lay out several scenarios and when I know who this person is, I can take action."

Sherry sat up straight. "Now that you have options and a plan to develop, we should have dinner before it gets cold." She stood up. "I hope you like roast chicken."

Stephanie let Leo pull her up from the chair. He slipped his arm around her waist.

"Sounds delicious."

Sam and Sherry stepped into the house.

"We'll be right in, Mom." Leo slid the door shut behind them.

He turned to face her. "I'm sorry if I overstepped by talking to Dad. I hate that someone has done this to you and I'm frustrated that I can't help."

She stepped closer to his lean, warm body. "Don't you see? You are helping me by listening and meeting with the security company. Knowing that you have my back means the world to me."

"I'd do anything for you. And when the person is caught, I'll be by your side when you make your next move."

She tilted her head back and looked into his chocolate-brown eyes. She really did discover a nice man on the worst day of her life. Maybe her dad was still trying to take care of her like he did when she was a kid.

"I appreciate that. Knowing you've got my back is what has gotten me through this mess."

He bent to kiss her. Hovering there, he said, "I'm always here for you."

She claimed his mouth with a fast, hot, searing kiss. "I know you are."

The last few weeks had flown by and today was Anna's wedding. Leo slipped into his tux jacket and adjusted his bow tie. Why on earth did Anna want him to get this dressed up? He wasn't really in the wedding. All he had to do was be in pictures.

He was excited to have Stephanie on his arm for this event. For so many years, he had gone stag, but not this time. He heard the click of her shoes before she walked into the living room. The moment he did, he sucked in his breath. His heart skipped. Stunning didn't begin to cover how she looked today. Maybe breathtaking was a better description.

Her smile went from ear to ear and she did a slow turn. The cream-colored slip dress made an unobtrusive background for the vibrant flowers scattered across the dress. He liked how it skimmed her shoulders, leaving her collarbone free access for his lips later when they danced. A belt accentuated her small waist. The dress flowed over her hips, following their curve, and the back slit gave him a peek of her legs as she moved. Amethyst earrings dangled from her ears and she wore a matching bracelet on her wrist. She was stunning and he couldn't believe his luck. "Are you trying to outshine the bride?"

With a soft laugh, she said, "Anna will be the center of attention."

"Not for me." He took her hand and turned it over, kissing the inside of her wrist. She shivered.

"You're so handsome." She leaned in for a kiss, then slipped her arm around his waist and turned to the mirror hanging on the living room wall. "We make a pretty sharp couple."

He kissed her cheek. "Are you ready to spend another day with the family?"

She pulled back and looked at him. "Everyone is so much fun and nice. You're fortunate to have been born into a family like this."

"Everyone loves you."

"It's been nice to be included." She stepped away and picked up a small leather clutch. She looked inside and snapped it shut. "I'm ready if you are."

He tugged on his tie. "I hate these things. I feel like I'm being choked."

She held out her hand. "Let me straighten that for you."

As she did, it reminded him of all the times he had witnessed his mom fixing Dad's tie. He waited until she seemed satisfied, a lump lodged in his throat. How could he convince her to move back to the valley, leave her career behind, and run her dad's shop? Or did he need to walk away from what he had built here for love? There was a part of him that couldn't believe he was even thinking of leaving.

She patted her hand on his lapel. "Perfect."

He ran a finger down her jawline, mesmerized not just by her physical beauty but the kind and gentle side of her that was so appealing.

"What do you say we enjoy ourselves today, from this moment to when we end our day here?"

She tipped her head to the side and gave him a sweet and saucy smile combined into one heart-racing look. "Is that a promise?"

"No. It's a sure bet."

She tenderly kissed him. "I don't want to rush the day, but it is something to look forward to."

Stephanie watched as Anna glided down the church aisle on Sam's arm, proceeded by Liza. She was radiant in a simply styled off-white lace gown with a stunning aquamarine necklace gracing her neckline. She had flowers in her hair and she carried a bouquet of roses and lilies. If there was ever a woman happy on her wedding day, Anna was the perfect picture. She watched as Colin saw her for the first time. A lone tear slid down Steph's cheek. Wiping it away, she reached for Leo's hand. He gave her a smile and then returned to watching the ceremony.

Anna and Colin recited their personal vows, and he wiped a tear from her face, a simple and sweet gesture.

Would she ever experience a day like this of her own? Steph was surprised to realize it was what she wanted. The career and the financial security that came with it suddenly seemed empty. Even being on the peripheral fringe of the Price family was nice. It had made bearing the loss of Dad easier.

The happy couple sealed their future with a kiss as the photographer captured every moment while they made their way back up the aisle. After the first few rows emptied, Leo stepped into the aisle, allowing her to join him. Hand in hand, they made their way outside, where guests and family were milling about. They joined the group of well-wishers and when it was their turn, Anna pulled her into a hard hug.

With a twinkle in her eye, she whispered, "Jump in. The water's warm."

Steph's stomach tightened. With a small laugh, she said, "I'm good on dry land." She moved to Colin and kissed his cheek. "Congratulations. You're a lucky man."

"Thanks, Stephanie. I'm glad you're here." With a wink, he said, "There's room for one more in the family."

Leo didn't hear what was said but shook Colin's hand and offered his congratulations. With his hand at the small of her back, he steered her out of the receiving line, helping her to avoid having to respond to the statement. She gave him a grateful smile.

They strolled over to Sam and Sherry. Leo said, "We're going to head to Sawyers. See you there?"

Sherry gave her a huge smile. "Stephanie, you look beautiful and Leo, I have to say it's nice to see you dressed up."

Sam said, "Son, I don't know about you, but I'm looking forward to taking this tie off."

He grinned. "Right there with you, Dad, and thanks, Mom."

"Thanks, Sam, and Sherry, your dress is lovely. Forest green is your color."

"Thank you, Steph. You two get things going at the reception and we'll see you there."

Leo and Stephanie took their time walking to the car. It was a warm late summer day and the sun was high in the deep-blue sky.

"Anna and Colin couldn't have asked for a better day."

"I'm hoping the rest of the day is as uneventful as it started."

She looked at his profile. "Why do you say that?"

He opened the passenger door to his car. "At Tessa's wedding, Dad was having chest pains. He didn't say anything until brunch the next day. That's when we rushed him to the hospital and Anna met Colin for the second time."

She got into the car. "Second time?"

He closed the door and got behind the wheel but didn't start the car. "Yeah, they'd met when Dad had his first heart attack."

"Sounds like fate had a guiding hand in putting them together."

"You know, I never thought about Anna and Colin's relationship as a positive from Dad's heart attack, but you're right." He turned the key and the car purred to life. "Do you think fate played a role in us meeting?"

"Yes, I do." Or did Dad also give them a push? Leo was the first guy she had met who used Dad as a subcontractor, and it wasn't something Dad usually did. "I'm sorry I gave you a hard time about painting the Chevelle. I know Dad would never have subcontracted with you if you'd had a poor foundation."

He turned in the seat and his eyes held a twinkle. "So why did you insist on coming to my shop before taking the paint job?"

"I'm not sure. I guess I wanted to see you again and that was the best way to do it. Although I thought you were married or at least involved with someone else."

He drew back. "Really?"

"The boys. The rapport you had with them—well, that you have. It wasn't something I expected from an uncle."

"Hmm. Makes sense. I never thought about it."

"Your relationship with Liza and the family is something I envy. The way you are there for each other even if you all overstep and meddle a bit. It's nice."

"And even though you thought I might be in a relationship, you still wanted to see me again?"

"Not like that. Seeing you with the boys made me miss my dad just a smidge less." She dropped her eyes. Missing him still hit hard from time to time.

"Steph, look at me."

She did as he asked. "I'm not much of a believer in fate or kismet or whatever you might want to call it. But that Saturday in April, I firmly believe I was in the exact spot I was meant to be."

She nodded. Tears filled her throat, leaving her speechless. As if understanding, he cupped her cheek.

"What do you say we skip the reception and spend the afternoon by ourselves?"

With a strangled laugh, she shook her head. "And miss out on dancing with you? Not a chance."

"I might step on your toes." The corners of his lips twitched. "You've been warned."

"Have you forgotten? We have danced many times in your house."

"That was in bare feet. Better suited for dancing. Not these spiffy black-tie shoes."

"Excuses. Just drive, Price."

He buckled his seat belt. "As you wish, sweetheart."

Steph rolled the window down partway to keep it from blowing her hair out of place. The wedding had given her a lot to think about, and things she didn't want to dwell on. It brought to reality that her time in New York was down to a few weeks.

"Tell me about Colin's sister Marie. I thought it was so sweet that she was her brother's best person instead of Drew."

"They're really close. I know everyone thought she and Drew were a couple, but it turns out they're best friends."

He gave her a sidelong look. "Did you happen to see how Drew couldn't stop looking at Liza?"

"I did. Are they friends?"

"Not really. I mean, he came to the barbeque Liza had a few weeks ago. Remember, we saw him show up with that plant?"

"Oh yeah. Do you think he's interested in her?"

It was a short drive to Sawyers and Leo backed the car into a space at the end of the lot.

"She hasn't shown any interest in seeing anyone other than friends and family since her husband died. I don't think she's ready."

With a smile, she said, "Is that your opinion? Because right now, you sound like an overprotective brother."

"She and the boys have had enough heartache. I don't want her to ever be hurt again."

"That would be her choice, not yours."

His voice held a touch of sadness and anger. "Maybe, but I lived through those first few days with her. She was a mess."

"Leo, everyone needs love in their life. It brings us alive, and to be without it is living half a life."

He took her hand and looked deep into her eyes. "For the first time, I understand exactly what you're saying. When we met, I felt what true love really is. And you're right. If and when Liza is ready to date, I'll be there encouraging her."

Steph knew what he meant. That day in April had been eye-opening for her as well.

"You really are the best guy I know." She kissed him and then grinned. "Come on. Maybe we can sneak in a quick dance before everyone gets here."

He held on and kissed her again. The look in his eyes spoke volumes; too bad they wouldn't get their happy ending.

$\mathcal{L}$eo held Stephanie close as they swayed on the dance floor. He wanted to ask her the question in his heart, but today was not the day. It was his sister's wedding.

Steph's head was resting on his shoulder, one arm circling his waist and the other hand in his. Leo couldn't ask for anything more today. Over her head, he saw Liza scolding the boys along with Owen and Ben. Steph was right. She was a good person and deserved to find love and happiness again. He was being honest with Steph when he said he'd support Liza any way he could.

The music ended and he looked at Stephanie. "Cake?"

"Mmm, sounds good. I wonder if they have coffee?"

"I'm sure we can rustle you up a cup."

Anna and Colin were working the room and now headed toward Liza. Leo steered Steph in that direction.

Liza smiled as Anna sank into a chair. "Come over and join us."

Leo held the chair out for Steph and sat next to her. "How's the cake?"

"Which one?" Anna asked. "There are four different flavors."

"Leave it to you, sis, to have options for your wedding cake."

"Liza, I got the idea from you." She grinned. "When you're the bride, everyone says yes." She beamed at Colin. "My husband"—her smile grew wider—"agreed we should have several cake flavors."

Marie and Drew were headed in their direction from across the dance floor. Colin stood up and met them halfway. After Colin slapped his friend on the back and hugged his sister, they came to the table.

Leo was watching as Drew's gaze stopped on Liza. She was oblivious to his attention, as Johnny took that second to come running over, asking if he could have another soda. He continued to watch Drew watch Liza until Marie pointedly said, "Drew."

"Sorry. I was, um, distracted."

Steph nudged Leo's leg and bobbed her head in that direction. He shrugged. He had no idea what was happening.

Marie dropped to a vacant chair. "Guys, this has been a great wedding. The food was amazing, the wine"—she kissed her fingertips—"unbelievable, and the cake choices awesome."

She looked at Liza and Leo. "Since Anna's my new sister, I guess that means we're all related now." She grinned. "I always wanted a big family and thanks to my favorite brother—and until today, my only brother—now we're all connected."

Stephanie smiled as Marie chattered away about being a part of the family. She had a wistful look in her eye. He was curious if Steph could be open to becoming a Price.

"Do you think they're going to bring coffee around or do I need to go to the bar?" Steph asked.

Leo looked around and then raised his hand toward a waiter. He made a motion like he was drinking a cup of coffee. The waiter nodded.

Everyone turned their cups upright.

Anna looked around the table. Her eyes stopped with Steph, and then she looked at Leo.

"Baby brother, you're the last sibling who hasn't tied the knot."

He shifted in his chair and didn't dare look at Steph, either because she was hoping for a proposal or praying he wouldn't.

He took Steph's hand. "We're happy just the way we are, so stop pushing. And don't forget it took you forever to get hitched, so I have plenty of time."

"Well, don't wait too long so we can all start to have the next wave of kids."

"Whoa. Anna."

Liza said, "It took you and Colin over two years to get married. Leo and Stephanie have only been dating for what?" She looked at Stephanie. "Five months?"

The waiter poured Steph's coffee and worked his way around the table. She added a splash of cream, thinking about how the conversation had been going. The last thing she wanted was for Leo's family to speculate about the long-term status of their relationship. After watching him with the family, she could never ask him to move to Portland. That was off the table.

"Don't forget I'm leaving in a few weeks, and then everything will go back to the way it was." She wanted to remove the knife she had just plunged into her own heart. But she continued without looking at the man she loved. "I'll be back from time to time and I'll make sure to check in with everyone. We'll keep in touch."

She could sense Leo's shock at her statement. She shouldn't have been so blunt, and she hated doing that to Leo in front of his family. It was the cowardly way out. She looked up to see the hurt in his eyes.

"Steph?"

Liza's coffee cup tipped over. Dark liquid splashed over the tabletop. Anna pushed back and Drew began to sop it up with his napkin, making sure to stem the flow before it reached Liza. Silently, Steph thanked Liza for causing a break in the tension.

She couldn't look at Leo. At least not right now. That's when she noticed a spot of coffee on her dress. Not speaking to anyone directly, she said, "I'm going to go wash this out before it sets."

Anna said, "I'll go with you."

She really wanted to be alone and not with the sister of the man she had just crushed, but so be it. There was no way she could gracefully get out of it.

On the way to the ladies' room, Stephanie picked up a couple of white cloth napkins from the table so she could use them to blot the coffee stain. Standing in front of the sink, Stephanie wrung excess water from one. She handed it to Anna, who refused it.

"Take care of your dress." She crossed her arms across her midsection. "Stephanie, are you okay?"

"Of course." She finished blotting the stain. She wouldn't look up.

"You can't hide how you feel about my brother. So why did you just blow him off out there?" She took the napkin away from Steph. "I promise to keep this conversation just between us, but has something happened? Did the two of you have a fight?"

Steph fiddled with her bracelet and chewed on her lip. She knew it was her tell, so she stopped the moment she recognized she'd started.

"No. We didn't argue."

"Then why did you just act like what you have is disposable?"

She squared her shoulders and stared into Anna's eyes. "Leo belongs in Crescent Lake, not in Portland. I'm not naïve enough to think that he'd be happy long-term away from your family."

"You should let Leo make that decision. By you deciding for him without even having the conversation, you wounded him."

"It wasn't my intention. It just kind of came out." She sagged against the sink. "I do love your brother, but we live completely different lives."

"That's a cop-out." Anna touched her arm. "Just think about what you might be giving up." She pointed to front of Steph's dress. "Looks like the coffee won't stain."

She turned to look in the mirror and caught Anna looking at her. "We should get back out there. I have some apologizing to do."

*L*eo waited for Anna and Stephanie to come back to the table. He had done some quick thinking and decided she had been dealing with so much that pushing her into deciding about their future was overload. He loved her and could be patient. They still had a couple of weeks and before she left, they'd have a long talk about their future.

The girls were walking toward the table. Leo stood and held out his hand. She took it.

"Dance with me."

She gave him a half smile. "I'd love to."

He twirled her into his arms. The music was slow and they moved in sync, swaying to "Can't Help Falling in Love

With You." He sang softly in her ear. She relaxed as they moved.

Looking into his eyes, she asked, "You're not mad at me?"

"Nothing to be mad at. My sisters are way too pushy for their own good and I'm glad you held your ground. It's just one of the reasons I love you." He kissed her forehead. "Look at my mom and dad dancing as if it's just the two of them."

She turned her head in the direction he indicated. "They're two peas in a pod."

"They've had a lifetime of experience. I remember as a kid watching them dance in the kitchen after they thought we had gone to bed. The first time I saw them, I was young. I heard music and crept down the back stairs. There they were, Dad dancing with Mom. They were talking low so I couldn't hear what they said, but I knew it was a special moment just for them."

"That sounds nice." She held him a little closer. "Is that why you like to dance around your house?"

"Can I be honest?"

She gave a soft laugh. "I hope you're always honest with me."

"You're the first girl I've danced with in my house."

A look of surprise flitted over her face. "You're kidding, right?"

"That one simple act is special." He stopped dancing. "Will you take a walk with me?"

She nodded. He slipped his hand in hers, interlacing their fingers. He opened the door and they stepped into the late afternoon sun, the warm air wrapping around them.

"There's a park down the street."

As they strolled hand in hand, he wondered if he should tell her that she was the love of his life. But no, that wasn't what he was going to do.

"Can we walk over to the pond and feed the ducks?" She clasped his hand a little tighter.

"Of course."

The late afternoon was still warm and Stephanie slipped out of her sandals as they walked through the grass. "My heels are sinking."

He took them from her and steered her to a bench next to the water. She settled into the crook of his shoulder.

"This is nice." She stretched her legs out in front of her and wiggled her toes. "I'm sorry about what I said before."

"It's okay." Leo continued to look in front of him. "You know, I used to be like a duck."

An amused look sparkled in her eyes. "Spend a lot of time swimming around?"

He chuckled. "No, I'm happy on a boat."

"So then tell me, how were you like a duck?"

"Before I met you, I'd date a girl for a few months at a time, like a season for a duck. Then I'd find myself in a new season with a new girl, never quite finding the one who was my goose." He pointed across to the other side of the pond. A pair of geese were swimming side by side.

"The difference between a duck and a goose is what?"

"Geese go through their lives with one mate. Even when one dies, they never take a new one."

"I had no idea." Her mouth formed a small O. And then he could tell she understood.

He reached into his pocket and pulled out a small jewelry box.

Her eyes widened and she shook her head. "Oh, Leo. I can't."

"Open it."

She flipped open the top and withdrew a silver necklace with a goose charm. "Oh, Leo." She pressed her lips to his. "I love it."

"I love you, Stephanie."

29

Sunday morning, Steph toyed with the goose charm on her necklace as she pulled out her laptop at Leo's kitchen table. She wanted to review the camera footage from the day before. Leo came over and handed her a mug of fresh coffee.

"Find anything yet?"

"Just starting to scan. So far, things are thankfully dull." She fast-forwarded through the morning footage with nothing out of the ordinary happening. She held her coffee mug to her lips and said, "Huh. Val just came in."

Leo scooted his chair closer to her. She took it off fast-forward mode and let it run in real time. Val was sitting at the computer and tapping on the keyboard. She seemed to be scanning the room and looking back at the computer screen.

"What do you think she's doing? Is she looking for someone?"

Steph leaned closer to the screen. With a laugh, she said, "I don't know why I'm getting closer; it's not like the camera angle is going to change."

He pointed to the screen. "Look. She's getting up and going down the hall."

"There is nothing down there on the weekend."

Val opened the back door and a man Steph didn't recognize stepped inside. She closed the door again. Then they went into the storage room. Steph switched the view to the interior of the closet.

"Thank heavens you decided to put a camera in there."

She glanced at Leo. "You don't think she's…" Her voice trailed off.

On the screen, Val was sorting through a stack of papers. She pointed to a printer and a laptop. The man pulled them from the shelf and counted out five bills to her. She double-counted, smiled, and tucked it into her back pocket. The man stacked the laptop on the printer box. She opened the storage room door and then walked him down the back hall and let him out the back door. She flipped the lock and returned to the desk and bent down, out of view, the papers in her hand.

"The shredder is under the desk." Steph banged her hand on the top of the table. "Look! The papers are gone. She shredded the invoices." She jumped up and began to pace the kitchen. "Can you believe that she just sold computer stuff I bought for the business?"

"Don't look now but she's going to the back door again."

Steph flopped in the chair and groaned. "Now what's she going to do?"

She brought in a woman this time and basically followed the same procedure. Only this time, it was a stack of basic office supplies and the woman seemed to go shopping off the shelves. Val rifled through a box, said something, and the woman handed over the money. Val walked her out too.

Steph watched, mesmerized, as Val did the same thing

two more times. It was like watching a car wreck in slow motion and she was grateful when Val walked out the front door and didn't return.

"How much money do you think she just made off me?"

"It's hard to say but I'm guessing a couple grand."

She flicked the lid shut. "I don't want to watch any more in case she comes back." She dropped her head to the table. "I wouldn't have suspected it was Val. Not in a million years. She and Dad have been friends—hell, according to Val, more than friends—for a long time. Why would she steal from me? And worse, from him?" She lifted her eyes to Leo. "I have to go down there and see if anything else is missing. Will you come with me?"

"I'll need to get changed."

"Oh, wait. We can't. You need to go to your parents' for the after-wedding brunch for Anna and Colin."

"We'll skip it."

With a shake of her head, she said, "No, it's a family event and you need to go. I'll check out the shop and we'll meet back here later."

"We'll go together and swing by my parents' after. I'll let them know something came up and we'll be late."

"Leo, no."

His face grew serious. "I'm not going to argue about this. I'm assuming you want to do inventory, and it will go quicker with two of us. When we're done, we'll stop and have something to eat at my parents', wish the happy couple the best, and then come back here and formulate a plan."

She felt herself relax. It was comforting to know he wanted to help, and he was right that it could be done faster with both of them and it was really all the evidence she needed to move forward.

"How soon can you be ready?"

He flashed her a wide grin. "The better question is how fast can you be ready?"

She was already hurrying down the hall. "You pick up the kitchen and I'll be ready before you're done."

*L*eo waited until Steph disappeared into the bedroom, and then he balled his hands into fists. Anger bubbled to the surface and for a minute, he lit it, then told himself to control it before she came back, so he loaded the dishwasher and wiped down the table. It was times like this when he'd call Dad to ask his opinion, but he wasn't about to make that mistake again. He would suggest Steph could ask Dad's advice on how to handle Val stealing from her.

He sent his mom a text, letting her know they'd be late and he'd explain later.

She immediately pinged back, *Is everything okay?*

Yeah, unavoidable.

Mom texted, *Come when you can.*

He strode to the bedroom and discovered Steph was sitting on the edge of the bed. She was wearing hot-pink capris and the tank top that she had slept in, and she was crying.

He was at her side with his arms around her in a flash. "Hey, what's going on?"

"I can't do this anymore."

"Can't do what?" Fear stabbed his gut. Did she mean their relationship?

"Run the shop," she cried. "It's too much, and how will anything work when I'm gone? If someone I trusted can steal from me while I'm here, what'll happen when I'm not?"

"You'll fire Val and once everyone knows what

happened, you can fill her position. Maybe Gary could be the general manager. He's more than capable."

"How do you know? You only met him a couple of times."

He wiped the tears from her cheeks with his thumb. Her eyes were troubled. "I've been told I'm an astute judge of character. And don't forget I'm here. I can check on things, if that will make you feel better."

That was until he made the move west. But now was certainly not the time to bring that up.

"You'd do that for me?" Her lower lip trembled.

He knew this was about much more than just the issues at the shop. It was hitting her all at once. Leaving. Her dad's death. Uncertainty at the shop, and of course, her own heart was breaking, just as his was. He didn't like the idea that they'd be apart for any length of time.

She brushed the hair back from her face. "Give me five minutes and I'll be ready to leave."

"Take your time. I let Mom know we'd be late."

"Why are you so good to me?" She ran her finger down the length of his arm.

"'Cuz I kinda like you." He gave her a light shoulder bump. "And you're awfully cute."

The corners of her lips quirked up.

He said, "How about tomorrow night we borrow Jack's boat and have dinner on the lake?" He tipped his head and squinted. "Might be a little cool, but I'll keep you warm." He pulled her up from the bed. "And if Jack is using his, there are several others in the family."

"The family that boats together has fun together."

He snorted. "Something like that."

She grabbed her blouse off the bed. "Give me two minutes and I'll be ready to go."

He watched as she closed the bathroom door. He stripped off his sweatpants and pulled on decent jeans and a deep-purple polo shirt. After he ran a comb through his hair, he'd be ready to do inventory. He certainly hoped there wasn't more missing than she had seen on the videos.

*S*tephanie finished checking the final column on the spreadsheet. She closed the door behind her and snapped the switch into the off position. Leo was coming in from the shop. He held up the clipboard.

"Inventory out there is on the nose."

With a forced smile, she said, "That's good news." She jerked her head toward the closet. "In addition to confirming our suspicion from earlier, there's a large monitor missing. I was planning on having that installed for Chuck. He's on the computer most of the day and that small screen is going to give him eyestrain."

"Any idea of the grand total?" He handed her the clipboard.

Stephanie double-checked the sheet. "Just under three thousand."

"That's grand larceny."

"Yeah, I know." She tossed the boards onto the desk and leaned against it, studying her short pink nails. "I honestly don't know what to do. Ever since I saw Val on that video, I've been dumbstruck. I want to see her charged but on the other hand, I wonder why she's doing it. She's paid well. From what I can tell, she lives a decent life. What could have motivated her to steal from me?"

"The only way you're going to have answers to your questions is to ask her."

"I want to drive over to her house and confront her, demand that she tell me the truth."

"You can't go off half-cocked. Take a few days to think about it, and then talk to her, or you can call the police now."

She had a hunch that since nothing had been stolen during the week, things would be safe for the next few days. "You're right. For the rest of the day, we're going to forget about this and spend some quality time with your family." That was another gut punch—she was running out of time. She corrected her thought process; no, they were also her new friends. Back home, she just had one close friend. No time to dwell on that today.

She picked up the clipboards. "I'm going to put these in my desk and we'll go."

Leo waited while she secured them in the file cabinet and locked it. She didn't want to take the chance that someone—no, that was wrong. She didn't want Val to come snooping around and stumble across them and shred these too.

She picked up the picture of her dad from the corner of her desk. She had always loved this one of the two of them. It was the last Thanksgiving they had together before she went off to college. "We had all the time in the world, Dad. At least that's what I thought. I'm really sorry for what's happened, but don't worry. I'm going to take care of it and make sure your company will continue to grow no matter where I live." She kissed her fingertips and placed them on the photograph.

She turned off the lights and walked back to the lobby where Leo waited for her.

"I'm done here." She took his hand. "I wonder if your dad has that wine I like on ice." She looked up at him.

"Are you kidding? He'll have a couple bottles waiting for you. You're his favorite non-family member."

30

*A*s soon as Steph and Leo parked their car, his four oldest nephews raced to the driveway. Her car door was pulled open and George said, "Stephie, come on! We saved you cake!"

She looked over her shoulder at Leo, who shrugged, but his eyes were filled with laughter. "We take cake very seriously around here."

She gave him a last look. "I can see that."

Ben took her hand and smiled up at her. "Don't worry. Mimi saved you a piece just 'cuz she knows we're bottomless pits."

Ben was the soft-spoken one in the group. Not that he didn't have his share of raucous fun but occasionally, like now, he was pretty quiet. He pointed toward the backyard.

"Mom said I should 'court you to the party."

She held back a smile at his choice of words. "That is very nice of you, but wouldn't you rather have fun with your cousins?"

"Mom said I need to practice my manners."

"Thank you, young man."

He beamed. They rounded the side of the house. The

backyard seemed to have people everywhere. Some were talking in small groups; others were filling plates from the extensive buffet.

She felt a hand at the small of her back. Leo whispered in her ear, "You're a good sport." He kissed her cheek.

Ben waved to Kate and pulled his hand away. "See ya later, Stephie." He took off running to the badminton net where his cousins were getting ready to play.

Out of the side of her mouth, she said, "Just another small family gathering."

He answered her with a low chuckle. "What can I say? The family keeps growing." With the pressure of his hand, he steered her toward the house. "There's room for one more, you know."

She laughed and hoped it didn't sound like a nervous cackle. "Good to know."

Before they could go inside, Sam called out to them.

"Hey, you two. What kept you?"

They changed course and walked over to Sam, who was sitting on a cushioned deck chair, keeping one eye on the boys and the other on them.

"Hi, Sam. Sorry we're late. We had to make a detour."

His eyebrows shot up. "Everything okay?" He looked at Leo.

She glanced around to make sure she wouldn't be overheard. "Remember that problem we talked about a couple of weeks ago?"

"Did something happen?"

"I have video proof now of who it is."

"By the look on your face, it was not who you had been expecting." He pulled a chair over. "Have a seat and son, why don't you get Steph a glass of wine? I have her favorite chilling."

She glanced at him. It was apparent Sam wanted to talk to her one-on-one.

"That sounds nice, Leo."

"Dad, can I get you something?"

"I'm all set."

Leo made his way toward the house, talking to people as he passed them. Stephanie wasn't sure what to say to Sam. His mouth was set in a firm line and his dark-brown eyes were like stone. She couldn't imagine what it was like growing up with him for a dad. He must have been intimidating.

"How can I help?" Sam patted her hand in a fatherly gesture. So much like Dad would have done.

She dropped her chin. "Thank you, but there is nothing you can do."

"Why don't you share with me what you saw? It might help you to talk with someone who isn't biased." He bobbed his head from side to side. "Well, I'm not completely uninvolved, as I don't like it that someone has hurt you."

Why would Sam want to help? Was he just being nosy? Or did he truly care about what was going on? The look on his face and the sorrow in his eyes told her he wanted to help.

"It's my front office manager. She's worked for Dad for years and I would never have even had an inkling that it would be her."

"Sadly, given the right circumstances, I think most people would commit theft. Do you think she has debts she can't pay?"

The way he said the word *debt* instantly conjured up an image of a loan shark and gambling issues. She knew Val loved going to the casino. Dad said they had gone together a few times but, like him, was a nickel slot machine fan.

"I don't think so." Slowly, she continued. "She doesn't seem to be sick, so no medical bills either."

"Do you have an idea how much she has taken overall, or just this last time?"

She clasped her hands in her lap. "It was a few thousand this time and overall, well, it's approaching fifteen thousand."

"That's a lot of money."

She gave a snort. "Yeah, and I have to stop her but I'm torn. Do I contact the police and give them the video, or do I confront her with the evidence and fire her and cut my losses?"

He asked in a quiet tone, "What does your gut tell you to do?"

"I don't want to have to deal with it at all. But I know that's not realistic." She looked around the yard and watched the boys waving rackets in the air, missing the birdie.

She turned her attention back to Sam. "What would you do?"

His face turned very serious. "I'd contact the authorities and have her arrested."

Steph felt her mouth drop open. It was not what she had been expecting from him. "You would?"

"This has been going on for months, hasn't it? And all this time, she has made herself out to be a model employee. Loyal and hardworking, offering to help you in any way she can, correct?"

"How did you know?"

"You never mentioned her as a suspect. And all this time, she's known you could uncover the truth, but she hasn't stopped. She's banking on your kind heart and vulnerable position. It hasn't concerned her for one moment that you could have her arrested."

"I never thought of it like that." Sam provided a fresh perspective. She had been feeling bad for Val, overlooking that she and everyone who worked for Black River were the victims, not the other way around.

Sam asked, "Do you have an attorney you can trust since you haven't lived around here in many years?"

"I'm going to use the woman my dad used for his business first thing tomorrow and see if we can meet right away. Once I talk to her, that should help me formulate my plan."

"If you'd like me to go with you, all you have to do is ask." Sam gave her a warm smile. "Not that you can't handle it on your own."

"Thank you, but I wouldn't want to bother you." She placed a hand on his arm. "Just lending an ear was helpful."

He leaned forward. "Don't tell anyone, but I'm a little bored, so I offered from a purely selfish standpoint. Helping to stir up a ruckus over something like this is right up my alley."

She couldn't help but smile. "There are times, Sam, when you remind me of my dad."

He looked pleased. "I'll take that as a compliment." He gestured over her shoulder. "It seems my son is itching to join us again." He waved Leo over.

In a few long strides, Leo was handing her a glass of chilled white wine and perched on the arm of her chair.

"Did Dad give you good advice?" He slipped his arm around her shoulders.

"Actually, he's offered to go with me tomorrow to my lawyer's office."

"Thanks, Dad, but I was planning on going with Steph."

"You have a car to work on," Steph said, "and I don't want you to waste a half a day dealing with this." She made a quick decision. "I'd like your dad to go with me. He has more experience than either of us in business. I think his insight will be valuable."

Leo's face dropped. "I want to see this through with you."

"I'm going to need you more at the end of the day."

Sam got up from his chair and moved away, giving them some privacy in the midst of a party.

She turned in the chair so she was facing Leo. "I really appreciate that you want to be there for me, but when your dad offered, at first I thought it would be a bad idea. It's growing on me."

"You know you have people who will help you. All you have to do is ask."

Steph did know all she had to do was ask; it was one of the first lessons an independent woman learned. What concerned her was that she was coming to rely on Leo and that contradicted who she thought she was; or was it part of being in a committed relationship? Or maybe it was because she felt alone and needed someone to lean on. If that was the reason, she'd better get a handle on her life. She didn't need to rely on any guy. Support was one thing but dependence was not healthy.

"I appreciate that you want to help but as I was talking to your dad, in some ways he reminded me of how Dad would be firm and wouldn't give Val the easy way out. Your father won't let me cave."

He nodded and gave her a small smile. "You've got this and we'll talk about it when you get home."

"Of course, and I'll need your support if I decide to have her arrested." She took his hand. "I don't want the rest of the employees to turn on me."

"When they know the truth, they won't. You don't have anything to worry about."

She glanced around and noticed they were getting some curious looks from his siblings. "We need to get up and mingle, especially before Anna and Colin take off for their honeymoon."

"Those two sure know how to celebrate their marriage. They took a trip before the big event, and now they're off again."

She picked up her wineglass. "Come on. I want to know their secret to all the vacation time." With a soft laugh, she took his hand. "I could definitely use pointers. I'm terrible about taking vacations."

e held her hand as they walked in Anna's direction. He could understand why Steph wanted Dad with her. He was a formidable man and he wouldn't let her give in to her soft side. But hell, he didn't want her to feel like she was alone. Not anymore.

Anna's smile widened as they grew closer. "Hi, guys." She noticed Steph's glass. "I see you're drinking the Chenin."

She held up the glass. "How did you know just by looking at it?"

With a laugh, Anna said, "I'm in the wine business." She tapped her glass to Steph's. "Excellent choice."

Colin said, "Do you play golf, Stephanie?"

"I have for work functions, but that's more business than playing for fun. Why?"

He said, "I thought maybe the four of us could play a round sometime."

Steph glanced over. "Leo, do you play?"

"I do from time to time."

"That explains why you're so good at mini golf."

His eyebrow arched. How did she know he was good? They had never played.

She grinned and jabbed a finger in the boys' direction. "They tell me all kinds of things."

"I need to talk to those kids about the bro code."

She placed a finger across her lips. "Don't say anything.

I just think they might like me, occasionally, more than they like you."

Leo slapped his hands together and laughed. "You might just be right."

He noticed Anna watching them.

"Stephie. Come 'ere." George was waving to her.

She handed her glass to Leo. "I'll be back."

She was walking away when Anna gave him a playful hip check. "What are you going to do next?"

Colin said, "Take it from me. Don't let her get away. She's a keeper."

"I have no intention of letting her go."

He watched as she joined the badminton game, laughing while trying to hit the little birdie. Leave it to George to take a shine to her. He had great taste.

Like uncle, like nephew.

31

*S*am was waiting for Stephanie outside her lawyer's office just before ten the next morning. She relaxed when she saw him.

"Hi, Stephanie. Are you ready to do this?"

"Thanks for coming, Sam. I'm as ready as I'll ever be." She straightened her sagging shoulders and stood tall.

"We're going to start the ball rolling. This is the beginning of the end of your problem."

He pulled open the door and Steph steeled herself as they walked into the foyer. The receptionist looked up and smiled and invited Steph and Sam to sit down while she told the attorney they were there.

Sam sat next to Steph. "Are you nervous?"

"A little. In an odd way, I'm embarrassed about this entire issue."

His brows furrowed. "Why? You did nothing wrong."

"I know there was nothing I could have done to prevent Val from stealing company property and reselling it, but what does it say about me? I gave her my trust, and Dad did too. From the financial records, this started around the time he got sick."

"It is obvious to me she was cunning and knew how to play the game with others. Then she got sloppy."

The receptionist reappeared, holding the door open. "Ms. James, if you'll come with me, please."

Steph and Sam were ushered into an intimate conference room. One wall was lined with books and a framed law school diploma. Another held a door, which Steph knew from her last trip here—for the reading of Dad's will —led into Paula's office. Paula was a business attorney who worked in the firm and had handled Dad's business needs. A large picture window looked out over a manicured lawn. She and Sam took a seat facing the door to Paula's office, thanking the receptionist but declining her offer for coffee.

Steph pulled out a manila folder from her shoulder bag and set it on the polished mahogany table.

The office door opened and a tall, slender, dark-haired woman came in. Her smile warmed her eyes. "Stephanie, it's nice to see you again." Her gaze shifted to Sam. She extended her hand. "Paula Adams."

He half stood and shook her hand. "Sam Price. I'm a friend of Stephanie's."

"Sam owns Crescent Lake Winery."

"Nice to meet you. Please sit." Paula placed a legal pad and pen on the table and pulled out a chair. "So Joyce told me the reason for you coming in today. How can I help?"

"First, thank you for working me in on short notice. I know you're very busy."

"This is a serious matter that should be addressed as quickly as possible. Not only does it threaten your financial security, but it adds undue stress to you."

She gave a half nod. "After Dad died, I wanted to familiarize myself with all aspects of the business. As you know, I plan to return to Oregon and have a manager take control of the day-to-day workings of the business."

"Which I thought was a sound idea." She had her pen poised over the top of her legal pad.

"When I started to review the financial records, I noticed a few discrepancies. At first, I thought it was just human error. No one is perfect."

Paula nodded. "Of course."

"Then there was a mix-up with a supplier where we were significantly overcharged. I did a physical inventory myself and discovered we were short product. I had Val call and clear up the matter with the supplier. But it was when my newest employee said she had money taken from her backpack on several occasions that I grew more concerned. These weren't simple mistakes." She took a deep breath and continued. "I had cameras installed to record everything twenty-four seven. The latest incident happened on Saturday. The office was closed but when I reviewed the video on Sunday, I discovered my front office manager had gone into the office and actually sold computers and other supplies to people she let in the back door." She kept her voice steady even though her throat felt constricted.

Sam poured a glass of water from the pitcher on the table and handed it to her. "Have a drink."

She tightened her fingers around the glass. She took a small sip and set the glass down on a piece of cork Paula slid across the tabletop.

"Take your time, Stephanie."

She lifted her eyes and noticed Paula had been taking notes while she relayed her story. She took two pieces of paper from the folder and handed them to Paula. "This was the inventory Val did on Thursday, and here is the inventory we did on Sunday."

Paula scanned the pages and looked up. "This would have made a tidy sum for a few transactions."

Steph nodded. "I have it all on video." She took a USB drive and handed it to Paula. "This is the footage."

"I'm assuming you saw Val this morning when you went to work? Did she happen to mention something, as in the door was unlocked?"

"No," Steph said. "Why would she do that?"

"On the off chance you went looking for something, she'd have her story in place."

"Not a word."

"As of this moment, she has no idea you might suspect her of any wrongdoing?"

"I don't think so." She looked at Sam and back at Paula. "Should I have spoken to her?"

"Confronting her would have been the wrong thing. She would have stopped until you left and then started up again." She looked at the pages again. "What do you want to do?"

"I was willing to talk to her, tell her I knew and if she repaid me for the items she had stolen, we'd go our separate ways. But now I'm not sure."

Paula laid the papers on the table and looked her in the eye. "And now? I'm guessing something has changed."

"Well, I want her to repay me, but I'm torn on getting the police involved and having her arrested and potentially charged. But if I do, then I could scare the hell out of her, have her repay me, and then drop the charges and move on."

"While I'm not a criminal lawyer, with the amount she has stolen, that will be hard to forgive and forget. And for the record, I believe you need to contact the police."

She made a fist under the table. "I just want this over with, but she should have to pay restitution. She didn't just steal from me. She threatened the security of my business, betrayed her coworkers—and she betrayed my father's trust. What kind of person does that?"

Paula stated flatly, "A criminal."

The comment hung heavy in the air. Steph felt the

weight of this decision was solely on her shoulders. Whatever she decided would change Val's life forever. She could go to jail and, with a record, have a much harder time finding a job when she got out or she could cut her a break.

"I'd like to have a meeting with Val and you, if you'll represent me. Lay out the facts and give her the option of paying full restitution before I fire her. I won't give her a reference to another job and she is never to darken my door again, and she needs to sign a document that agrees to never try to come back on me for loss of wages. In other words, she can't claim that I fired her unjustly."

"Why do you want to be lenient?" The attorney cocked a brow.

"At one time, she was a good friend to my dad. I want to know what changed." She narrowed her eyes. "I want to know why she was hell-bent on stealing from my father."

Paula tapped her pen on the legal pad. "And if she doesn't?"

"I contact the police, turn over all the evidence, and fire her. She can deal with charges and jail time. But I'll wash my hands of the entire situation."

"As I said before, this is not my area of expertise. I can make a couple of phone calls and get someone to work with you." She placed her palm on the table. "Are you sure you don't want to have her arrested?"

With a firm shake of her head, she said, "If I have her arrested, I may never know why, and to me that's more important than having her tossed in jail."

Paula pushed back her chair. "Give me a few minutes and I'll see if I can make a connection for you today."

"Thank you, Paula. I do appreciate your help." She was relieved to know this situation was going to get resolved and in addition to Sam's support, now Paula was doing all she could to help.

"Your father was a good friend of mine. I hate the fact

that someone took advantage of him and now you." She strode from the room.

Steph didn't want to look at Sam, as she knew he had wanted her to go in a different direction. Instead, she looked out the window and watched a bird fluttering at the feeder.

She addressed him directly. "I know you encouraged me to have her arrested and charged. Maybe I should, but for me, this feels like the right thing to do."

"Will you be able to sleep at night?"

She was taken aback. "You mean when this is all over?"

Sam nodded. "The most important piece of advice I've tried to instill in all my children is that after the decisions we make, both in business and in life, we have to be able to sleep at night knowing we always tried our very best."

Her heart hardened. "Then I've made the right decision." She looked him in the eye. "Make no mistake. If Val doesn't recognize this is a gift of her personal freedom or she says she can't make full restitution"—she emphasized the word *full*—"I *will* have her formally charged. That is non-negotiable."

Paula came back into the room and handed Stephanie a business card. "Scott Neilson. He's expecting your call and can meet with you today. With a bit of luck, you could wrap this up by the end of the week. He's one of the best criminal lawyers I know and he'll advise you as well as be with you during the conversation with Val."

Stephanie and Sam stood up. "Paula, I appreciate your help."

"Just do me one favor. Before you go back to Oregon, give me a call and let me know how everything worked out. I'd really like to know." Her smile was genuine. She must have liked Dad. It was good he had surrounded himself with good people. Once again, Steph was reminded there was a lot she hadn't known about her dad and it was something she couldn't change. Now all she could do was stand for what was right.

She shook Paula's hand. "You'll be hearing from me soon."

Sam shook her hand and thanked her for her help.

They stepped outside into the cool and cloudy day. Steph shivered against the fall temperatures and buttoned her jacket.

"Thanks for coming with me. I'm going to give this guy a call to see when we can meet."

"I didn't do much. But you're very welcome."

"Moral support was a huge bonus. In a small way, it was like Dad was with me." She withdrew her phone. "If you want, I can call you later and let you know what he says."

His eyes opened wider. "You don't want me to go with you to the next appointment?"

"Sam"—she forced a small smile—"I do appreciate that, but I can't ask you to spend more of your day hanging out with me. Unless you'd like to have lunch?"

He pointed to her cell phone. "Set up the appointment, and then we'll talk lunch."

She dialed the phone. A deep voice said, "Scott Neilson."

Stephanie introduced herself and Scott said he'd been expecting her call, then asked if she was still at Paula's office.

"Yes, we're in her parking lot." He certainly was direct and to the point and she was surprised he answered his own office phone.

"If you're facing down the hill, turn around. Do you see the large brick building behind you at ten o'clock?"

"Does it have a yellow door with white trim?"

"That's my office. When you come inside, just let May know you have an appointment with me."

"Thank you." She looked at her phone and then at Sam. "Well, that was an odd call but he's waiting for us. It's just across the street."

"Let's go and wrap this up." He gave her shoulder a fatherly pat. "I'll just need to let Sherry know I'll be a little later than planned." He tapped the center of his chest and gave her a grin. "She gets worried if I don't check in occasionally."

Steph said, "Fair warning: We're not going for salad. I'm in the mood for a burger and maybe even a beer."

"Now you're talking!"

As they crossed the street, Steph looked at Sam out of the corner of her eye. He was a tough guy with a soft heart. Leo had more in common with his father than he realized.

32

$\mathcal{I}$t was before eight on Friday morning, and it was the day of the big showdown. Steph had dressed as the boss today, in dark-gray slacks, a simple dove-gray blouse, and a floral scarf, with black flats. Her jacket was ready on the back of her desk chair, possibly more ready for this meeting than she was.

Steph met Scott at the front door when he arrived. "Good morning," she said, relieved Val hadn't been the first to arrive. "We're going to have our meeting in the conference room just down the hall."

She led the way and then stepped to one side. To settle her nerves, she had thought out each detail. "I was thinking if you sat at that end of the table"—she pointed to the far side—"I'll be here and Val will be across from me. Also, I'm going to ask Gary, who is currently the shop manager, to keep everyone in the shop so that we won't be interrupted."

"What about foot traffic?" Scott began pulling out documents from his briefcase and setting them aside.

"I'm going to have the closed sign on the door, and I'll lock it. Then, once I know how Val is going to play it, I'll

246

assemble the rest of the team, let them know about the change, and the locksmith will be here by noon."

"You do know you can't tell the specifics. Just that she will no longer be working here. Period."

"Stephanie?" She started, her heart hammering. She should have hung the closed sign already as she hurried into the lobby. Sam was standing next to the front desk.

"I didn't expect to see you today."

"Well, it's like this. If you were my daughter, I'd want to be nearby, just in case you needed moral support. Not beside you, but maybe in a spare office where I'm not visible. I talked it over with Sherry and she encouraged me to get over here." He gave her a wide smile. "Got a spare office I can hang out in?" He patted his shirt pocket. "I've got my phone and I love playing solitaire. I'm up to level six."

She rushed over to him and hugged him hard. With a chuckle, he said, "I'll take that as a yes."

"You can hang out in my office. It's just down the hall from the conference room but you'll be out of sight."

He gave her a sidelong look. "You're not going to protest and try to get me to leave?"

"Heck no. Besides, Sherry's probably enjoying the peace and quiet at the house." She was grateful to have his support even though she could do it on her own. "I'll show you the way."

Once Sam was sequestered, Steph paced the lobby, waiting for a glimpse of Val's car. She checked her watch; the damn thing didn't seem to move. Maybe the battery had died. To eat up a few minutes, she walked into the shop and gestured for Gary.

He was wiping his hands as he came over. If he took notice of how she was dressed, he didn't give it away.

"What's up, boss?"

"I have an important meeting in the office and I'd like

for you to keep everyone in the shop. When I'm done, I'll be out."

His right eyebrow arched and any questions he might have never came from his lips. "You got it." He began to walk away and stopped. "If you need me, holler."

"Thanks."

With one look at the clock on the wall, she hurried back into the lobby just as Val's car pulled in. She wiped her damp palms on her slacks and took several deep breaths to steady her nerves. Her career in pharmaceuticals had not prepared her for this, that was for sure.

Val came through the door with a huge smile and a box of donuts in her hand.

"Hi, boss lady." She gave her the once-over. "You look sharp. Checking to make sure your fancy work clothes still fit?"

She set the box on the counter and walked around it, setting her bright-red handbag on the counter. Steph took a hard look. Designer and new. It wasn't hard to guess where that had come from.

"Nice bag." She couldn't help herself.

Val gave her a cautious look. "Every girl deserves nice things from time to time."

"Would you come with me? I'd like to talk with you for a few minutes."

This time, Val didn't look her in the eye. "Just let me get my computer booted up and check voicemails."

Steph stiffened her spine. "That can wait."

Her tone must have captured Val's full attention, as the smile faded from her lips. "Sure thing, Stephanie."

"We're going into the conference room."

Val fell in step beside her. "Well, aren't you all formal-like. Is something wrong?" A slight waver in her voice betrayed her nerves.

Stephanie had her walk in first. "Have a seat."

Val looked at Scott at the end of the table and then at Stephanie. "I didn't know we were having a supplier in today. I would have been on time."

Steph changed her mind and took the chair closer to the door. With Sam in her office, she knew no one would come down the hall.

Val turned to Scott. "I'm sorry, but I don't recall seeing you here before. What company do you rep?"

"Val, this is my attorney, Scott Neilson."

Her face paled. She licked her lips and clasped her hands together in front of her on the tabletop. "I'm sorry," she said. "I don't understand why I'm meeting with you and your attorney."

"I've discovered we have a problem here at Black River. Someone has been stealing from the business." Steph's voice was flat, devoid of emotion.

"What?" Val's eyes grew wide and her pupils dilated. "That's shocking."

"Yes, it was very upsetting to discover that money is being stolen from employees right out of their lockers and equipment has been stolen along with office supplies."

Val's hand flew to her mouth. "How awful. Do you have any idea who did it?" She leaned forward and with a conspiratorial whisper, she said, "I'll bet it's Zira. You know she's new and well, she was hired when your Dad wasn't feeling well. He must have misjudged her character."

Stephanie couldn't believe her ears. Val was seriously trying to blame someone else? She wished she had called the police instead of trying to be civil. Maybe if Val talked a little longer, she'd hang herself in the process.

Val looked at Scott. "Is that why you're here? To make sure that when Stephanie fires her, it's done all legal-like?"

Scott shifted his gaze from Val to Stephanie.

"Yes, Val. Scott is here to provide legal counsel." She wished she had a glass of water. Her mouth felt like the desert at high noon. "But we won't be talking to Zira. I was able to catch the person on camera—in the act, you could say."

The stunned look on Val's face was all the satisfaction Steph needed to keep going. "You see, the new cameras I had installed actually record twenty-four hours a day. Every day."

"The door cameras only activate if there's a break-in." Val snapped her head up. "What? You lied to us?" Her eyes darted from Scott and back to Steph.

A half smile slipped out. "I own this business and I don't need to tell you every detail of how I choose to run it." She was taking a small measure of pleasure as she watched Val squirm in her seat. "Be that as it may, imagine my surprise when on Sunday morning, I'm enjoying a cup of coffee and I pull up the footage from early Saturday night and within a short time, I see you enter the building. Would you care to explain to me what you were doing here that late?"

"You know me, just trying to be proactive. I did a little tidying in the storage room, moved things around so they're a little more organized."

"Interesting. Did you talk to anyone while you were here?"

Val pushed back the chair so hard, it kicked against the wall. "I don't like your tone. If we're done, I'll go and ask Zira to come in and you can grill her."

Anger seethed in Steph. Her voice was razor-sharp. "Sit down."

Like a scared little mouse being stared down by the feisty feline, Val did as she was told.

In a carefully controlled tone, Steph said, "You sold items from my storage room. It was you who took money from your coworkers. It was you who fudged inventory numbers and lined your pockets with my money."

Val thrust her chin up. "Prove it."

"You left a very nice trail of breadcrumbs for me to follow. Did you think I was so grief-stricken that I wouldn't see what you were doing?" She leaned forward. "Don't answer that. The question I really want you to answer is why would you do that to my father? He was very good to you. Paid you well and gave you excellent benefits, and you stole from him. Why?"

"I deserved it all." She smacked the tabletop. "If he hadn't gotten sick and died, this business would be mine."

"How do you figure that?"

"I was going to convince him to marry me and eventually he'd cut you off. As his loving wife, it would be all mine. Then he got sick and I knew I'd never get a dime. So I took what was rightfully mine."

Stephanie was stunned beyond words. Scott cleared his throat, pushing her forward.

"Val, you have two choices. You can sign these papers agreeing to pay back the money and, of course, you're fired."

"Or what?"

Stephanie set her phone on the table. "I call the police now and have you arrested for grand theft, which will carry one to three years in jail. And I have proof." She set the USB drive on the table next to her phone and looked at her watch. Her eyes narrowed as she slowly brought them back to Val. "You have one minute to decide."

33

*L*eo sat on the sofa with Stephanie at Sam and Sherry's. He held a glass of sparkling wine aloft and gestured for the others to do the same. "To Stephanie"—he smiled as she felt her cheeks get warm—"and the end of a long and stressful event."

They all drank to her success. She looked at Leo, Sam, and Sherry, grateful she had them in her life. "Thank you for your support. I couldn't have gotten through these last two weeks without you."

Sam beamed with pride. "You are a very strong young lady, and when Val tried to weasel out of the very generous opportunity you gave her, I don't think I would have stayed the course. I'm confident I would have called the police and washed my hands of her entirely."

"To be honest with you, it is easier for me that she took the deal. Now I don't need to ever think about her again."

Sherry topped off their glasses. "Do you think she'll stay in Black River?"

"No. Gary stopped in the office before I closed up and said he heard her house was already on the market."

"That didn't take long."

She took another sip. "Thankfully, she's really gone and once she pays restitution, it will be behind me."

"You never did say if anyone at the shop approached you about her leaving."

"Funny you should bring that up. Chuck came into my office, and he was hemming and hawing like he had something on his mind. He finally said he wished he had spoken up about the problem with his inventory and then when the invoices were magically cleared up, he'd been afraid I'd blame him."

Sherry said, "So people did notice things. Interesting."

"I guess so. I told him in the future, if he noticed any discrepancies, he should let me know right away and that he's a trusted member of our team."

Leo touched her leg. "If we're going to have dinner on the boat, we should take off. The days are a lot shorter and it's going to be cool on the water."

She set her glass on the table and touched the arm of Sam's chair. "I was very serious when I said that you helped me more than you'll know. It would have been extremely tough to deal with Val and the lawyers if I hadn't had you by my side."

Color crept up his neck and flushed his cheeks. Sam muttered, his voice gruff, "No big deal." She thought it was cute she had embarrassed him a little.

Leo pulled her up, picked up their glasses, and took them to the sink. "Mom, Dad, I'll talk to you later."

Sherry took Sam's hand, a gesture that didn't escape Steph's notice. "You have fun this afternoon. If you want, grab a couple of sweatshirts from the hall closet so you'll be warm enough."

"Thanks, Mom. Steph packed a huge tote with extra coats."

He took her hand and steered her out the front door.

Before they could walk down the steps, she stopped him with a tug on his hand.

"I didn't want to say this in front of your parents, but you giving me the space I needed to handle the problem showed me that you know I am strong and can take care of myself."

He gave her a long, sultry look. "With the exception of the women in my family, you are the strongest woman I have ever met and to be honest, you're every bit as strong as they are."

That was high praise. Leo admired and respected the women in his life and she was glad he counted her in that elite group.

In an effort to lighten the mood, she asked, "Do you think Jack would mind if I drove the boat?"

He slung his arm around her shoulders and held her tight against his side. "I'll teach you, but if you run us aground or hit something, you're on your own." He chuckled as they walked to the truck.

"What kind of man are you, letting your girl take the fall?"

"An honest one." He opened her door. "Now put a wiggle on it before the sun sets on our dinner cruise."

*S*tephanie carried a canvas tote and Leo had the cooler as they made their way down the dock to Jack's boat, a sleek open bow rider. Next to it was Don's forty-foot boat. His was a sleek motorboat with room for the family to comfortably sleep below deck and spend the night on the lake.

"Pick one."

She was confused. "I thought you asked Jack if we could borrow his boat?"

"I asked both of them. Do you want to spend the night on the lake or just a few hours?"

"What do you want to do?"

He grinned. "Make you happy."

"Well, if it's really okay with Don, we could take his boat out and if we decide to stay out all night, we can. Otherwise, we can come home too, right?"

"Again, whatever makes you happy works for me."

She grinned.

"Put the tote bag down and I'll hand it to you once you're on board."

Steph did as he asked, but paused when she lifted the cooler. "What's in here, the entire kitchen?"

"Let's just say I'm prepared to have breakfast on the water."

"Does he have a kitchen?"

With a chuckle, he said, "A galley and a head." He gave her a wink. "Bathroom."

"Good to know."

Leo got the boat ready to leave the dock, suggesting Steph sit back and relax; he had everything under control.

Slowly, the boat eased backward and Leo turned it to face the lake. They cruised ahead at a slow and steady pace.

"Why are you going so slow?"

"We're in a no wake zone. Once we pass those markers, we'll be able to pick up speed. And then I'll show you how to drive it."

"No rush. I'm enjoying the view." She slid close to him on the bench seat.

"Are you comfortable?"

The sun was still high enough in the sky to be warm. "I'm glad we got out here early. It's going to be fun tooling around before we have dinner."

"We'll explore the shoreline, and there is a small island I

thought we could anchor near to have dinner and if you like, we can stay right there until dawn."

She sighed. "It does sound romantic."

"Darling, you ain't seen nothing yet. Just wait."

She laughed. "Love the little drawl."

Leo eased the throttle forward and the boat began to pick up speed. The breeze teased the loose strands of her hair and whipped through his. She could feel the tension of the last several months carried away with the wind. She closed her eyes and turned her face up to the sun. Freckles be damned. This felt amazing.

She could feel the boat skim over the water's surface. She had no idea boating could be relaxing and exhilarating at the same time.

"Ready for your first lesson?"

She opened her eyes. The shoreline had grown distant behind them and the lake appeared endless. She stood and gained her balance. Leo switched sides with her. With her hands on the wheel, he went through the explanation that she didn't need to do anything as they cruised along. The power under her hands was unexpected and the way the boat was responsive was a nice surprise. She had spent her fair amount of time in the driver's seat of a muscle car, but this was totally different. She grinned up at Leo and he kissed her softly.

"I'm not going to be a distraction." He pointed to the left. "Turn the boat slightly and let's go that way."

She eased the throttle forward and they went faster. But he never asked her to back off. She could see herself looking to drive the boat again; this was a blast.

A tiny island slowly began to take a distinct form and he said, "We'll stop there."

A shiver of anticipation raced over her. There were a few things they had to talk about regarding their future. Time was growing short and talking out here with no distractions was ideal.

After the anchor was set and Steph had set the table with flameless candles, a bottle of red wine, and a plate of nibbles, she and Leo sat holding hands on the bench seat. Leo pulled a throw over their legs, as the air did have a bit of a bite.

"Is it too cold to sleep out here tonight?"

He held her close. "There's heat below deck and I have no intention of letting you get cold." He nuzzled her neck, his lips leaving her nerve endings sizzling.

Breathless, she placed a hand on his chest. "Leo, can we talk for a few minutes?"

He looked at her with soft brown eyes and his mouth curved into a sexy smile. "What do you want to talk about?"

"The one subject we've both been avoiding. When I leave, what happens next."

He took her hand and looked out over the water and then back at her. "What do you want?"

He seemed to hold his breath as if afraid of her answer.

"I have never loved anyone the way I love you. Despite meeting you on one of the saddest days of my life, you've brought me so much happiness. But my feelings aside, I made a commitment at the beginning of the year that I would go back and pick up my responsibilities."

"Do you want to go back?"

"It doesn't matter. I made a promise.'

"Steph, our choices do matter." With his thumb, he wiped a tear that had slipped unnoticed down her cheek.

"I want what I can't have. To be here with you *and* continue my career in Portland."

"What if you could have both? To continue our relationship and Portland. It doesn't have to be one or the other."

She hesitated to ask but plowed forward. "You'd be willing to try a long-distance relationship? You know I'm planning on coming back every three months to check on the business, and I can set up my schedule so I can work remotely from here during those few weeks. And maybe, like every six weeks or so, you could steal away from Vintage and stay with me for a week. Or however long you want." She sat up and half turned on the bench. "My town house is spacious, so there is plenty of room for the both of us. We can explore the city. It'll be great."

He was watching her but didn't bubble over with enthusiasm. Her heartbeat sped up in her chest. Did he want to break this off, not continue to be committed to her?

"Leo?"

"I'm surprised you want to try a long-distance relationship. I was thinking maybe one of us could move."

"I don't think we're ready for that yet."

He looked out over the water into the growing darkness.

With a flash of annoyance, she wondered if he expected her to give up her job and move back after she'd given her word to her boss? If she didn't get back soon, she might not have a job to go back to and while on one level that was okay, on the other she honored her obligations and promises and she controlled her career. She wasn't going to lollygag until the decision was made for her. As for Leo, his response was not something she would have expected from him. He had always seemed to understand Portland was a reality.

"We're not, or you're not?" His tone cut her to the quick. This was not how she expected this conversation to go.

"Leo, I love you and I want our relationship to continue to grow, and we'll see where it goes. For now, I'm asking we both take time to see what we can do long-term. Don't you want that?"

For several long minutes, he was silent. If they were on

dry land, she'd get up and walk away. On a boat, there was no place to go.

When he looked at her, she could see the hurt in his eyes. But she didn't understand why. Not really. She had never hidden the fact that she had to leave. Had he expected her to change her mind?

"I love you and if this is what you want, then we will see how things go over the next few months."

Relief washed over her. She put her cool hands on his warm cheeks and pulled him close. She could smell the sweet aroma of wine on his breath. "It will all work out. I'm sure of it."

His lips claimed hers and the worry that niggled at the back of her brain was shoved away. At least for tonight.

34

Stephanie treasured every day of her last week in New York; it had been bittersweet for her and Leo. They went to a family dinner so she could say goodbye to everyone. Amidst the tears, there were plenty of laughs. Without Leo knowing, Stephanie had taken some office time and built Johnny and George replicas of her Bronco and for Ben and Owen, she had built model boats that matched their dads'.

It was their final day together. They both had taken the day off from work and tomorrow he would drive her to the airport. They lingered over coffee and small talk.

"Gary seems to be doing great, running the place. It was a good idea to move Chuck to the front desk. But you'll stop in from time to time and check in on them? Not that I don't think they can handle it but…"

"I know you'll feel better." He gave her a strained smile. Making plans like this was hard.

"And you're coming out in three weeks, right?" She sipped her coffee. The smile in her eyes made him think everything was going to be fine. "That will give me time to wade out from emails, get the condo cleaned, and the refrigerator stocked."

"I arrive late Thursday, on the ninth, and then I'll leave on the red-eye Tuesday."

Steph pushed her mug to the middle of the table. "Come on. It's Saturday and we shouldn't be stuck in the house. We're going to go out and have some fun." He allowed her to pull him up and down the hall. "Get dressed, Price. We're leaving in ten minutes."

He couldn't help but laugh. "*You* can't get ready in less than fifteen."

She put her hand on her hips. "It's called motivation. Now. Go." She flicked her hand in the direction of the bathroom.

He made short work of getting dressed. There was no need to shave; she liked the scruffy look. He could hear her singing in the bedroom, and he paused to listen. It was an old classic, "My Girl," but she had changed the words to *my guy*. Her voice was clear but soft and he waited until she was done before stepping into the room.

"I'm ready."

She spun around and grinned. "You do look handsome." She cocked her head and tapped her chin. "You need one thing." In a few long strides, she was in his arms, laughing while he twirled her around. When he set her down, she looked into his eyes. He was expecting a long, sensual kiss and maybe a tumble on the freshly made bed.

But she pulled back and said, "I'll drive."

"What are you up to today?" He allowed her to pull him down the hall. She tossed him a jacket before grabbing hers.

"You'll see." The garage door slid up. Her eyes were shining. Then he glimpsed the classic candy-apple-red-with-red-interior Chevy Z16 sitting in his driveway.

"Where did that come from?"

"Gary dropped it off for me late last night. I wanted us to spend our last full day driving around in this."

"Whose is it?"

"Dad's. It was the first car he restored for himself. It's been in the garage and sadly it hadn't been driven in a while, so with a little help from my crew, they checked her out from nose to tail and we're ready to roll."

"You never said anything about this car."

"A girl has to have some secrets." She held up the keys. "Wanna drive?"

"Yes." With a low wolf whistle, he walked to the car while his hand trailed over the side, down the length of it. The paint job was flawless, and he looked in the side windows. It was in mint condition and he hoped he wasn't fan-boying over a car. He glanced up "Did you know there were only two hundred of these that came off the assembly line in sixty-five?"

Her laugh was low and throaty, like the sound the engine would make in a few minutes. "Huh, you don't say." With a sexy grin, she opened the passenger door. "Time's a-wasting."

He slid into the red leather bucket seat. The chrome on the dash gleamed in the sun and never in his wildest dreams would he have thought he'd be sitting in the driver's seat or getting ready to rev the engine. This was as close as he'd ever get to owning a rare Z16; they were never seen outside of car collectors. Driving this amazing machine would be a highlight of his year—heck, maybe life. Well, that was an overstatement, but this definitely ranked right up there. He ran his hand around the steering wheel, thinking of the person who had driven this car off the lot in '65.

With a playful poke, she said, "Earth to Leo?"

His grin couldn't get any wider. "Where to?"

"You choose. Either right or left and we'll go with the flow." She smiled at him. "I just want to spend the day with you, doing what we both love. We'll stop when the whim strikes us, with no agenda."

Steph watched as Leo drove. The grin he wore was priceless. She didn't know how to show him that he was important to her, the most important person in her life. Until yesterday, when Gary had delivered it to her, she and Dad were the only two people who had ever driven this car after it was restored. She should have pulled it out sooner. With one hand on the wheel and the other resting in the open window, it was obvious Leo was having a blast, and he handled the car with ease as he moved through the gears.

Driving with no destination took them over small two-lane roads, past vineyards, breweries, and farms. "Do you want to stop anywhere?"

"Driver's choice. I'm just riding shotgun."

There was a sign for a park up ahead. He slowed as they approached it. "Let's go back to the town we just went through, get some sandwiches, and sit in the park."

"Sounds nice."

It didn't take long before they strolled hand in hand to a picnic bench. The park was empty. Leo placed the bag on the table. "Eat first or walk?"

What she really wanted was to slow time. The day was evaporating before her eyes.

She saw a few ducks waddling around near the pond and she pointed to a table. "Let's eat and then take a walk."

They ate in silence while holding hands. Mentally, she was reminding herself they would see each other very soon. It wasn't forever.

*L*eo pulled the car into the driveway. "I'll pull my truck out and we'll park the Chevy inside."

"I appreciate that."

He got out of the car and she scrambled into the driver's seat.

She hadn't said much on the drive back to his place. He understood exactly where she was coming from; sadness snaked around his heart like a vise. Tomorrow he had to let her go and all he wanted was for her to say, *Come with me to Portland.*

He opened his side of the garage and eased the truck out, leaving her enough room to pull in. He pulled in next to her.

She locked the car and handed him the key. "Would you mind if I left it here? I'll need to drop the Bronco off at my place so you can have your garage back."

All of these details were breaking his heart.

"Sure." He tried to keep it light. "I have a little surprise for you."

When they walked inside, he snapped on a small table lamp in the hall. In the living room, a bottle of wine and glasses were on the table. "Come."

He grabbed matches and proceeded to light candles scattered around the room.

She gasped. "How did you do all of this?"

He smiled. "You're not the only one with helpers."

She said, "Liza."

"I'll be right back." In the kitchen, Liza had left a plate of sliced fruit. A small warmer plugged in on the counter held melted fudge sauce. Perfect. He carried the tray into the living room. "I thought we'd have dessert first."

She placed a hand on her heart. "Liza brought my favorite wine."

"It goes best with fruit and chocolate fondue." He placed the tray on the table and flicked the music on. Soft, romantic piano music filled the room. He held out his hand and she stepped into his arms. They danced in the candlelight. For the first time today, time stood still. It was just the two of them.

When the song changed, Steph said, "We should enjoy dessert."

"Will you dance with me again?"

With a hitch in her voice, she said, "Yes. All night if you want."

"I have other plans for the remainder of the night."

"I like where this is going." She poured them each a glass of wine and handed one to him. Her eyes glistened. She took a small sip. "I'm going to miss this."

"I'll have Peyton ship you some."

"Leo, not the wine. You and me, together. Sharing unforgettable moments."

She took a strawberry and dipped it in the sauce and then fed it to him. He savored the sweetness of the gesture. His tongue teased the tip of her finger. It was exactly what he wanted to hear, that she was going to miss him, miss them. Should he speak up and tell her he was ready to walk away from Crescent Lake? Not yet. He didn't think she was ready.

He then fed her a small square of cake with sauce. He leaned in and kissed a small drip of chocolate from the corner of her mouth. Leo wanted tonight to be a night she'd always remember. In one slow motion, he eased her from the sofa and into his arms. Holding her close, she laid her head on his chest and they began to move in time to the music.

• • •

*S*tephanie loved being in his arms. Dancing with him in the glow of candles was the most romantic thing she had ever done. The wine and dessert were just as sweet as he was. He held her close and she knew she was loved and treasured.

She was in no rush to get to the bedroom; if they stayed here, maybe the night wouldn't end. She knew she could ask to stay and he would say yes. The unspoken words had been lingering in his eyes all day. But she was a woman of her word. The road home had been paved before she came east to spend Dad's last days with him. She lifted her face, inviting a long, slow, toe-curling kiss. It was what she wanted—no, needed.

He lowered his mouth to hers, exploring the softness of her mouth. She nibbled on his lower lip; his low groan in response was audible. If it was possible, he held her closer as they become one. Now they were barely moving. They were lost in the rhythm of their heartbeats, in time with the other.

The kiss deepened and he ran his hands down her back and, in one slow movement, pulled her shirt off and tossed it into the darkness. She returned the favor. Eyes closed, she ran her hands over his lean back, down his muscled arms, memorizing how his skin felt under her fingertips. She would not cry.

He brushed her hair off her face. "I love you." His whispered words were like silk as they wrapped around her heart, binding her heart to his. Unbreakable.

He scooped her into his arms and waited.

She slid her arms around his neck. "Yes." It was all she needed to say.

He carried her down the hall and placed her in the middle of the bed. His gaze roamed over her.

A small smile played over her lips. She couldn't wait to show him the depth of her love.

35

*L*eo scanned baggage claim. He had taken the late-day flight, so the airport was fairly quiet. The last three weeks had been hell, but he had kept busy working on Stephanie's truck and a '72 Corvette. At night, he had also started looking online for garage space in Portland. His goal was to check out the competition in Portland and any available real estate while Steph was working.

"Leo!"

He turned. She ran to him, threw her arms around his neck, and pulled him into a searing kiss.

With a small chuckle, he murmured, "It's safe to say you missed me?"

"It's been forever since I've touched your handsome face." She grazed his jawline and chin with her fingertips while looking into his eyes. "And those molten chocolate eyes. Mmm." She kissed him again before saying, "Did you get your bag?"

"I didn't check one. We can roll."

She looped her hand through his arm with a possessive grip.

"How was the flight?"

Or was it that she thought he might disappear? He didn't care; all that mattered was that they were together.

"Uneventful."

They strolled through the parking garage. Considering it was approaching midnight, it wasn't busy. Stephanie was giving him facts about the city and the weather forecast for the upcoming weekend.

"It's going to be in the low fifties and sunny for most of the time you're here. I booked tickets for tomorrow night for a sunset river cruise; being it's Friday, it shouldn't be too crowded. They serve dinner and we can see the city skyline and some famous landmarks all from the Willamette River. There's live music too. Then on Saturday—if you want, of course—there is a guided tour of Multnomah Falls and the Columbia River Gorge, or we can check out some wineries instead."

She guided him to a luxury SUV. The hatch slid open with the touch of a button. This was another side of her he hadn't expected. He tossed his bag inside. "Where's your convertible?"

"In the garage. This is more practical for airport pickups."

"How far is your town house?" He got into the passenger seat and buckled up.

"Traffic is light, so about a half hour." She whisked through the parking garage and merged onto the highway, then glanced his way. "I am so happy you're here."

She kept two hands on the wheel, as traffic was fast, with lots of lane changes, a few cars sliding in and around them. Despite the darkness, Steph mentioned points of interest as she drove. He could her the pride in her voice; it was clear she was at ease in the city as well as the small town back home, and this had been her home for a long time.

"I wanted you to meet Maggie this trip, but she's away visiting family."

"Next time. We can enjoy our time together and explore Portland."

Did she hope he might fall in love or at least like the area? It was going to take some getting used to. He was a small-town guy but he could adapt to a city of cement, steel, and glass. It was true the things a man would do for love.

"Are you hungry? I put together a snack for when we get home and then—" Her voice trailed off when she glanced his way.

Could she see the desire in his eyes? Her eyebrow arched. With a suggestive laugh, she said, "That is definitely on tonight's agenda."

"With all the plans you made, I was beginning to wonder." He could feel the corners of his mouth twitch.

She slowed and took an exit. "We're just another mile."

With all the streetlights, he could see a river to his right. "Do you have a water view?"

"Yes, and that's the river we're going to cruise on."

He slowly nodded and watched the passing scenery. He wasn't in his comfortable neighborhood now. The street was lined with well-manicured lawns and pristine town houses. He guessed she did well but wow, she had to be killing it to live in this part of the city. Could he live in a community like this? His gut tightened. The commute might be tough to a shop location but he could make it work as long as they were together.

"You're pretty quiet over there."

Her voice caught his attention.

"Just looking around." He looked at her as she slowed and pulled into a short driveway. The garage door slid up. Inside were a couple of shelves with very little on them and a covered car.

"Home sweet home." She opened the driver's door. "There's my toy." She bobbed her head in the direction of what he took to be a low-slung car, hidden by its protective cover. It must be one hell of a toy. "We'll take it out tomorrow if it's not raining."

He was curious about the car, but more so about her place. This was not what he had expected. Where was his Steph, the woman with the small house who drove an old classic Bronco, at home in the garage or in her office, which had a faint smell of paint and grease. He grabbed his bag and followed her inside and was not surprised the interior was just as tidy as the garage. The first floor walls were a pale tan, and the few decorative accents around the room were black and glass, very contemporary. It was an open floor plan, with two sets of sliding glass doors leading to an outdoor seating area and on the deck was an open-air table for two. There was a gas fireplace and deep, cushioned chairs in front of it. It couldn't be more opposite her home in Black River.

After showing him the first floor, she said, "There's a bathroom at the end of the hall. Let's go upstairs and I'll show you the rest."

The first room held a large desk with an oversized screen and keyboard with a leather desk chair, clearly her home office, and the next room, decorated in soft greens, must be the guest room. On the opposite side of the hall was the oversized master suite, complete with a fireplace and sitting area. It was like a magazine spread, including a lack of personal items except for a framed photo on the dresser, whom he guessed were her parents.

"Nice place."

In answer, she pulled on the front of his shirt and walked him back to the bed. He dropped his bag on the way.

"Consider this your home away from home." She

unbuttoned his shirt and kissed his exposed skin. With a catch in her voice, she said, "I've missed you."

That was music to his ears. He didn't need to respond with words. He showed her by his actions.

*L*ying side by side, completely relaxed, Leo kissed the palm of her hand and worked his way up her arm to her lips, leaving a trail of kisses. She sighed.

"Happy?"

"Yes. You?"

He rolled over to show her again just how much.

*T*he next morning, Steph had to spend a few hours in the home office, but she said she would be done by noon. She offered Leo her SUV keys if he wanted to go explore, and he took her up on the offer. It would give him time to check out locations to relocate his business. He hadn't discussed it with her, but once he had a better idea of where it might be, then he'd talk to her. He knew she'd be thrilled they would be able to be together. Then after some time, they could sell her place and buy a home large enough to raise a family.

He smiled as he pulled up to the first garage on his list, just happy to be less than an hour from the woman he loved. His smile dimmed as he looked around at the aging neighborhood. A few old tires had been cast aside on the sidewalk and across the street, the building had boarded-up windows. He didn't want to have to worry constantly about the security of the cars he was working on and didn't even bother to get out. He drove by three more locations, and only one was a remote possibility. Maybe talking to

Steph would help him find a suitable and affordable location. Everything he had seen today had been stupid expensive; were homes also more pricey than he expected? Portland was a beautiful city and despite all the people and traffic, he'd find a way to be happy here. And maybe if he said it enough to himself, he'd be convinced.

On Friday night, Steph and Leo were going on a sunset cruise. It was a dressy event and she'd asked him to wear a blazer. He said he was always happy to accommodate her requests and his pale-yellow shirt, jeans, and black blazer even complemented her floral print dress.

"You look beautiful tonight, but are you going to be warm enough?"

She smoothed a hand over her dress and matching jacket. "I should be comfortable. And don't forget, my boyfriend can always hold me close to warm me up." She batted her eyes at him. "Very romantic."

He put his arms around her waist and nuzzled her neck. "That would be the highlight of the evening."

She placed a hand on his chest and could feel her cheeks flush. "I've never taken the boat cruise. But I've heard it's a lot of fun."

"How long have you lived here? Is the weekend going to be filled with firsts with me?"

"I work a lot but I've made some time for fun too." She squeezed his hand. "However, I'm looking forward to all you have planned. Did you decide what you want to do tomorrow?"

They got into the boarding line at the boat.

"We should do the winery. That way, we won't have to get up too early."

"Am I tiring you out?" She laughed softly.

"I don't intend for us to sleep."

She didn't have a chance to respond before the line moved to board. After being escorted to their table near a large window, she said, "We're going to have stunning views." The previous men in her life hadn't been that romantic, or maybe it was because she hadn't felt that way about them so she'd never suggested something like this. Either way, she was glad to be experiencing this special night with Leo.

They were handed a glass of champagne, and a plate of appetizers was placed in the center of the table.

"Do you want to go outside and watch as we pull away from the dock?" he asked.

"That sounds nice."

They crossed the dining room and stepped out into the crisp air.

He held up his glass. "To us."

She clinked his glass and sipped. "Today has been wonderful."

He drank and smiled. "This isn't too bad."

"I forgot I'm in the presence of a wine heir."

"Not really. I just know what I like." But she could see the smoldering desire in his eyes and felt the same; he wasn't talking about the champagne. She softly brushed his lips with hers.

He leaned against the rail and watched her instead of the skyline. A small smile played on his mouth. "I've been doing a lot of thinking these last few weeks, but I wanted to wait before I talked to you."

She took another drink. Her heart thudded in her chest. Was he about to change their lives?

"While you were working, I went and looked at a few possible locations for a garage."

What was he talking about? "Oh?"

"I would like for us to drive by one tomorrow and get your opinion."

"You want to close your shop in Crescent Lake and move here?"

He took her hand. "Steph, I have walked through the last three weeks in a haze, thinking about this time with you and imagining how great things had been with us. And after being here, I don't want to leave. If you'll allow me to move in with you, I can work and we can be together. Down the road, we can look for a house. It'll be great."

He was serious. As much as she wanted them to be together, she wasn't ready to have this conversation. At least, not tonight. She wanted to have it on her terms; she was still working through if she even wanted to stay in Portland, and if he was already thinking of packing up and relocating, that was a huge decision to make without discussing it with her before looking for garage space.

"Sure." She hesitated. "We can swing by the place you're considering. If not there, I'm sure there will be others in the coming months." They should be talking about the possibility of them taking their relationship to the next level, not the location of a new garage.

He gave her a quizzical look. Before he could ask any questions, she said, "We should go inside. Dinner will start soon."

Leo didn't bring it up again for the rest of the evening, even though it was an elephant between them, and Steph did her best to push it from her mind. The night was for romance.

*M*onday was a cloudy, overcast day that matched Stephanie's mood. She had given the idea of Leo moving to Portland so much thought, her head hurt. She kept coming back to his connection to his family. She knew what it was like to live without one, and there was no way she was going to have him resent her at some point. She decided that after today—well, really tomorrow afternoon—she was going to tell him they couldn't see each other anymore. Today was her last full day with the man she loved and she planned to make the most of it.

"Steph." Leo called up to the bedroom. "Come on down; I have a surprise for you."

"Be right there." She double-checked her makeup. It was funny. In Black River, she never gave a thought to checking her lipstick, but here she didn't leave her bedroom without it. It was as if she were two different women.

She ran down the stairs and, at the bottom, she stopped and looked at the dining table. He had set it with her good dishes, which were covered with aluminum foil.

Her heart ached. "What's all this?"

"Breakfast for my love." He pulled out her chair. "Just sit back and relax. I'll get your coffee."

"You didn't need to do all of this." She sat in the chair he held. "It's very sweet."

"Nothing's too good for the love of my life." He wouldn't be saying these kinds of words in thirty-six hours. Not after she told him her decision. Her heart wept. She was going to break his heart, and hers too. Was it even fair to keep up the pretense? She didn't want to miss a moment before he left so she pushed everything aside to enjoy breakfast with him.

He brought over the insulated coffee carafe and filled her mug. "I made bacon, French toast, and orange juice." He gave her a feather-light kiss.

"We could have gone out for breakfast. I know several good places within walking distance."

"We can go out tomorrow." Before he sat down, he

passed her the syrup and butter. With a dramatic flair, he peeled off the foil. "Ta-da!"

She could feel tears fill her eyes. "It looks delicious." She wanted to lay her head on his chest and cry. Was she a fool for destroying the best relationship she'd ever had?

"Hey, what's going on?" He pulled his chair close and handed her a cloth napkin.

He had even found her linens. She had to give him credit; he knew how to romance a girl.

"You're too good to be true." She leaned in and kissed him, then waved her hand toward the table. "Thank you for all of this."

"You know I'd do anything to see your smile."

She picked up her fork. "Breakfast is getting cold."

He dropped a kiss on her cheek. "I love you, Steph."

She looked into his eyes. "I love you more."

eo finished packing his bag. One final dinner together and they'd be off to the airport so he could take the red-eye home. The days had gone by too fast. He wanted to have another conversation about the garage location with Steph, but when he had tried, she had changed the subject. Was she opposed to the idea? No, that was crazy.

He hoped Steph could run down a couple more possibilities and if one had a lot of potential, he'd fly out for a few days. He was anxious to get things in motion. Moving the garage in winter would be a pain but manageable.

He had stashed a small velvet drawstring bag inside his shirt pocket. Tonight, he was going to ask Steph to marry him.

He went downstairs to check the main living area. The lights were low and the space empty. Steph was sitting on the deck with two glasses on the small table in between the wicker chairs.

He crossed the deck and kissed her upturned cheek. "Hey, beautiful. I'm all packed and checked in online. I can head right to the gate after security." He was making small talk since she seemed miles away.

She gave him a sad smile. "I thought we could have a glass of wine and talk."

That would work to his advantage. He pulled the stopper on the bottle and poured.

He looked at the label. "This is my favorite Cab from CLW. How did you manage to get this vintage here?"

"Before I left, I arranged for Peyton to send me a couple cases of our favorites."

"Always thinking. I like it." He handed her a glass and then gave her another kiss before sitting down. "I like the lipstick; your lips are the same color as the wine." He was getting used to seeing her hair and makeup always perfect, unlike back home where messy buns and a t-shirt and jeans were her daily attire.

She gave him a weak smile. He knew just how she was feeling. As if a piece of her was getting ripped away.

He took her hand. "It's going to be okay. We won't be doing this long-distance thing forever."

"I wanted to talk to you about the garage."

"I'm hoping you'll be able to look at a few with the Realtor while I'm gone." He sat back in the chair and grinned. "I know it's a lot to ask, but what I saw on this trip won't work. Hopefully it won't take long to find a place. Then I can pack up and make the move."

She sipped her wine and set the glass aside.

Leo continued. "It's good that you know the ins and outs of the restoration business. It'll make the move that much easier."

She gave him a half nod.

"The next trip out, I'll bring extra clothes and leave them here, if that's okay."

"Leo."

"When do you think you're coming back east? I know

you've been really busy playing catch-up, but the holidays are right around the corner and it'd be nice if we spent them with the family. You're going to love the craziness. The kids are a blast."

"Leo."

The sharpness of her tone caused his next words to die.

"We need to talk."

"About?" The word hung in the air.

"You shutting down Vintage and moving to Portland."

His heart thudded in his chest. He did not like the serious tone of her voice. He reminded himself not jump to conclusions.

"I don't want you to relocate to Portland."

His breath was sucked from his lungs.

"If you feel like I'm rushing you," he said, "we can slow things down. Put a pause on my plan to set up shop here." Or was she about to give him the best news, that she was moving back home?

"It's not that." She looked away from him. "Now that I'm back, I'm not the girl you met in Black River. We have very different lives, and I can't see us having a future."

"Stephanie, you've got to be kidding." He got up from the chair and paced to the deck rail. Leaning against it, he tried to search her eyes, but she skillfully avoided him.

"Would you look at me, please?"

She stared at his chin.

"Look me in the eye and tell me you aren't in love with me." He could hear the demand in his tone but he didn't care. He wanted to fight for her. For them.

"This isn't about love. We aren't a good fit. End of story."

"This is just the beginning." He thought of the ring in his shirt pocket. His heart hammered in his chest and a cold sweat trickled down his spine. She couldn't possibly mean what she was saying. She loved him.

In a few long strides, he knelt next to her and took her hand. "Stephanie, we don't need to rush into anything. We can take our time. Slow things down."

She shook her head. Her eyes glistened with unshed tears. "No. After I drop you at the airport, we won't see each other again."

He heard the finality in her voice. His thoughts scrambled. How could he change her mind? Tears glistened in her eyes, and the heart-wrenching words were killing him. This wasn't how he had thought tonight would go. The ring was heavy in his pocket.

"There's no changing your mind?" His heart thudded in his chest and the pit of his stomach was a stone. But worse, he was gutted. All he wanted was to love this woman sitting in front of him and have a future with her. Why was she doing this? It didn't make sense.

She pulled her hand away and averted her eyes. "No, I won't change my mind, and look around. We are two very different people." Softly she said, "I'm sorry."

With a heavy heart, he stood up. "I'll find my own way to the airport. Goodbye, Stephanie."

He crossed the living room and picked up his bag. He didn't stop when she called for him to wait. He closed the door with a thud.

Stephanie looked around her bedroom. It was devoid of life, just a place to sleep. Nothing more. With Leo gone, so was the spark she had felt for the first time in this house. He was the beam of light she had been missing.

She left a trail of her clothes as she walked into the bathroom, too drained to pick them up. Stepping under the steaming hot water, she let the tears flow. Deep, racking sobs were muffled by the sounds of the water. But what did it matter? She was alone.

For over two weeks, since Leo left, Stephanie went through the motions of living her life. Other than work, where she was fully focused, the rest of her days and nights were devoid of energy. She missed her father more than ever and all of the Prices, too. The large and nosy bunch had made her feel like she belonged and now she was even more alone than before she fell in love with Leo and discovered what it was like to be part of a family.

Another long weekend was in front of her when Maggie stopped by for coffee. They were relaxing in front of the gas firepit, bundled up to ward off the damp air, when the doorbell rang.

"I'm not expecting anyone."

Maggie smiled and waved her hand at the door. "Go see who's there, and then we'll get back to catching up. I want to hear more about the status of things in Black River. After all, we need to make a trip out there, and soon. I wanted to get out there during the summer but my schedule was slammed."

"It's okay. There was a lot going on and our phone calls and emails kept me going during those difficult days in the beginning." She was lucky Maggie had stopped by. It was good to have her best friend to hang out with. "I'll be right back."

Steph checked the peephole, shocked to see Anna standing on her doorstep. What was she doing here? This couldn't be good—or heaven forbid something had happened to Leo. Her heart pounded in her chest and with a deep, ragged breath, she opened the door. "Hi, Anna. What are you doing here?"

"Hi, Stephanie. I'm sorry I didn't call, but may I come in?"

She swung the door wide and stepped to the side, but she didn't meet Anna's eyes.

"I thought you'd avoid me if I called first."

Jeez, Anna had her pegged.

"Is Leo okay?"

She tipped her head to the side. "He's as good as can be expected," she said and she gave Steph the once-over. If she noticed the dark circles under her eyes or that her jeans weren't as form-fitting as a few months ago, she didn't mention it.

"What brings you to Portland?" This was so hard, having Anna here. She wanted to ask her a thousand questions about Leo, home, and more about Leo.

"I'm consulting with a winery about an hour from here and I wanted to see how you were doing." She scrutinized Steph's eyes and face. "You look about as good as my brother."

"Would you like a cup of coffee? Maggie and I were just having one on the deck."

"I'm sorry to interrupt." Anna glanced to where Maggie was sitting. "Are you sure? I can come back."

"Stay. I'd like for you to meet Maggie."

"Then yes, thank you."

"Make yourself comfortable." She gestured to the deck. "How do you take your coffee?"

"Just cream if you have it." Anna walked through the room and stopped to look at a photo on the mantel before going out to the deck.

Steph cringed and her heart sank. It was a picture of her and Leo from the river cruise. Why had she left that up?

Because she had never imagined anyone from his family would see it.

"Here you go." She handed Anna a mug. "This is my best friend, Maggie Stafford."

Anna gave her a warm smile. "Nice to meet you. I'm Anna Price-Grant."

They sipped their coffee in silence.

Anna looked back at the mantel. "Nice picture of the two of you."

"I, um, forgot to put it away."

Anna held the coffee cup. "I'm going to be blunt." She gave Maggie a small smile. "One of the more annoying traits in our family." She looked at Steph. "What happened? Looking at you and seeing Leo, you're both miserable. And should I remind you about a certain conversation we had regarding Leo being hurt?"

"Yeah, you said it wouldn't be pretty."

Anna gave her a hard look. "Well, not pretty just showed up, so explain to me why you broke his heart."

"We're not right for each other and besides, he'll get over me." She stared into her mug. "He just needs more time."

"And you. Will you be able to forget about him and move on with your life?"

Stephanie didn't answer her. She swallowed the tears in her throat and the blood roared in her veins. She focused on her coffee as if it were the most fascinating thing in the world. That was a joke; Leo was the only man she'd ever love with all her heart, and getting over him wasn't an option. It didn't matter how many months passed; he had taken her heart when he boarded the plane for home.

Anna placed her hand on Steph's arm. "I have seen how you look at each other."

There was no way she was going to tell Anna. It would

get back to Leo and he'd come back to Portland. That was how he was. "It's better this way."

"I beg to differ."

The women sat in uncomfortable silence. Maggie watched Steph. She opened her mouth to say something and then closed it.

Anna set down her still full mug on the side table. "Can I give you a piece of unsolicited advice?"

Stephanie fought back the tears. She would not cry in front of Anna.

"Call him. It's not too late."

She felt the lump in her throat grow so big, it seemed to strangle her.

"Whatever excuse you manufactured in your head to protect him has devastated him." Anna stood up. She smiled at Maggie. "Nice to meet you." She gave Steph a quick hug. "Take care, Stephanie." She stopped at the front door and looked over her shoulder. "I'm as close as your phone and no matter what, I will always be your friend, but I had hoped we'd be family."

Stephanie heard the front door close, and with the back of her hand, she wiped away the tears that slid down her cheeks. For the last ten months, her life had been in a turmoil. Dad dying, keeping the garage afloat, and dealing with Val had been the hardest things she'd ever lived through, but the one person who eased her burden was Leo. At first, she had been worried she was using him to fill the void since he was a lot like her dad. But soon, he had made his own spot in her heart. On the flip side, she had spent years working to achieve success in the business world and if she walked away, it was career suicide. If she went back and took over the garage, she'd have to make it a real success. And then there was the Price family. Seeing Anna was a sharp reminder that she missed them all, and having people who were in her corner was very important to her. But she had thrown that away to protect Leo. Surely Anna understood.

After a few long minutes, Maggie said, "Anna's right. I've never seen you this torn up over any guy. Leo has to be something special. You're great at your job, but being a pharma rep is just a job. Think about what your heart really wants and needs."

She lifted her head. "Anna was right. The Price family is opinionated, but they welcomed me like family. I wasn't an outsider with them. Sam helped me when I was dealing with the Val situation, and I never expected to have that kind of support from anyone who wasn't my dad."

"And Leo?"

"I've never felt about anyone the way I feel about him, and this place—" She looked around her, exhaled, and placed her hand over her heart. With a catch in her voice, she said, "This isn't my home."

The Monday before Thanksgiving, Stephanie took a last walk through the town house. The moving company was coming in a couple of hours for a few family antiques and boxes with her personal things. She had already shipped the Benz a week ago. She couldn't bear to part with it so when it arrived in Black River, Gary would put it in storage for her. The rest of the furniture was staying. Thank heavens the new owners liked her interior designer's style. The SUV was packed and she was ready to hit the road. Not that she'd get far today, but she was anxious to begin the next phase of her life. She planned to take the week to drive to Black River. That reminded her she needed to call Gary and let him know everything had fallen into place.

Chuck picked up the phone and said, "I heard the good news. You're gonna come back and run the place!"

"I am. Is Gary around?"

"Sure, boss. Hold a sec."

She listened to the hold music and made a mental note to change that. It was boring.

"Hi, Steph." Gary sounded happy to hear from her. For the first time, she really felt like she was going home. He was the closest person she had now.

"I wanted to let you know I'll be in the shop on Monday."

"Good. The place hasn't been the same without you."

That put a smile on her face and lightened her heart. With a laugh, she said, "Turns out I miss the smell of motor oil." For the first time, she knew exactly where she belonged. She'd never had this kind of easy relationship with her former coworkers. Maggie was the exception, and she was the only person she'd miss.

"Kind of gets in your blood and heck, Steph, you were born with it in your veins."

"Catch me up on what you're working on, and is there anything major coming up?"

Gary rattled off a list of new cars he had scheduled and what they were wrapping up before year's end.

"We've had a good year. I want to talk about bonuses when I get back. How about Tuesday? Give me a chance to get into the day-to-day swing of things."

"I'll be here."

She could picture his friendly grin. "Also, what do you think if we gave everyone a turkey for Thanksgiving or maybe a gift certificate to the market for their meal? I know it might be kind of late, but I want to do something." After all, these people were the closest thing she had to a family.

"That would be really nice. And I can tell you it'd be appreciated by everyone."

"Alright, can you ask Chuck to check with everyone and then call in the orders for turkeys and the gift certificates. Then see what the church needs. Well, that's if they still do the community dinners."

"They do, and that's something your dad did every year and I'm going to guess the market is just waiting for our call."

She smiled. She was going to carry on the tradition.

"Well, you drive safe and check in if you want," Gary said. "You have my cell, right?"

"I do. Thanks, Gary, and I'll see you soon."

"Don't forget to watch the weather." His tone was full of fatherly concern.

"I won't." The doorbell rang. "I gotta go."

She stuck her phone in the back pocket of her jeans and checked the peephole. The moving guys were early. She rubbed her hands together in anticipation. This was the last step in putting her plan into action, and then it was time to head east. Soon she'd be back in her tiny family home and working on cars again, as well as running the garage. She might not have family living under that roof, but she'd make it her home. For the first time in years, she felt good about her decisions.

She watched as the men made the final trip to the truck. With one last look around, she picked up the framed photo of her and Leo from the mantel. She touched his face and placed it in her tote bag. Time to go home.

37

For mid-December, it was more like early October, with sunny days and moderate temperatures that dipped low at night. Leo thought about Steph every day as he had finished the final coat of wax on her Chevy truck. If he couldn't be with her, the least he could do was finish the truck as a Christmas gift. The interior had come out better than he had hoped, an exact replica of the pictures she had shown him. He had it loaded on the flatbed and covered for the drive to Black River. While he was there, he wanted to talk to Gary about an iridescent paint job.

He pulled the flatbed around to the back of Black River Restoration. Gary greeted him with a wave and a smile. He must know that Steph had broken it off with him, but Gary wasn't letting on.

"You got her done."

"It came out better than I had hoped. Wait until you see."

Gary rubbed his hands together. "Let's get it unloaded."

Leo tossed him the keys. "You can drive it off."

He held up both hands. "Not on your life. I'm not getting a spec of grease in this cream puff." He pulled off the fabric cover and gave a low whistle. "She's going to be surprised. It looks great."

"Where can I park it?"

"We got the last bay ready. If you head that way, I'll get the door."

The truck almost purred when he parked it in the garage. Gary closed the overhead door and Leo covered it back up and again handed him the keys. "Do me a favor and don't tell her I finished it. Let her think it was you."

"Leo, as soon as she looks at the project logs, she's going to know we didn't have time to do this too. Besides, you should tell her."

With a firm shake of his head, he said, "I have a GTO that needs an iridescent paint job, and that is the specialty here. Can you fit me in before Christmas?"

"I can take a look. Come on inside."

The men walked into the center of activity. Zira waved to him and smiled. He returned the gesture. "How's she doing?"

"Good. She said you are a good teacher. Thanks for working with her on the paint prep."

"All she needed was a little more experience." He looked directly at one of the cameras. Did Steph still check them on a regular basis? He looked at the concrete floor and figured since there was nothing going on, probably not.

Gary was looking at a computer screen. "Any chance you could bring the GTO over next Wednesday?"

"Yeah, that'll work." He patted Gary's shoulder. "I appreciate the help."

He nodded. "This partnership is working out for both businesses. You're a good wrench man. If I didn't know any better, I'd swear Eddie had taught you himself." He looked toward the lobby door. "You remind me of someone else I know."

With a shake of his head, Leo said, "I'll see you Wednesday, about eight."

It was like déjà vu. Leo was backing the flatbed through the chain-link gate with the GTO on the back. He had worked like a madman to have it ready. Getting ahead of schedule meant he could work on his Mustang.

Gary greeted him just like always, with a wave and a grin. He helped get the car unloaded and they parked it in the side lot.

"We'll get it inside in about ten minutes. Why don't you go in, grab a coffee, and then you can talk to me about the paint? I need to pull the colorants and make sure we nail it for your client." He pointed to the door. "You know the way. Oh, and can you tell Chuck I need him for a minute on your way in?"

"Sure."

Leo strode through the door and let Chuck know he was needed in the shop. Then he made the short walk to the coffee pot. A light was spilling from Steph's old office. It was almost like old times. He heard a drawer slam. Who was in there? Curiosity got the best of him and he crept down the hall.

He stepped into the doorway and froze. Sitting behind the desk was Stephanie. She had her hair up in a messy ponytail and was wearing a Rosie the Riveter long-sleeved t-shirt.

Her eyes grew wide and her mouth went slack. She stuttered, "Leo, what are you doing here?"

He held up the coffee cup.

"You came for coffee?" Confusion filled her eyes.

It dawned on him. Gary had wanted him to get coffee because Stephanie was in the office. His breathing slowed and his mouth went dry. She was as beautiful as always.

"How have you been?"

"Okay."

He pointed toward the shop area. "I gotta go. I need to talk to Gary before I leave."

"Wait."

"I gotta get back out to see Gary. He's doing a paint job for me, but if you prefer, I can load up and take it someplace else."

"No. You don't need to go elsewhere." Her voice was sharp. She was all business and it was all he could do to not close the distance between them and touch her cheek.

"Um. Thanks." He was going to leave and then hesitated. "You look good, Steph."

He dropped his coffee cup in the garbage on the way to the shop. The desire for caffeine was gone.

Gary had some explaining to do and Leo wasn't in the mood to listen to any flimsy excuses. The mechanic straightened when Leo walked into the shop, turning and wiping his hands on a rag. "By the look on your face, you bumped into Stephanie?"

"You should have told me she was here."

"You need to know she's here permanently."

His heart slowed. Could it be there was a chance they could get back together? "Did she want you to tell me that?"

"No, and if she knew, she'd kick my butt. In all fairness, she's my best friend's daughter and Eddie would want me to meddle."

Leo turned on his heel and half ran back into the office

and down the hall. He burst through her door just in time to see her wiping her eyes with the backs of her hands.

"Stephanie. Is it true you're back full-time?"

Her head snapped up. "Yes."

He almost didn't hear her. "You're back. Does this mean you've given up the Portland gig and that sterile town house?" His heart slowed.

She nodded and looked around her office. "I'm happy here and at heart, I'm a small-town girl. I loved the city for a while and if I'd never stretched beyond these walls, I would have regretted it. My dad was a wise man. He gave me roots and wings." She gestured to her outfit. "This is the real me, not the designer suits and shoes, or the expensive dinners out with clients and spending time at the salon for facials and all the other upkeep it takes to look perfect for a job. The slower pace, friends who are like family is what I want out of my life. I'm no longer willing to have just one person I can call when something good happens. Maggie is like my sister, but she was the only anchor I had to Portland." She pushed back from the desk and stood up. "It took me too long to figure out where I belong but I'd rather spend the next forty-plus years working in this garage with these people, working my butt off, than live a cushy life of retirement after thirty years in my former career."

By this time, Leo's heart was a steady beat in his chest.

"When you said you wanted to leave Crescent Lake and move to Portland for me, I didn't want you to live with regret like I have. I can't get back the time I lost with Dad, but I can honor his memory by keeping his legacy alive and I'm doing it because for the first time in a very long time, it's what I want for my life."

"Is that all you want, to run your dad's business and be successful?" Could he dare to hope that she wanted him back in her life too?

"Partly. But there are a couple of other things." This

time, a smile spread across her face. "I happen to be in love with a brilliant mechanic and I'm not sure if he'll forgive me, but when he got on a plane a couple of months ago, what he didn't know was he packed my heart in his bag and took it with him."

"Maybe you need to ask if this brilliant man still has feelings for you." He wanted to say the words she needed to hear but the first thing she had to do was ask him.

"Leo, can you understand I needed to figure out what I wanted without you clouding my judgment? I had to make the decision for the right reason—for me. It's not that I didn't love you, but I've been on an emotional journey and I needed to be ready."

"At first I didn't understand. I thought if I relocated Vintage, everything would be perfect, that our love would conquer everything. But after Anna saw you, I knew you were suffering as much as I was. I hoped you'd change your mind and reach out to me."

"I wasn't ready. Again, it wasn't about you. It was about me."

"It seems Gary had another idea and decided to play matchmaker."

Her face relaxed into a wide smile. "I'll have to speak to him about that since I don't want him to think it can be some kind of a side business."

His laughter lightened his heart. "In Gary's defense, his intentions were good."

"I saw my truck." She tipped her head and smiled. "It's beautiful, Leo."

"How would you feel to know I'm completely in love with you and I've been devastated without you?"

She came around the side of her desk. With a catch in her voice, she said, "I'm so sorry."

He held his arms open and she ran to him. "Loving

someone means you forgive them, but for the record, I'm never letting you go."

She lifted her face. "I love you, Leo."

"Stephanie, I love all sides of you, and I'm thrilled you're here in my arms."

EPILOGUE

The next six months were a whirlwind. Stephanie sold her father's house and officially moved in with Leo. Both businesses were booming, but there was only one thing Leo needed to do.

He had chosen her favorite foods and wine. The candles were lit, and all he had to do was wait for her to get back after spending the day with Liza and the boys.

He heard the garage door open and close. He could visualize her truck parked next to his. The new and the old.

He met her at the door. "Welcome home, love." He gave her a kiss.

She looked around and a slow smile spread over her face. "Hon, what's going on?"

He took her handbag and set it on the table. "You look beautiful." He gave her another look. "Come with me."

She walked into the living room and took in all the minute details. Vases of flowers were on every surface, and so were flameless candles. She smiled. Her favorite white wine was chilling in the bucket. Her heart hammered in her chest and she was having trouble taking a slow, deep breath.

"You went all out."

He slipped his arms around her waist from behind and nuzzled her neck. "Do you like it?"

She leaned back into him. "It's perfect."

He led her to the sofa and pulled her into his lap.

"Wine." It wasn't a question but a statement. He handed her a glass and then picked up one for himself. "Can we talk about last fall, when I came to see you?"

Her heart thudded in her chest. "I'm sorry I hurt you."

"You were right. We did need time. To have our relationship deepen, sinking our roots in this region, not on the coast." He brushed the hair from her face. "But you've never talked about your thoughts about me."

"Your family, this home, your life. I didn't want you to leave this and have regrets."

"You're my family. You're my home. You're my life."

He pulled a ring from his shirt pocket and held it at the tip of her ring finger. "Say yes and marry me. We can have our own family. Help me make this house our home. Live your life with me and together we'll fill our lives with happiness."

Her hand trembled as he slipped the ring on her finger.

She was not going to cry. She blinked back the tears. "Yes. I'll marry you." With a catch in her voice, she said, "On one condition."

His eyes twinkled. "Name it."

She took his face in her hands. "Dance with me always."

"Forever and a day."

She kissed him and breathed, "I'm going to hold you to that."

He rose to his feet and held her in his arms. "Dance with me now?"

She whispered, "Yes."

***

Thank you for reading Leo and Stephanie's story. I hope you enjoyed the story. If you did, please help other readers find this book: **Please leave a review now!**
Are you ready to read more about the Price family? Check out this sneak peek into Bouquet Book 5 in a Price Family Romance series:

Sweet second chances for a widow and the handsome billionaire...

Liza Bradford never dreamed she'd be a widow, raising two boys and starting an event business. It wasn't part of her life plan, but neither was crushing on the handsome billionaire Drew Cameron. Her life was too busy to even think about dating; she helped at her family's small town winery and the boys were busy with sports and activities. Besides Drew wouldn't be interested in her, she was just average compared to the women he dated. She was better at planning weddings than finding her own happily ever after. After all she thought, you only get one chance at true love.

Drew Cameron is handsome and rich. He fell hard for Liza the first time he laid eyes on her. He has been patiently waiting until she was ready to go out with him and she took his breath away when she asked him out on their first date. He liked a woman who knew what she wanted and went after it, even if that meant he moved at her turtle pace. But he's worried about her struggles and, he has the means to make her life effortless. As a bonus, her boys fill a void he hadn't realized was there. Maybe he can have the family he always dreamed of. He's finished with the glamorous but empty life, all he wants is a chance to show Liza she's the only woman for him.

Here's a sneak peek at Bouquet
Featuring lovely Liza Bradford and handsome billionaire, Drew Cameron.

Sweet second chances for a widow and the handsome billionaire...

Liza Bradford never dreamed she'd be a widow, raising two boys and starting an event business. It wasn't part of her life plan, but neither was crushing on the handsome billionaire Drew Cameron. Her life was too busy to even think about dating; she helped at her family's small town winery and the boys were busy with sports and activities. Besides Drew wouldn't be interested in her, she was just average compared to the women he dated. She was better at planning weddings than finding her own happily ever after. After all she thought, you only get one chance at true love.

Drew Cameron is handsome and rich. He fell hard for Liza the first time he laid eyes on her. He has been patiently waiting until she was ready to go out with him and she took his breath away when she asked him out on their first date. He liked a woman who knew what she wanted and went after it, even if that meant he moved at her turtle pace. But he's worried about her struggles and, he has the means to make her life effortless. As a bonus, her boys fill a void he hadn't realized was there. Maybe he can have the family he always dreamed of. He's finished with the glamorous but empty life, all he wants is a chance to show Liza she's the only woman for him.

Order **Bouquet Now…**

Have you enjoyed Vintage? Not ready to stop reading yet? If you sign up for my newsletter at www.lucindarace.com/ newsletter you will received **Blends**, the love story of Sam and Sherry, right away as my thank-you gift for choosing to get my newsletter.

Can two hearts blend together for a life long love..

His mother's final illness waylaid Sam Price's college dreams, but he's content working in his family's vineyard in a small town in upstate New York. When he finds a woman with a flat tire on a vineyard road, he's stunned to discover it's the girl he'd had a crush on in high school. He'd never been confident enough to ask her out back then. He'd been a farm kid. Her daddy was the bank president. Way out of his league.

Sherry Jones is tired of her parents' ambitious plans for her life. She'll finish her college accounting degree like they want, but how can she tell them about her real love: working with growing things? Then a flat tire and a neglected garden offer her an unexpected opportunity, with the added bonus of a tall, gorgeous guy with eyes that set her senses tingling.

What does a guy with dirt under his nails and calluses on his hands have to offer a woman like Sherry? It will take courage for her to defy her parents and claim her own dreams. Sam and Sherry's lives took different paths, but a winding vineyard road has brought them back together. Are they willing to take a chance to create the perfect blend for a lifelong love?

Blends is only available by signing up for my newsletter – sign up for it here at www.lucindarace.com/newsletter

LOVE TO READ?

CHECK OUT MY OTHER BOOKS

Cowboys of River Junction

<u>Stars Over Montana</u>
The cowboy broke her heart but he never stopped loving her. Now she's back ready to run her grandfather's ranch…

Hiding in Montana

Orchard Brides Series
<u>Apple Blossoms in Montana</u>
Twenty years later Renee and Hank are back where they fell in love but reality is like a spring frost and is a long-distance relationship their only option for their second chance?

The Sandy Bay Series
<u>Sundaes on Sunday</u>
A widowed school teacher and the airline pilot whose little girl is determined to bring her daddy and the lady from the ice cream shop together for a second chance at love.

Last Man Standing/Always a Bridesmaid

<u>Barrett</u>

Has the last man standing finally met his match?

<u>Marie</u> *May 2023*

Career focused city girl discovers small town charm can lead to love.

The Crescent Lake Winery Series

<u>Breathe</u>

Her dream come true may be the end of his...

Crush

The first time they met was fleeting, the second time restarted her heart.

<u>Blush</u>

He's always loved her but he left and now he's back…the question, does she still love him?

<u>Vintage</u>

He's an unexpected distraction, she gets his engine running…

<u>Bouquet</u>

Sweet second chances for a widow and the handsome billionaire...

Holiday Romance

<u>The Sugar Plum Inn</u>

The chef and the restaurant critic are about to come face to face.

Last Chance Beach

<u>Shamrocks are a Girl's Best Friend</u>

Will a bit of Irish luck and a matchmaking uncle give Kelly and Tric a chance to find love?

A Dickens Holiday Romance

<u>Holiday Heart Wishes</u>

Heartfelt wishes and holiday kisses…

<u>Holly Berries and Hockey Pucks</u>

Hockey, holidays, and a slap shot to the heart.

<u>Christmas in July</u>
She's the hometown girl with the hometown advantage. Right?

<u>A Secret Santa Christmas</u>
Christmas just isn't Holly's thing, but will a family secret help her find the true meaning of Christmas?

It's Just Coffee Series 2020
<u>The Matchmaker and The Marine</u>
She vowed never to love again. His career in the Marines crushed his ability to love. Can undeniable chemistry and a leap of faith overcome their past?

The MacLellan Sisters Trilogy
<u>Old and New</u>
An enchanted heirloom wedding dress and a letter change three sisters lives forever as they fulfill their grandmothers last request try on the dress.
<u>Borrowed</u>
He's just a borrowed boyfriend. He might also be her true love.
<u>Blue</u>
Will an enchanted wedding dress work its magic one more time?

The Loudon Series
<u>Lost and Found</u>
Love never ends... A widow who talks to her late husband and her handsome single neighbor who has secretly loved her for years.
<u>The Journey Home</u>
Where do you go to heal your heart? You make the journey home...
<u>The Last First Kiss</u>
When life handed Kate lemons, she baked.
<u>Ready to Soar</u>
Kate will fight for love, won't she?
<u>Love in the Looking Glass</u>

Will Ellie's first love be her last or will she become a ghost like her father?
<u>Magic in the Rain</u>
Dani's plan of hiding in plain sight may not have been the best idea.

Cozy Mystery Books
A Bookstore Cozy Mystery Series 2023
<u>Books & Bribes</u>
It was an ordinary day until the book of Practical Magic conked Lily on the head causing her to see stars. And then she discovered her cat, Milo, could talk.

Catnip & Crimes
Tea & Trouble
Scares & Dares

SOCIAL MEDIA

Follow Me on Social Media

Like my Facebook page
Join Lucinda's Heart Racer's Reader Group on Facebook
Twitter @lucindarace
Instagram @lucindraceauthor
BookBub
Goodreads
Pinterest

ABOUT THE AUTHOR

Award-winning and best-selling author Lucinda Race is a lifelong fan of reading. As a young girl, she spent hours reading novels and getting lost in the fun and hope they represent. While her friends dreamed of becoming doctors and engineers, her dreams were to become a writer—a novelist.

As life twisted and turned, she found herself writing nonfiction but longed to turn to her true passion. After developing the storyline for A McKenna Family Romance, it was time to start living her dream. Her fingers practically fly over computer keys as she weaves stories of mystery and romance.

Lucinda lives with her two little dogs, a miniature long hair dachshund and a shih tzu mix rescue, in the rolling hills of western Massachusetts. When she's not at her day job, she's immersed in her fictional worlds. And if she's not writing romance or cozy mystery novels, she's reading everything she can get her hands on.

Visit her at:
www.facebook.com/lucindaraceauthor
Twitter @lucindarace
Instagram @lucindaraceauthor
www.lucindarace.com
Lucinda@lucindarace.com

www.ingramcontent.com/pod-product-compliance
Lightning Source LLC
Chambersburg PA
CBHW071211210726
48293CB00002B/387